# A CONVICTION OF GUILT

Murdoch Finnegan's death poses a mystery for Horatio T. Parker, chief crime reporter of the *Hampstead Explorer*. Not only is the murder apparently motiveless, but Finnegan has left Parker a curious house in Golders Green. Parker begins a dangerous investigation which leads him back to the horrifying abduction and murder of a little girl in London in 1972. How is Murdoch Finnegan's death connected to this unsolved crime and what dark secret binds him to her wealthy and powerful family?

# A CONVICTION OF GUILT

# A CONVICTION OF GUILT

*by*
Lew Matthews

**Magna Large Print Books**
Long Preston, North Yorkshire,
England.

British Library Cataloguing in Publication Data.

---

Matthews, Lew
  A conviction of guilt.

  A catalogue record for this book is
  available from the British Library

  ISBN 0-7505-0896-5

First published in Great Britain by The Crime Club an
imprint of HarperCollins Publishers, 1993

Copyright © 1993 by Lew Matthews

Lew Matthews asserts the moral right to be identified as
the author of this work.

Published in Large Print December, 1995 by arrangement with
HarperCollins Publishers Ltd., and the copyright holder.

Magna Large Print is an imprint of
Library Magna Books Ltd.
Printed and bound in Great Britain by
T.J. Press (Padstow) Ltd., Cornwall, PL28 8RW.

This one for Vivienne

# CHAPTER 1

Rosie Ferreira sighed as she took the key out of her apron pocket and put it into the door. She hated Wednesdays, when she cleaned for Mr Finnegan.

Actually, she quite liked Mr Finnegan. He was always pleasant and paid her well and in cash but, like so many bachelors, he lived like a pig. It wouldn't have been so bad had he paid her to come in two or three mornings a week so that she could keep control of the mess before it built up. But he didn't like that idea. He wanted her to come in for the whole day on Wednesdays, and by then the small flat was littered with dirty clothing, the bathroom was filthy, and the kitchen was a disaster area with greasy plates, cutlery, pots and pans piled up in the sink.

This morning she groaned quietly as she opened the door and was assailed by a new stale odour that she had not encountered before. The flat was in darkness, with the curtains still drawn shut, which was odd because Mr Finnegan was usually an early *riser and was always up and about when she arrived at seven o'clock.*

*Perhaps he was drunk and has been sick somewhere, she thought to herself as she began picking up bits of clothing. When she opened the bedroom door, the strange smell suddenly became overpowering. The room was dark, and even as the cleaning lady reached for the lightswitch some sixth sense told her that something was very wrong.*

'You're fired,' Arnie Bloch told me as soon as I got to work that Wednesday morning.

I could have said, 'You can't fire me, Arnie, I own this newspaper,' but I didn't, because only three or four people in the whole world knew about that arrangement. And my colleagues, who included Arnie Bloch, were not among them.

What I did say was: 'What?'

'Yew hurd me, man, yew're fiyad.' Arnie was a large South African with an accent as ripe as it was on the day he had arrived in England twenty-seven years before, after swimming across the great green greasy Limpopo River with Pretoria's security forces and bloodhounds snapping at his heels. Something to do, I believe, with

12

his outspoken journalistic condemnation of apartheid.

And during those twenty-seven years he had lost none of the belligerence that had so endeared him to the old Afrikaner regime. In fact he was a downright ornery cuss, and there were times when I wondered why I had ever made him editor of the *Hampstead Explorer.* This was one of those times.

Eloquent as ever, I countered with: 'Why? What have I done?'

'It's more to do with what you haven't done; like any work for the past few months, for example.' He took a bite from his sandwich. There was always a sandwich or some other form of essential sustenance within reach of Arnie Bloch.

'I've been warning you for months that your production of copy has been unacceptable, and you responded by disappearing from the office for days on end. When I ask you where the hell you have been, you get all mysterious and tell me you are working on a big story. But do we ever get to see this big story? We do not. And when I ask you to tell me about this big story, do you do so? You do not. You get even more mysterious, and then disappear from the office for more days on end.'

He paused to take another bite. I remained silent because, frankly, there was not a lot I could have said.

'And then I find out that you have been lying to me. Last Thursday you told me you were off to see an important informant in Hendon, and then someone tells me that they saw you skulking around Gray's Inn. It just came up in conversation, you understand. Someone recognized you, and just happened to mention it to me.' Crumbs sprayed everywhere as he spoke.

'I can explain,' I said, aware of a small speck of egg mayonnaise which had landed on my tie.

'No doubt you can, but I haven't finished yet. Then there is the writ.'

'The writ?'

'Yes, the writ we have received from a certain Labour councillor in Camden, of whom you wrote, and I quote: "He only lies when he moves his lips." '

'That was a joke,' I said lamely.

'Well, I can inform you that neither he nor his lawyers are rolling about on the floor laughing. Nor am I, for that matter. I don't see any joke at all; all I see is a very seriously defamatory statement that is going to cost this newspaper thousands of pounds in damages and legal fees.'

'No, I meant I wrote it as a joke. It was supposed to be edited out by the subs.'

'Well, it bloody wasn't! The story was handled by a sub-editor who was busy, someone who doesn't spend his time swanning around doing bugger-all or writing jokes, someone who has a lot of work to do in a limited amount of time. Yes, he overlooked your little facetious comment, and yes, he shouldn't have, and yes, I have shat all over him for that, but at least he didn't write the stupid comment. You did.'

'What can I say, Arnie? I'm sorry.' I really was, and I deserved all this. I also knew that what he was really upset about was not the threat of financial damages, but the fact that the paper would have to run an apology. He hated that more than anything.

'What can you say? You can say goodbye!'

'Isn't this a bit extreme?'

'I don't think so. If I can't trust you, I can't employ you, it's as simple as that. You'll get three months' pay in lieu of notice, and you've got fifteen minutes to clear your desk.'

'No appeal?'

'No appeal. I've cleared this with the general manager who has full powers in the day-to-day running of this company. You can appeal to the mysterious owners, if you like. If you can find out who the hell they are, that is. I've tried, I can tell you, and got nowhere. There's just this Ambrose Pendleton geezer who represents them, and he's saying nothing.'

'What about my record, Arnie? I've written some blockbuster material for the *Hampstead Explorer*. There was all that stuff about the Tory MP who was accused of killing his wife, and all the exclusive coverage about how I was present when he got shot. I solved the whole damn case and they were massive scoops!' I protested.

'Yes, they were. But that was a year ago, and what have you done since then? Nothing. We gave you a pay increase, your own office, and relief from general reporting duties because you were our star investigative reporter. And you just took advantage of the whole situation. Sorry, Parker, I warned you again and again, and now it's goodbye and good luck.'

I seemed to have exhausted all avenues of argument, and further protest seemed pointless. I walked through an embarrassed and silent newsroom to the little glassed-in enclosure that Arnie had called my office, and cleared my desk. There wasn't all that much to clear, when it came down to it. I had worked on the *Hampstead Explorer* for twelve years, but all I ended up taking were a few pens, my contacts book, a diary, one or two letters, a photograph of myself, a cracked mug and half a bottle of Scotch. There wasn't even a half-finished novel in the bottom drawer.

I left the building in an intrigued state of bewilderment. The fact was that I did indeed own the newspaper, but at that moment I couldn't think of a way of getting myself reinstated without revealing myself, or at least creating suspicions that would lead some of my colleagues in that direction. For it had been a central pillar of my philosophy that none of them should ever know that I was the boss.

I had been in that unusual but happy state for just over a year, since a very dear little old lady by the name of Edwina Llewellyn had died and left me—Horatio

Thorpe Parker—all her money. That, when they finally managed to count it all, came to approximately fifty-two million pounds. That in turn produced income of more than three and a half million pounds a year—the unimaginable equivalent of forty-five thousand pounds a week, after tax.

It had, as you can imagine, come as a considerable surprise to me, especially as I had actually believed that the poor dear was a bit short of dosh. There had even been an occasion when I secretly paid one of her gas bills—something which had given no end of amusement to Ambrose Pendleton, the elderly lawyer whose duty it had been to break the news of Edwina's bequest to me.

I had been incredulous that someone like Edwina could have had that degree of wealth without it being widely known, but Pendleton and a certain Mr Douglas of Rothschilds had made it clear to me just how many quietly secret multi-millionaires there were, and just how easily and quickly money flowed into the coffers of those who already had more of the commodity than they could ever spend.

For my part, I did two main things with the inheritance. The first was to buy the *Hampstead Explorer,* using an offshore holding company fronted by Pendleton, set up in such a way that even the most inquisitive of my newshound colleagues would not be able to trace the real ownership past Pendleton and a London-based company called Golden Daffodils Limited. I paid three million pounds, cash.

I realized from the first that if the rest of the staff knew that I was the boss, it would be impossible for me to continue doing the one job I had ever really enjoyed—being a reporter on the *Explorer.* No one could have felt comfortable working alongside me, and I would inevitably have been edged into a management position and forced into behaving like the multi-million-pound tycoon that I was.

I was more than content to lead my rather quiet and lazy life, now and then exerting a little pressure on the tiller of the company through Pendleton and the general manager, Bob Price. I had, for example, ensured that Arnie Bloch was appointed editor. I gave the staff large pay increases and a generous annual slice of the profits, all of which had gone a long way towards comforting those who might otherwise have spent much more time worrying about, and perhaps even investigating, the real ownership of the paper.

In all the time I had only told the truth to one person, an extraordinarily beautiful person with startling green eyes called Andy Ferris—and the confession had cost me the relationship. Andy had tried to ignore the millions and to forget that I was both her lover and her boss. But, shortly after I made her news editor—in effect my daytime boss—Andy realized that the situation was far too complicated for her to deal with and we went our separate ways.

She was snapped up by the *Observer*, which knew a first-rate journalist when it saw one. We remained good friends, and occasionally we had lunch or dinner, but I could see now how the constant strain of knowing and staying silent had been too intense to allow the relationship to flourish.

The other thing I did was to establish the Edwina Llewellyn Memorial Trust in an attempt to deal with the income that my capital generated. The trust, administered by Pendleton and a small staff of professionals (including a doctor, two social workers, an ex-policeman and an accountant) specialized in providing funds to groups, and individuals who had been turned down by other charitable organizations or didn't otherwise qualify for help.

We trod a careful road of trying to assist those at the bottom of the heap who were not catered for in the system, while at the same time trying not to attract too much publicity, so as not to swamp our resources. And, so far, we had done pretty well.

My personal standard of living had, of course, improved somewhat. I paid off my ex-wife, redeemed my mortgage, ate in the best restaurants regularly, mildly upgraded the quality of clothes I wore and found that I could now afford the exotic holidays of my dreams. But I had felt no urge to buy a palace, live in the opulent luxury I could certainly afford, or buy flashy cars. I also knew that if I didn't go on working I would quickly become a disgusting human being.

My one ostentatious act had been to hire on a permanent basis my very own black taxi with its own mobile telephone. I had an expensive arrangement with a cheeky cockney cabby by the name of Frankie Price who picked me up every morning, drove me around during the day, and took me home at night. The deal suited him perfectly. Frankie was always taking courses through the Open University, and was delighted to have the time between my journeys to study his books and write his essays—while being paid handsomely for doing so. After he dropped me in the evening, he would turn the meter on and go looking for real customers, the greedy bastard.

I had thought that everything had been working perfectly, but I now realized that I had been spending much too much time dealing with trust business in Pendleton's office in Gray's Inn, and this is what had brought me into conflict with Arnie Bloch.

I couldn't blame Arnie, now that I thought about it. I had spent very little time at my desk in recent months, produced little useful copy, and had indeed been very stupid to write a facetious comment in a news story. The problem was, how was I going to get myself re-hired without undermining Arnie's authority?

I walked out of the building and then

around the corner to where Frankie always parked with apparent immunity on the double yellow lines. I told him to take me home, which is a house in Estelle Road, NW3. That's in Hampstead or in Gospel Oak, depending on who you are talking to and the kind of impression you want to make. Or maybe even Hampstead Bottom.

It wasn't even ten o'clock yet.

'Long, tiring day at the office, guv?'

'Beware, driver, your employer is not in a good mood.'

'What's up?' asked Frankie, always keen to listen to people's problems. He had a degree in psychology, and was now working towards an MSc.

'I've been fired,' I informed him.

'Oh dear, does that mean our arrangement is off? You know...should I turn the meter on?' I knew he wasn't being serious, though, and I didn't bother to answer.

Frankie didn't know about my millions, but he was shrewd enough to deduce that what I earned on the paper would not pay his wages on top of everything else and that there had to be, therefore, another source of finance. He was also shrewd enough to be discreet about his status as my employee, and was careful to appear like any cabbie when I had someone with me.

I didn't quite know what to do with myself when I got home. I made tea and then went out into the garden holding the steaming cup. March was just turning into April, and all around me there were demands for attention. Roses required pruning, next door's creeper needed hacking back severely, the apple tree needed attention, last autumn's leaves were still rotting in piles and, worst of all, the grass looked like it needed cutting. Just the kind of things one could do on an unexpectedly free day. I beat a hasty retreat, and made two phone calls.

The first was to my friendly neighbourhood garden maintenance service to ask them to send a man round right away.

The second was to Ambrose Pendleton, to inform him of the termination of my employment and to ask his advice on a tricky legal matter.

'Can I appeal to an industrial tribunal for my job back without actually revealing to the tribunal that I own the company that sacked me?' I asked. 'Would that be perjury?'

'Hmm. I doubt if there can be too many

precedents on this, but I'll think about it and come back to you,' he replied.

I was just wondering what to do next when the telephone rang.

'Parker, get back to the office right away!' It was charming Arnie at his most mellifluous. It sounded like: git beck to thu orifice rah awai.

'Hello, Mr Bloch,' I said sweetly. 'Is there something I can do for you?'

'Don't fuck me around, Parker. Do you want your job back or not?'

'Arnie, I would kill my best friend to have my job back. What's happened?'

'Don't make jokes about killing your friends. Murdoch Finnegan was found murdered this morning.'

There was, indeed, nothing funny about that.

# CHAPTER 2

Murdoch Finnegan was not one of my best friends. He was only an acquaintance. But that didn't entitle anyone to put the muzzle of a twelve-bore shotgun close to his chest and pull the trigger.

I didn't see the body, of course, but the unpleasant manner of Murdoch Finnegan's death was among the facts provided three hours later by Inspector Theodore Bernstein, the recently promoted press liaison officer at Hampstead police station in Rosslyn Hill who was, as always, not pleased to see me.

'The victim was discovered at around seven o'clock this morning by his cleaning woman, a Mrs Rosario Ferreira. She would clean for him once a week, on Wednesdays,' Theo told the handful of reporters who had turned up to the hastily called press conference.

The last big murder in Hampstead, the killing of the sexy celebrity actress Monique Karabekian, had attracted scores of journalists, but the death of poor Murdoch had only brought out the local papers, one news agency and a scribe from the *Evening Standard*.

'She was pretty hysterical and got a neighbour to ring us.' Theo continued.

'Any time of death established yet?' I asked. Theo sighed.

'I have no doubt, Parker, that if you had been one of Job's afflictions he would have been somewhat less patient.' Our Theo was somewhat of a Bible scholar, and an expert on the Talmud, the teachings and deliberations of the Babylonian rabbis in exile. 'Kindly exercise some patience, and all that I am able to reveal will be revealed.' I smiled at him in an encouraging way. It was my belief that Theo's antagonism towards me was entirely feigned.

'A police surgeon's preliminary report suggests that the murder took place some days before the body was found, so there is no possibility of pinpointing the exact time of death,' Theo continued.

'However, further inquiries lead us believe that he was shot at some time on the previous Friday morning. He was seen alive by Mrs Ferreira on her last visit, and was also seen and heard by neighbours on the Thursday night. The doctor said that the degree of decomposition of the body indicated that he had been killed at least four days before he was found, so that rules out any time this week.

'Working backwards, we can also rule out the weekend, since the building was full of people and no one was aware of a gunshot, which they would certainly have heard. That leaves us with Friday, when we have established that there was a period in the morning, between around ten o'clock and noon, during which none of the other tenants in the building were at home. That's when we think it happened. That would also account for the fact that no one in the building appears to have seen anyone unusual around.

'Now, before Parker can ask this question, I can also tell you that there is at this stage no indication whatsoever as to what the motive for the crime could have been. Our own search of the flat and the opinion of the cleaning woman leads us to conclude that nothing was stolen. Valuable items including cash, credit cards, cameras, VCRs, etcetera, were left untouched. Furthermore, the flat does not seem to have been searched. Filing cabinets were still locked and apparently undisturbed.

'We have not, at this stage, been able to trace Mr Finnegan's movements on the days before his death, but inquiries, as they say, are being made. You will note, therefore, that we do not have a great deal to go on, and we would appreciate an appeal through your newspapers for anyone who had any dealings with Mr Finnegan, or who knows where he was in the last week or two, to contact the incident room which has been set up in this station. Similarly, anyone who saw, or even think they saw, anyone or anything suspicious in the vicinity of the flat on that Friday morning. They should ask for Chief Superintendent Harrison.'

I winced, because Harrison was another policeman who seldom exhibited any signs of joy when he cast eyes on me.

'Sounds to me like a mob hit,' said Leon Kypriades from one of our give-away rivals, the *Kentish Town Courier*. We all called him Kippy, because most of the time he seemed to be fast asleep.

'Aah. Just the kind of erudite comment I would expect from the gutter press. I can see your headline now, Kippy: MOB WAR IN BELSIZE PARK. The fact that there is no evidence whatsoever of any involvement by organized crime shouldn't hold you back at all. But then you don't have to worry about selling your newspapers, do you? You just stuff them through people's doors whether they want to read your lies or not.'

I loved all that, of course, but it was just water off a duck's back to Kippy, who really loved his job and gave every sign of expecting to win a Pulitzer prize for journalism at any moment. In his fantasies he worked for the *Washington Post.*

'You sure you're not holding anything back?' he growled at Theo.

'Like what?'

'Like maybe whoever offed him cut off his dick and stuffed it in his mouth. That's what the Mafia do to people who break the *omertà* vow of silence.'

'Oh, for heaven's sake! I'm not even going to answer that. Anyone else got any questions?'

'Yes,' said Jacqui Thingummy from the *Evening Standard,* whose surname I could never remember. 'You haven't told us what this Murdoch Finnegan did for a living.'

'He was, I understand, a private investigator. And, before you ask, we don't know what cases he was currently investigating. As far as I know, he did a little divorce work and some debtor location for credit companies. Not exactly a Philip Marlowe.'

'Was he an American?' Kippy jumped in.

'As a matter of fact, he was.'

'Wow!' said Kippy, scribbling in his notebook. Theo closed his eyes for a

30

moment and sighed.

'He had been living in London for twenty-one years and was a permanent resident, although he had retained his US citizenship and passport.'

'How old was he?' Jacqui Thingummy asked.

'Forty-five.'

'Did he have a carry permit?' Kippy chipped in.

'A what?'

'You know, a permit for carrying a concealed weapon, a Walther PPK or something like that.'

'If you mean did he have a firearm licence, the answer is no. Come back down to earth, Kippy, this is not New York or Detroit.'

'Did he die immediately, or was he tortured?' Kippy asked.

'That's it! Press conference over!' Theo picked up a few papers and left the room.

'A cover-up if I ever heard one,' said Kippy breathlessly as he followed suit.

I turned to Jacqui Thingummy and asked if she fancied joining me for a late lunch. She looked at me as if she was an evening paper reporter and I was a mere weekly hack.

'No,' she said, and followed Kippy. Well it was succinct, anyway.

When I got to where Frankie was waiting with the cab, I was still hungry. I didn't want to eat alone so I invited him to join me for lunch. He loved these little perks.

'You choose where,' I said. He usually chooses Ed's Easy Diner in Hampstead, but this time he suggested we try the new American restaurant at the Chalk Farm Hotel, the big building above the tube station overlooking the famous Round House Theatre.

It turned out to be decorated like a Louisiana swamp, with canoes and stuffed alligators nailed to the walls and mangrove fronds hanging from the ceilings. The menu was full of Cajun dishes, and things called 'blackened' fish and steak. I wasn't quite sure just how they went about blackening the food, so I ordered a double New Orleans Jazz-burger, medium rare, with Fresno Fries and Oklahoma Onion Rings, noting in my mind that Fresno was in California and Oklahoma cuisine could not really be described as Cajun. I also ordered something called a Double Thick Shawnee Mountain Shake. Frankie was so impressed by my decisiveness that he ordered the same.

Our order was taken efficiently by a cheerful young waitress with a lapel badge that said 'Pam' who repeated the items back to us and disappeared towards the kitchen.

Nearly half an hour later she returned, looking very embarrassed, to apologize for the delay, caused by a shortage of staff in the kitchen. And ten minutes later she brought the 'food'. I use the word 'food' only in its figurative sense, because what had been put on plates in front of us was not only disgusting but an insult of monumental proportions.

Frankie, who ate regularly in disgusting workmen's cafés and knew disgusting food when he saw it, said: 'This is disgusting.'

'It's not only disgusting,' I replied, 'it's an insult of monumental proportions.'

The onions and the French fries were burnt and limp and cold, a condition that takes not a little concentration to get the timing right. The burger was a blackened disc of what looked like overcooked grey oatmeal. The buns were stale, soggy and scorched, a feat which nearly matched the production of the fries. And the milkshake was thin, curdled and so sweet that you got toothache just looking at it. I motioned for Pam.

'This,' I explained to her quietly when she arrived at the table, looking a little pale and uneasy, 'is not only disgusting, but an insult of monumental proportions.'

'Sir,' she replied quickly, 'I think the best thing I can do is call the manager, and you should complain to him.' Then she ducked her head, conspiratorially and whispered: 'Personally, I wouldn't eat *anything* here. I really should have warned you, but I'm new here, and I need the job.' And then she was off.

A minute later she was back with a slim man in a natty black suit who had a dangerously thin moustache and a badge which declared him to be Bud Hawkins, the Restaurant Manager. 'Well, gents, how can I help you?' he drawled in an American accent.

I explained to him, quietly and as pleasantly as I could, that the food was not only disgusting but an insult of monumental proportions. And to my surprise, he bristled vigorously.

'I take it, then, that neither of you two gents has ever been to the deep south of United States?' He pronounced it 'Yooonited States', and he did not wait for an answer. 'Because it seems to me that if y'all *order* Cajun food and then turn round and tell us that you don't *like* the Cajun food we bring ya, that's a pretty tough break for the restaurant, don'tcha think?'

'Come on,' I said to Frankie, 'We're going.' I had no intention of arguing with a man who clearly had the brain of a newt. But Bud had other ideas.

'I must ask you gents to pay for your meal before you leave,' he said.

'Ask away,' I said, standing up, 'but we're leaving anyway,' Frankie followed suit.

Newtbrain Hawkins headed for the doorway, where he stood with his arms folded. 'Pam, call the police!' he barked. Pam was looking pale and scared.

'Good idea, Pam,' I said. 'Call the police. The local station numbers is 431 1212. I'm sure they'll love to waste their time having to explain that our refusal to pay for this uneatable food is not a criminal but a civil matter. If you like, you may sue me for the amount involved, including interest and any damages you can prove. Here is my card, and I look forward to our day in court.'

'Get out, then!' he spat at us. 'And don't come back. We don't want your kind of trash here.'

Outside Frankie looked at me and said, 'Jeez, Mr P, that was a speech and a half.'

'Never mind that,' I told him, 'I'm starving!' The trouble was that we had run out of time. I had to get back to the office to write my Murdoch Finnegan murder story in time for Wednesday afternoon deadlines, and I certainly didn't want to be fired for the second time that day. So we bought some chicken and chips from the Kentucky Fried place across the road from the hotel and ate them on the way back, Frankie complaining all the time that the cab would then stink of chips and vinegar for days and his tips would suffer in the evenings.

I wasn't listening to him. I was sitting there wondering if I wanted to get into the hotel and catering business. I picked up the telephone and dialled Ambrose Pendleton's direct line.

'It's me,' I said. 'Do we know anyone who knows anything about hotels?'

36

# CHAPTER 3

My return to the office was less than triumphal. There was no avenue of cheering colleagues; just a load of reporters and sub-editors glued to their computer screens, busily working towards the Wednesday evening deadline.

'I want five hundred words in twenty minutes,' was the only greeting I got from Arnie Bloch. But still, it felt good to get back into my office, return my meagre possessions to the drawers of the desk, and switch on my computer terminal. It had been a tough life being unemployed.

The story was easy enough to write, and it didn't take me very long. And it was as I tapped away at the keyboard that anger began to replace my journalistic detachment about the death of Murdoch Finnegan.

Hell, I wondered, who would want to shoot such an inoffensive and, let's face it, ineffectual guy? He was, as Theo had said, a private investigator, but a less likely candidate for the job would be impossible to visualize.

I had met him some years ago, just a few days before he had been arrested by Hampstead police as a Peeping Tom. A woman in Redington Road had seen Murdoch clamber over her garden wall and climb a tree that gave him a clear view into the bedroom of the house next door. She had, of course, called the cops immediately.

Murdoch's protestations that he was engaged in the lawful activity of checking on the marital fidelity of the wife of a client did not impress the arresting lawmen, and the intrepid tree-climbing private eye for a while became part of the rocketing crime statistics of the area.

It was only the next morning, after Murdoch had spent an uncomfortable night in a police cell, that he was released with a warning. This was because the objects of his attentions, having heard the commotion of the arrest outside the bedroom window, and, horrified by the prospect of court-room publicity, had arrived at the police station and begged the forces of law and order not to prosecute anyone. I too had brought to bear what meagre influence I had at Hampstead police station in the cause of leniency.

My connection was that I was Murdoch Finnegan's client, and the people in the bedroom had been my wife, Julia, and her smouldering Welsh mechanic who, she later explained, could do things to her carburettor that no other man could.

It had been the end of a bad marriage and the beginning of a peculiar relationship with Murdoch which had endured because of, rather than in spite of, his apparent inexorable incompetence at his chosen profession. His periodic blunders and indiscretions were a source of huge amusement to his friends, and he could hold an entire pub spellbound with tales of his disastrous escapades.

'Murdoch,' I once asked him, wiping tears of mirth from my eyes, 'Why do you persist in this hopeless endeavour?'

'There is always hope, Parker, and I enjoy it. Anyway, a man's gotta do what a man's gotta do. And besides, it's driving my parents crazy.'

Murdoch had arrived in England in the early 'seventies, having politely declined Mr Richard Nixon's kind invitation to go and kill small oriental people in Vietnam. An

English-born grandmother had bequeathed to him the immigration status as a 'patrial' which had enabled him to remain in Britain indefinitely.

But his parents who lived wholly patriotic lives in some small town in New Hampshire, had been outraged by what they regarded as his cowardice and desertion from the country of his birth, and had cut him off without a cent.

My view was that the US Army had had a narrow escape. With Murdoch in Vietnam the war would have become even more chaotic than it was, and who knows how it all would have ended. They should have given him a medal for evading the draft.

But, to be fair, while he was no Philip Marlowe, Murdoch did have certain essential qualifications for his job. Firstly, he was the most patently honest person anyone could ever meet. There was an instantaneous understanding on the part of everyone he met that this was the kind of guy to whom one could safely entrust a brown paper bag chockful of fivers, secure in the knowledge that he would not even open the bag, let alone make off with the lolly.

Secondly, he was persistent. No, he was more than that, he was downright dogged. It didn't matter that he might be following the wrong person, but he would follow him to the ends of the earth. And if it meant standing all night in the rain outside the wrong house, that's what he would do, without complaint.

Thirdly, and perhaps this was the clincher, he was cheap. Murdoch charged his clients absurdly low fees, probably because no one would have paid him more, and it was certainly this factor which had enticed me to call upon his services.

That was back in the days before Edwina Llewellyn had dropped her 52-megaton nuclear bombshell on me, and I had spent a lot of my time wondering where I was going to find the money for a new starter motor for my car.

I had asked Theo Bernstein to recommend a private investigator who specialized in marital work. It wasn't as if I still had any hope of saving my marriage; it was just that I felt that I had to know who she was sleeping with. Theo asked me how much I intended to pay and when he heard my answer he had no hesitation in mentioning Murdoch's name.

The three qualities had kept Murdoch in business. He was never overwhelmed with clients, and there was not a great deal of return business, but by and large the cheap people who hired him were satisfied with his cheap service.

As far as I was concerned, Murdoch became a source of off-beat stories. In his business he came upon the oddest things, and characters, and there had been many articles in the *Hampstead Explorer* which had started off as snippets gleaned from Murdoch in a pub. There had also been times when we had been able to publicize injustices suffered by his clients, and that hadn't done his business any harm either.

I was deep in this kind of reminiscence when the telephone rang. It was Ambrose Pendleton, the elderly but razor-sharp solicitor who handled my affairs and ran the Edwina Llewellyn Memorial Trust for me.

'You asked about hotels,' he said.

'I did.'

'I've found an excellent person. Someone who used to work for Southern Counties Hotels. Highly recommended.'

'Good. Ask him to go and spend a

night at the Chalk Farm Hotel, eat in the restaurant, have a look at the place—at our expense, of course—and come back to us with a proposal for a bid. I think we're going into the hotel business.'

'It's not a he, it's a she,' Pendleton said.

'I don't care what she is, as long as she knows about hotels.'

I put the telephone down and was about to put on my jacket and go home when a courier arrived with a large envelope for me. I signed for it and put it in my desk, intending to open it in the morning.

Then I noticed the distinctive handwriting on the address label, and my blood ran cold. My name was printed in haphazard capital letters in peacock blue ink in a way only Murdoch Finnegan could achieve.

## CHAPTER 4

Inside the envelope were two more envelopes. One was a sleek white envelope addressed to me on a typewriter, and the other was a chunky brown one, again addressed to me in Murdoch's distinctive shaky hand. I opened the white one first.

Out came a letter from Mo, Murphy and Forbes, solicitors, with an address in King's Cross. It was addressed to me in my full glory as Horatio Thorpe Parker, and I wondered ruefully for a moment how Murdoch had found out about my middle name, before I remembered that he was, after all, a detective.

The letter, dated that day, read:

Dear Mr Parker,

We were distressed to learn this morning of the death of our client, Mr Murdoch Finnegan, whom we have been representing on a number of matters over the last few years.

Two months ago Mr Finnegan deposited with us the enclosed envelope with instructions that it should be sent to you as a matter of urgency in the event of his death or incapacity.

We regret very much that his instruction must now be carried out, although we should stress that we have no information about the contents of the envelope.

Yours sincerely,
Arnold Mo

My imagination proceeded to run riot as my slightly trembling fingers began to open the larger envelope. Pornographic photographs? Money? Drugs? Blackmail material? An unpublished novel? Love-letters? But what I really hoped would be in the envelope was a clear indication of who had shot him, and why.

What emerged was a small bundle of official-looking documents, including letters from Mo, Murphy and Forbes, the Halifax Building Society, and a firm of estate agents by the name of Portman and Renbourne, all to do with the obtaining of a mortgage and the purchase by Murdoch Finnegan two months before of a house in Lemon Grove, Golders Green.

I looked briefly, through the papers and gleaned that he had put down £60,000, and obtained a further £80,000 from the Halifax, to buy a freehold property described by the agents as 'a former gatekeeper's cottage' with a total of four rooms (bedroom, 'parlour', kitchen and bathroom) as well as a basement on a piece of ground in the middle of a road mainly full of semi-detached houses.

The photograph on one of the agency

lists showed a mournfully small cottage of no architectural distinction. The particulars revealed that the house, built around 1855, had small rooms, and was 'in need of substantial modernization'—agent-speak for 'close to collapse'. The price obviously reflected the fact that it was detached, stood on a little plot of ground, and thus had development potential.

I looked at all this in bewilderment. Not only had Murdoch never mentioned anything to me about buying a house, but I couldn't remember him showing even the slightest inclination towards becoming a person of property. He had lived in the same squalid unfurnished flat in Belsize Park where he paid an absurdly low rent, for as long as I had known him, and he had frequently pronounced himself delighted to be living in what he described as the 'working-class end of Hampstead'.

I picked up the telephone and dialled the number for Arnold Mo at the firm of solicitors, and when there was no answer, I looked at my watch. It was nearly six o'clock. I locked the documents in my desk drawer and reached for my jacket.

Downstairs, parked on the double yellow lines as usual, Frankie was getting edgy.

My agreement with him expired every day at six, and he would usually go off and take commercial fares for two or three hours before going home. As if I wasn't paying him enough. I defused the atmosphere immediately.

'Turn on the meter,' I sighed.

He smiled. Frankie was never happier than when the meter was clicking away in his left ear. 'Where to, guv? Home?'

'No, I'm hungry. The Bluebell.'

The famous Bluebell Restaurant in Mayfair was another of my little indulgences. I had once been thrown out of there because my credit card limit had been reached and I had not been able to pay the bill. I hadn't minded being thrown out so much, but what had irritated me was the over-priced food and the snooty treatment I had received even before they found that I couldn't pay. The *maître d'* had tried to put me at the worst table in the house, next to the kitchen door.

So I bought the restaurant. My accountants had protested that the price demanded by the previous owners was too high, but I went ahead anyway, and as soon as the place was mine, I made some dramatic changes. The old manager and *maître d'* were given instant marching orders with golden handshakes just large enough to stop them from suing for wrongful dismissal.

I made one of the smart young waiters, the *maître d'*, and offered the manager's job to a friend of mine, Hazel Cowan. She had previously been a hack on the theatre magazine, *Spotlight*, and knew nothing about food (then) but she had one of those personalities which convinced me that she would be perfect in the place.

I didn't offer her the job personally, you understand, but through Pendleton, who would protect my identity with his life. We offered her an outrageous salary and carte blanche to make whatever changes she wanted—on two conditions. The first was that the menu prices were to be reduced by one-third across the board, and that staff salaries were to be increased by one-third. The staff were also told that half the annual profits would be added to their salaries in the form of an annual bonus with a special bonus to the chefs for each year they managed to retain the three Michelin rosettes.

Hazel hesitated seriously for about four microseconds before accepting the job, and even my accountants had to admit within a few months that we were on to a winner. She attacked the old-fashioned stuffiness of the place, swept away the traditional cobwebs and, backed by a startled and suddenly highly motivated staff had transformed the restaurant into *the* place to eat in London. Her numerous contacts in the theatre world also hadn't done the place any harm at all.

Profits came rolling in from the rich and famous, went straight into the coffers of the Edwina Llewellyn Memorial Trust, which distributed it to those who most needed it. Talk about the redistribution of wealth!

'I dunno how you can afford to eat here so often,' she said, grinning at me when I walked in that evening. She was a bouncy, slightly overweight lady with a lot of fluffy hair, who knew precisely how much creamy white bosom to reveal and still look classy.

'It's all a question of priorities, Hazel. Other divorced men spend money on expensive cars and fast women. I have no need for either.'

No matter how booked up the restaurant was, Hazel always kept a table free for odd friends and important people who might turn up unannounced, so it was rare that she would have to turn me away.

'Bullshit. You're a horny old goat. I've seen some of the women you bring here,' she said.

'I sincerely resent your use of the word "old".'

'You're thirty-five, right?'

'That is correct.'

'Then you're old in my book. Not that you aren't a bit sexy, mind you. You are. Sexy and old.'

It was true that my birthday cake would never again display thirty-five candles. I had thought that very old until a few weeks before when Arnie Bloch, who was pushing fifty, had looked at me with arrogant pity in his eyes.

'Jeez man, Parker, you missed the 'sixties!'

Well, I hadn't really missed the 'sixties. I mean, I was there, even if I was only five years old when the first Beatles record made number one, and was eleven when Woodstock went down. But I knew what he meant, and it had hurt.

Most of the tables in the restaurant were

in use but everything appeared to be well under control, so I asked Hazel to join me for dinner. Her eyes narrowed.

'This is not just a ruse to get me into bed with you, is it.'

'It could be.'

'Well, it could work,' she said, 'as long as you don't get too tired.'

'Tired? Me? C'mon, Hazel, they don't call me marathon man for nothing, you know.' I think I must have looked a little defensive.

'I didn't mean in bed, you prat! I'm talking about staying up late. I never get away from here before about two o'clock in the morning.'

Well, that put the lid on that potential night of passion. I contented myself with telling Hazel about my long hard day getting fired and then having to cover the murder of a friend who then posthumously sent me a letter. All this while I was eating my favourite dish: pig's trotter stuffed with sweetbreads, washed down with expensive Pouilly Fumé.

When I left she kissed me on the cheek and whispered, 'Good night, marathon man.' I felt like an ass, and caught a taxi home.

Lying in bed, something occurred to me, and I began to worry about it. Where the hell had Murdoch Finnegan got hold of £60,000 to put down on that house?

## CHAPTER 5

Thursday mornings are a mixture of tension and relief at the *Hampstead Explorer*. For the first hour or so there are last-minute changes being made before the paper goes to bed. Errors on proofs are corrected and occasionally a late-breaking story is inserted.

I checked with a rather tetchy Theo Bernstein at the police station that nothing new had come up on the murder investigation, and with some of the other police stations to make sure that nothing important had happened overnight.

Then when the final pages had gone, the whole mood changed to one of relaxed preparation for the week to come. Wastebins were filled with the formerly vital notes and pieces of paper which created that week's hot news, letters lazily opened, contacts calmly telephoned, appointments made, and the fat chewed in the vicinity of the coffee machine.

Not me, though. Having been fired only the day before for not doing any work, I was eager to appear busy. I picked up the telephone and called Arnold Mo of Mo, Murphy and Forbes, Murdoch's solicitors.

I was expecting a Chinese accent, but I was mistaken. Arnold Mo came on the line with a perfect public schoolboy drawl and, of course, knew who I was immediately. I asked some questions, and there was a slight pause.

'Are you the sort of journalist that takes people out to lunch?' he inquired, ever so politely. 'I mean with an expense account and all that?'

'It has been known to happen,' I answered, although the truth was that the most expensive lunch Arnie Bloch would ever sanction was a cheese roll in a cheap pub.

'In that case,' Mo went on, 'I'm free for lunch today, and there's a lovely little restaurant in Farringdon Road called the Quality Chop House which serves the best bangers and mash in London.'

The thought of bangers and mash did not appeal to me, but a happy Mr Mo did, so I agreed to meet him there at one o'clock.

Then I telephoned Pendleton. 'What can you tell me about Mo, Murphy and Forbes?' I asked him.

'Ethically sound, professionally competent, but very unpopular in the business,' he said.

'How come?'

'Four or five young solicitors, very left wing, lots of legal aid work, race relations, industrial tribunals, damages against the police. That sort of thing.'

'So why are they unpopular?'

'They are also one of the few firms ready to take on cases from clients wanting to sue other solicitors for negligence.'

'Ah,' I said. 'Sounds like the sort of firm I would use. If I didn't already have you, that is.' The last sentence was added hastily.

'Nice of you to say so,' Pendleton said, a little drily, I thought.

I put down the telephone and looked up to find Arnie Bloch filling the doorway. He had interrupted progress through a cheese Danish to heap praise on my report of

54

Murdoch Finnegan's murder.

'Your story was OK,' he muttered. That was heaped praise.

'Thanks, Arnie.'

'Don't thank me. Thank Finnegan. Otherwise you would've stayed fiyad.'

My telephone rang. It was Rosemary, the receptionist downstairs.

'There's a Mr Wallace here to see you. Says you know him,' she said.

I didn't know any Mr Wallaces. 'Does he have a first name?'

A few seconds later she said, 'Albert Wallace,' and then she added in a whisper, 'Mr Parker, I think he's drunk.'

'In that case, tell him I don't know him and ask him to go away.'

'He says you might know him as Wheezy.'

Indeed I did. 'Ah, Wheezy Wallis. Can he walk?'

'Well, he walked in here,' she whispered.

'OK, send him up. Let's see if he'll make it up the stairs.'

Contrary to the implications of his nickname, Wheezy Wallis was not asthmatic. He was, not to put too fine a point on it, a professional burglar whose slight physical stature and legendary ability to squirm his way into tightly locked houses and offices had resulted in him being dubbed 'The Weasel'. Over time that had been corrupted to the affectionate and alliterative Wheezy.

He was a cheerful and popular little chap, not averse to buying a round for his friends and associates, and apparently successful in his chosen career, even if he did periodically disappear from the scene as a guest of Her Majesty for varying periods of time. He was one of my network of informants, ever ready to drop a name or a piece of gossip for the odd tenner or twenty here and there. But not on all subjects, mind you. He regarded himself as a hard-working traditional criminal, preying only off people who had more than he believed they ought to have, and he had no time for the breed who dealt in drugs, prostitution and extortion.

But he wasn't looking cheerful when he walked into my office that morning and lowered himself shakily into the chair opposite my desk.

'Parker,' he said by way of greeting.

'Wheezy,' I responded cleverly. Then I added: 'I've never seen you pissed at eleven o'clock in the morning before.'

'Yeah,' he said, 'I'm really sick.'

'Have you been to a doctor?'

'No, not that kind of sick. I woz stung.'

'Bee, wasp?'

'No, conned. We woz all conned.'

'By whom?'

'I dunno.'

I could see this was going to be a complicated interview, so I got up and shut the door of my office. That was a sign that I shouldn't be disturbed, and it would be respected, even by Arnie.

'OK, Wheezy, tell me the story.'

He fished about in his jacket pocket and then handed me a tape cassette. 'You got a tape-recorder?' I nodded. 'Well, listen to that for a start.'

I slipped the ordinary-looking cassette into my little portable recorder and switched it on. For a few seconds there was just a hissing noise, and then a deep gravelly voice with a faint Irish accent came on.

The voice said: 'Newcastle, number four, April four. First, special offer, second, Carlton dancer.' There was a muffled sound to the voice, as if whatever machine it had been recorded on had not been working properly. Then the hissing came back.

'That's it,' said Wheezy. 'That's all there is.'

'What does it mean?' I asked patiently. I switched off the recorder.

'Horses. They're the names of horses. That's first and second in the fourth race at Newcastle on April the fourth. Special Offer and Carlton Dancer, one and two, just like he said.'

'You're going to have to start at the beginning. I don't know what the hell you're talking about. Hang on,' I said, and I went out to get him a large mug of black coffee.

I can't say it sobered him up immediately, but after a few minutes he began making more sense. He took a deep breath.

'It was about a month ago, Friday night, this big Irish geezer comes into the pub—' I knew which pub he meant; one of those places in Kentish Town with sawdust on the floor where nice people or honest policemen do not feel at home—'and 'e buys a few drinks and starts talking to some of the boys.

'Anyroad, after a while 'e asks if there's anyone wants to make some serious cash.

58

Now, as you can imagine there is a certain amount of interest in that kind of proposition. The fellas gather round, although they're a suspicious bunch, and everyone has a sharp eye out for the con.

'But 'e don't ask anyone for any money or anything like that. 'E just pulls out this cassette, and a big brown envelope 'E puts the cassette in the envelope and then licks the glue and closes it. Then 'e gets us all to sign our names across the seal, which about six of us do. Then 'e sort of folds the envelope around the cassette, and winds sticky tape around it so it's well wrapped up. And then 'e gives it to Ferdie, the barman, and says, "You got a safe?" As it 'appens, there is a safe in the office and Ferdie nods, so the geezer says, "You go and put that in your safe. Two weeks tonight I come back and we'll listen to it."

'Well, the guys ask some questions and that, but 'e's not answering. 'All will be explained in due course. See you in two weeks,' and 'e's gone.

'As you can imagine, the matter causes a certain amount of interest in the community, and when 'e comes back two weeks later, there is a bigger than normal crowd in the boozer. At first we think 'e's not coming, but then he comes in about ten o'clock, with one of those ghetto blasters, you know, a radio cassette thing with two speakers, which he puts up on the bar.

' 'E says to Ferdie: "You had any break-ins?" No. "Anyone been in your safe?" No. "OK, let's have it out, then." So Ferdie goes off and gets the parcel. When 'e comes back the Irish geezer, who says his name's McGuire, suggests we check it over, see if it's the same one, with our signatures on and all, and whether it's been interfered with. So we look at it, and no question it's the one, exactly as it was when it went in the safe. No way anyone could have opened it without tearing the paper. Anyway, so we tear it open—'

'Did he handle the cassette?' I interrupted.

'No, that's the thing, 'e didn't go bloody near it.'

'And this Ferdie the barman, you trust him?' I asked.

'With my life. Ferdie's one of us. 'E's married to a cousin of mine. Anyway, I was the one took it out of the envelope, and 'e says to me, "Put it in the machine," which I did. Then I pressed the play button, and we 'eard what you just 'eard.' Wheezy paused.

'And?'

'And it was the correct result of the fourth race at Newcastle on the Saturday, a week AFTER he gave us the tape to put in the safe.'

'Wow,' I said.

'Yeah, we were well impressed, I can tell you. But the guys are still suspicious, and no one is exactly reaching into their wallets. This McGuire guy explains that he has this 'source', a friend of 'is who every now and then gets wind of an absolutely sure bet. Not very often, mind you, but every now and then.'

'So how come he's not a millionaire?' I asked.

'That's exactly what we asked 'im, and 'e says that 'e's skint, doesn't have enough money to put on a worthwhile bet, and in any case, until now 'e's not been sure enough about the accuracy of the source to risk the little bread 'e has. What 'e's after, 'e says, is some partners with enough stake money to make a few big hits, where 'e can take a few points on the winnings

61

for providing the information.'

'Points?'

'You know, a percentage. We're still well suspicious but some of the guys ask 'im if 'e's heard anything about the races the next day. No, 'e says, 'e doesn't have anything, but 'e's expecting to hear from 'is source later that night, and if anyone wants to put up some cash, 'e'll be happy to take it, listen to what 'is man says, and put the money on the correct horses. 'E'll bring the winnings over the next night, 'e says.

'Naturally, the boys laugh at 'im. They don't know how it works, but they can smell the whiff of a con and they aren't going to trust any Irishman that they've never heard of before to walk out of the bar with any of their dosh. Except for Whiskey Robinson.'

'Who?

'You know, Len Robinson, 'e's a blagger out of Kentish Town. Call him Whiskey 'cause 'e's pissed 'alf the time. Anyway, 'e rushed out and came back about half an hour later with five 'undred quid, in cash.'

'I don't believe this!'

'Straight up, Mr P. We all thought 'e was crazy, and we told 'im so, but

Whiskey's pissed as a newt, and a bit crazy anyway since 'is wife snuffed it. 'E gives McGuire the money and, whoosh, the geezer's out of the door. We never thought we would see 'im again.'

'And?'

'You're not going to believe this, but the guy walks back into the boozer the next night, with a grin all over 'is face. We'd been sitting there telling Whiskey to wave goodbye, to 'is bread, and every single one of us is gobsmacked. But there's nothing compared with our reaction a minute later. The guy's got a briefcase, and 'e pulls out ten grand, in fifties, and hands it to Whiskey.'

'Ten thousand pounds?' There was incredulity in my voice.

'Yeah, well, we couldn't believe it either. 'E says 'is tip was for a double on two nags in a race in some place in Ireland that we'd never heard of, and 'e'd managed to get just over twenny to one odds, which 'e'd spread around the bookies. I tell you, we were all sittin' there like Jesus Christ 'imself just walked in the door, with the Holy Ghost an' all. Anyway, this McGuire tells Whiskey that 'e wants two grand for 'is ten point cut, and of course Whiskey gives it to 'im right away.'

'Was the money good, I mean was it counterfeit?' I asked.

'C'mon, Parker, there were at least three good forgers there that night. That stuff came straight from the Old Lady herself.'

'Old Lady?'

'Of Threadneedle Street. The Bank of England.'

'Oh. What happened then?'

'Pandemonium! There's loads of guys trying to get 'im to place bets for them, wanting to hand 'im wads of cash—and 'e's refusing!'

'Refusing?'

' 'E says no, for Christ's sake! 'E says 'e doesn't need it any more. 'E's got 'is stake from 'is cut off the ten grand, and 'e's not looking for anyone else to risk their dosh. But now we're not having that, are we? The guy has given us a taste of big money, which we are convinced is on the up and up, and no one's going to let a golden goose like that walk out of the door for ever. Some of the guys are getting heavy with 'im, suggesting that 'e might not walk out of the door in one piece unless 'e agrees to place more bets for us.

'Finally 'e agrees. What choice does 'e

have? People go rushing off to pick up their cash, and the next thing there's a bloody queue in the back room with McGuire writing down the names and amounts in a little book, and stuffing the bread into 'is briefcase.

'I tell you, Parker, there must have been more than thirty grand in that briefcase when 'e left. Must have been about fifty or more guys pushing money at 'im, handing 'im wads of notes.'

'How much did you give him?'

'Eight hundred. Then we were all sittin' there laughing, talking about how we were going to spend the dosh. Must have been about an hour before we began to feel sick about it. Once we calmed down we knew we'd been done. We didn't know the guy's address, we had no idea where 'e'd gone. Some of the guys went out to try and find him, but of course it was 'opeless. We never saw 'im again.'

'He made an instant profit of twenty thousand on his ten thousand investment,' I ventured. 'He was good.'

'The best I ever saw ' Wheezy said ruefully. 'And it was twenny-two grand, including the cut 'e took back from Whiskey. I dunno how 'e pulled that tape-recorder stunt, but that was nothing to the way 'e played us. I mean, the guy sat there for ten minutes refusing to take anyone's loot until we bloody forced 'im to do it. 'E knew exactly when to start taking the money, and exactly when to leave before the excitement faded.

'I've been hitting the bottle ever since. Wife's giving me bloody murder, screaming that she's got no money for the housekeeping and the kids, and the way I am at the moment I couldn't break a beer bottle let alone carry off a B & E, could I?'

Wheezy was less shaky now, and the coffee had clearly helped him sober up a little. Getting the tale off his chest had also clearly improved his state of mind.

'Presumably no one has gone to the police about this?' I asked.

'Come off it, Parker, you know how it is. I mean, with who we were, and the fact that not a fiver in that pile was known about by the taxman, no one was reporting anything to the Bill.'

'So why come to me?'

'Well, we thought you should put this in the paper, no names and places, mind you, to warn other people about this geezer. Maybe someone will catch 'im at it, but I doubt it. 'E's long gone from here by now.'

I sent Wheezy away with a promise that the scam would be written up in the paper—it was, after all, a great story—and with a recommendation that he apply to the Edwina Llewellyn Memorial Trust for some money to give to the wife and kids. I told him to mention my name. I also gave him twenty quid which he promised not to spend on alcohol.

Then Frankie drove me down to Farringdon Road and my lunch date with Arnold Mo.

# CHAPTER 6

Arnold Mo turned out to be Chinese after all, and the Quality Chop House was a delightful restaurant—an old working men's caff where only the menu and food had been changed. The woodwork, benches, tables, signs on the wall and shopfront had all been left charmingly intact.

They did indeed serve bangers and

mash, egg and chips and sausages of all descriptions, but in a manner which ensured that the place was packed with City gents and more than a sprinkling of journalists from the *Guardian*'s building across the road. The bangers, for example, were from Toulouse.

Mo was a breezy little chap who wafted in about five minutes after I got there, stood at the door and called 'Parker?'

When I waved he came over and stuck out his hand. 'Arnold Mo, short for Moshinsky. Ha ha.' I laughed politely with him. He ordered more food than his slight frame could possibly encompass, mineral water and a very expensive bottle of wine. Then he put his hands behind his head, and took a deep breath while looking around.

'I say,' he said in his plummy accent, which I was beginning to be suspicious of, 'it really is good of you to treat me like this! Most of my clients can't afford to buy me a sandwich.'

'I'm not one of your clients,' I reminded him.

'Well, no, of course you aren't. But your name has cropped up so often that I feel as if you are,' he said.

'Where has my name cropped up?'

'In our dealings with Murdoch Finnegan, and particularly in the last few months.'

'I don't understand any of this,' I said to Mo. 'I was one of his clients once, and we had a passing relationship, but I was never very close to him and I don't believe that he regarded me as one of his close friends, so how come my name kept cropping up?'

'You're right, he didn't regard you as a close friend, but he did describe you as extremely honest and reliable. He told me that you were one of the only people in London that he would really trust.'

'What about you? Didn't he trust you?'

'I never asked him that. Not my place, you see.'

'Oh,' I said. 'Anyway, what can you tell me about that envelope you sent me?'

'Nothing.' I looked at him blankly until he went on: 'I have no idea what was inside the envelope. All we did was carry out his instructions to send it to you in the event of his death or incapacity.'

'You know nothing about a house in Golders Green?'

'Aah. I didn't say that. I know quite a lot about a house in Golders Green. Am I to assume that the envelope contained the documents relating to the house in Lemon Grove?'

'It did,' I replied.

'In that case, let me press on with something else I need to tell you. Finnegan left you that house in his will. It's yours now.'

The food arrived at just that moment, and Arnold Mo set about shovelling great mounds of mashed potatoes, egg, chips, sausages, beans and slices of bread into his mouth. My own mouth remained inactive. It was open and immobile.

My entire life until a year before had been spent without the expectation of any inheritance. Even when my parents had died, it had almost cost me more to cart away the contents of their little rented house than they had been worth. Most of it went to junk shops, and the personal items that I kept weren't worth anything at all. Then within the space of a year Edwina Llewellyn leaves me a fortune, and Murdoch Finnegan leaves me his house.

I was more than astonished. Was I becoming something of a professional inheritor? Was there something about me which made casual acquaintances and friends reach for their wills when they saw me? How long would this go on? Would I be forced to advertise in the newspapers: 'Horatio Parker would like to inform his friends and acquaintances that he is already more than adequately provided for and need not, therefore, be considered as a recipient of any further bequests'?

'Wait a minute,' I said, finally. 'Start at the beginning. Tell me what you know about Finnegan.'

Mo stopped shovelling food for a moment, and looked at me. 'Not all that much, really. He became a client of the firm about ten years ago, before I joined, anyway. He used the services of my partners who deal with court and criminal work.'

'Not you?'

'No, I deal with contract matters, house conveyancing, wills, that sort of thing.'

'Go on.'

'Well, if you know anything about Finnegan, you will know that he was constantly getting into trouble. Not that he was dishonest but, you know, he was always getting into scrapes of one sort or another.'

'I know,' I said.

'Yes, well he occasionally needed to be bailed out of police cells, and he frequently needed legal advice about subpoenas, writs, and various actions for damages issued against him by the objects of his attentions.

'I became involved with him a few months ago when he bought the house in Golders Green. I did the conveyancing. And then a few weeks later he asked me to do his will. He left you the house, and everything else to his parents in America.'

'Did he give you any idea why he was leaving it to me?'

'No. As a matter of fact, I actually asked him, but he was evasive, and said something about you knowing how to deal with things, but when I tried to get him to expand on that he clammed up. Became quite short and irritable, and told me just to do what he asked. Perhaps he intended to explain it all to me, but in the end he didn't have time.'

'Did he seem nervous, as if he feared for his life or even that he expected to die soon?'

Mo hesitated for a few seconds. 'Not exactly.'

'What does that mean?'

'Well, he seemed tense about things, and insisted that the will be drawn up quickly, but he gave no impression that he was worried about anything specific.'

'What do you know about the house?'

'Nothing more than was turned up by the surveyor and local authority and land registry searches. It was built some years before the other houses in the road, and it seems to have been a gatekeeper's cottage for an estate which predates the general development of the land. It's very small, unmodernized, and needs a lot of work.'

'Who owned it before?'

'The vendor was a deceased estate. A Mrs Maureen Baker had lived there for many years as the freeholder. Apparently she had been a retired housekeeper or governess or something old-fashioned like that. Her will had instructed that the house be sold and the proceeds, together with the rest of her estate, was bequeathed to various charities, chiefly the National Society for the Prevention of Cruelty to Children, the NSPCC. She had no relatives that anyone knew about. The house had been on the market for some months, and Mr Finnegan bought it at auction—for a very reasonable figure, we thought, despite the age and condition of the house. The land alone was worth what he paid.'

'Where did he get the £60,000 he put down?'

'I haven't the faintest idea. And, before you ask, no, I did not ask him where he got it. It was absolutely none of our business.'

Despite the conversation, his plate was empty. Mine was almost untouched. 'Are you using that sausage?' he asked. I shook my head and he speared it deftly with his fork, leaving a neat hole in the mashed potato.

'So now it's mine,' I said. The house, I meant, not the sausage.

'Yes. Well, there are certain legal formalities, the whole process of probate and registration and all that but, essentially, yes, it's yours. We'll need the name of your solicitors to arrange some of the legal details.'

I gave him Ambrose Pendleton's name and address, and then asked: 'Can I go and see the place? Where can I get some keys?'

He put his hand in his pocket and pulled out a little ring with three keys on it. 'Here you go. Finnegan left these spares with us. I can't see any reason why you shouldn't have them and go and look at the place. It's not as if anyone is living there. Just don't do any damage or start work there before the legal processes are complete.' He handed me the keys.

Mo proceeded to have a rice pudding dessert while I nibbled at a fruit salad and drank a cup of black coffee. I found I was holding the keys tightly in my left hand, almost as if warming them might induce them to impart information to me, a message from Murdoch Finnegan perhaps, explaining this whole perplexing business.

Having eaten enough to fell a horse and having consumed most of the bottle of wine, Arnold Mo remained as sprightly as ever. At two o'clock he jumped up, displaying not the slightest bulge on his dark-suited abdomen. He took his leave of me as briskly as he had arrived and disappeared through the door. I ordered a cognac and sat thinking for a few minutes. But nothing made any sense.

Frankie was in his taxi, buried deep in a book called *Psycho-motor Factors in*

*Behavioural Conditioning.* I used the cab's telephone to check in with Arnie Bloch, who snorted when I told him I was working on the Finnegan murder and would not be back in the office that afternoon. But he didn't protest. Thursday afternoon was a quiet time on the *Hampstead Explorer,* and even Arnie was known to relax a little.

I asked Frankie to head for Hampstead police station, and on the way I turned my mind to the incidents recounted to me that morning by poor old Wheezy Wallis.

It was without doubt a great con, but I couldn't figure out how this McGuire person had worked the tape-recorder trick. Wheezy had been positive that the tape inserted into the cassette recorder had been the same one left there the week before, and he had been equally adamant that the man had not touched it. Wheezy himself had taken it out of the sealed envelope, inserted it into the machine and pressed the play button, so that ruled out the possibility of the con artist switching the tape for one he had brought with him.

So how had he managed to forecast the winners of the horse race so accurately—a week before the race? The more I thought about it, the more I became convinced that it had something to do with the tape machine he had brought with him.

We were going up Tottenham Court Road and I asked Frankie to make a little detour into Goodge Street, where someone I knew had a small electronics shop.

Mohan Mistry had a small business behind one of those shop windows packed with doodahs which had meaning only for those with an advanced degree in electronics. He made a very good living reconditioning and upgrading used computers and other electronic equipment, and he owed me a favour.

Someone had started daubing his windows with racial abuse and sending him threatening letters of the 'Piss off Paki' variety—a message all the more absurd since Mohan was a Hindu from Mauritius. Finally, a brick had been thrown through the window with a death threat wrapped around it with a rubber band.

Holborn police had expressed sympathy and made some perfunctory inquiries, but came up with nothing. Then Mohan came to me at the *Explorer*, and I had put Murdoch Finnegan on the case. And for once, he hadn't screwed up.

Murdoch had waited patiently in the

back of his little panel van for nine nights until the spray can artist had finally appeared early one morning. Murdoch filmed him at work with a video camera with a special low-light intensifier (supplied by Mohan, of course) and then followed him for two blocks to his car, the registration number of which was also filmed.

We promptly handed the evidence over to the police who established the perpetrator was the proprietor of a rival electronics shop in nearby Whitfield Street —another Asian man. A raid on the shop later that day revealed a back room filled with stolen television sets and video recorders, and that had been the end of Mohan's ordeal—and much of his competition. It had also made a very good story for the *Explorer*.

When I walked in that afternoon Mohan beamed at me and instantly stopped work on what looked to me like an omelette of circuit boards, chips and other components.

He listened carefully to what I had to say, asked a few questions along the lines of the ones I had already asked myself, looked thoughtful, and said he would think about it.

Then he sold me a gizmo to connect to the expansion port of my computer which, he said, would double the memory and the speed of my machine.

When I got back to the cab I gave the gizmo to Frankie. My computer was already too fast for my liking.

# CHAPTER 7

Inspector Theo Bernstein was never pleased to see me. Perhaps it had something to do with that time I had told him there was to be an armed robbery at a post office in Willesden—information I had received through Wheezy Wallis, who disapproved of anyone who carried guns.

Scores of police had been drafted in, most armed to the teeth, and an operation of monumental proportions had been mounted involving officers pretending to be road diggers, newspaper vendors and the like. As a special favour, in return for the information, I had been allowed to witness the whole thing.

We had all hung about until bank

closing time on the coldest day of the year, all of us slowly turning into blocks of ice—as the robbery went down entirely unmolested by police, two miles away in Harlesden. Not Willesden.

My protestations that I had only been wrong by the small matter of one syllable had not redeemed my stock, and although I had subsequently forced Theo to agree never to refer to the incident again, it nevertheless felt as if he relived his personal humiliation resulting from the incident every time he laid eyes on me.

'What is it, now, Parker?' he said when I was finally shown into his office.

'Hello, Theo,' I said chirpily, sitting down in his visitor's chair.

'OK. Hello, Parker. Now what do you want?'

'I have some information for you about the Finnegan case.'

Theo closed his eyes and took two deep breaths. 'It seems to me that I have warned you on a number of occasions about interfering in police murder investigations. "Take care not to pervert justice, for by so doing you shake the world." '

'Is that from the Talmud or the Met Police handbook?'

80

'What do you think?'

'What I think,' I said quietly, 'is that you are neglecting to remember that without my "interference", as you call it, in the Karabekian case, you would never have solved the murder.' The fact that that was true, and he knew it, let me win this little confrontation hands down.

'All right then, what is it?' he sighed.

'You have to agree to something first.'

'Oh yes? Like what, pray?'

'I want to look around Finnegan's flat.'

'What for?' There was a suspicious tone in his voice.

'Background. For my story. It wouldn't do any harm, Theo. Your scene of crime and forensic people must be finished with the place by now and in any case I'm not going to disturb anything. I just want some journalistic colour.'

'And in return for this you are offering...?' The question hung in the air. So I told him about the letter from Mo, Murphy and Forbes, showed him the documents about the house in Golders Green, and recounted my meeting with Arnold Mo.

'He left you a house in his will?' Theo sounded incredulous. I didn't blame him; I was still finding it hard to believe myself.

'Apparently so,' I said.

'We knew nothing about this house,' he said.

'So I see. But presumably you will want to look at it?'

'As soon as possible. There could be something there which would explain why he was murdered. Do you know who has the keys?'

I dangled them from my finger. 'We can go now, if you like. I have a cab waiting outside.'

'It's not just me, you nitwit. Chief Superintendent Harrison will want to go, and we'll need some of the lab people again.'

'Well, I'll meet you there, then,' I said.

'In about half an hour. But Parker...' There was a tough edge on his voice.

'Yes?'

'Don't even think of going in before we get there.'

'Of course not. Theo.'

It was about four o'clock when we all met up in Lemon Grove. Theo and the Chief Super had arrived in a smart Rover, closely followed by a van full of men in overalls who emerged carrying various holdalls and bags for their equipment.

I was with Frankie, of course, and the *Explorer*'s photographer, who got a lovely shot of the police all trooping through the front gate in an orderly line. Harrison had greeted me unenthusiastically, clearly unhappy at my presence, but obviously unable to do anything about it since I was holding the keys.

From the outside, the house was not impressive. It was a rather square and unadorned early Victorian cottage without any detail or features to break the monotony of its workmanlike lines, standing on its own in the middle of a small plot of ground. There was only one storey, a pitched roof with uneven-looking tiles, and two chimneys with blackened chimney pots sticking up in the middle.

The area around the house appeared to be completely neglected and was knee- and even waist-high in places with tangled weeds, woody shrubs and prickly brambles which had clearly been growing without hindrance for years. But around the perimeter of the plot, with a break only for the front gate, someone had planted a dense hedge, now perhaps twenty years old and eight or nine feet high, which did a very effective job of screening the house from its neighbours and the road, and vice versa.

The short path from the gate to the front door had, however, been kept clear, although recent neglect had allowed some young weeds to begin taking hold in the cracks between the slabs of York stone.

The key ring contained two worn Yale keys and a more modern mortice key. The second Yale key I tried unlocked the front door, and I stood back to let the police enter first. Five or six men clumped into the house, their boots ringing on the bare wooden floor. One or two others were picking their way through the weeds and brambles, having a look at the outside of the house, and Theo had sent a further two PCs to talk to the neighbours.

I waited impatiently for about two minutes before Harrison reappeared.

'Nothing,' he said succinctly. 'You can come in.'

'Nothing' was not an understatement. The house was completely bare. From the tiny hallway there were doors to the left and right. The one on the left led to a small sitting-room with another door leading to the kitchen at the back of the house. The door to the right off the hall led to a bedroom and then a tiny bathroom next to the kitchen.

Each room, including the bathroom, had a small fireplace, obviously well used, and there was no sign of any other form of heating. The kitchen had a deep stone sink and an ancient coal-burning Aga-type cooker with a large chimney flue and thick pipes leading to what looked like a small zinc hot water cylinder mounted on the common wall with the bathroom.

There was no furniture at all. Here and there were worn places on the floor along frequently used routes, and the walls displayed a few squares and rectangular patches where the dingy wallpaper was slightly less faded. There were also a few marks on the floorboards to denote the positions of beds, tables and the odd cupboard, but otherwise there was nothing of any interest.

There was also no sign of Murdoch Finnegan's ownership, and no clue as to why he might have bought the house. Someone with more money than Finnegan could have modernized the place and, with a little imagination, turned it into a rather cute studio house—although any smart operator would have demolished it instantly and applied for planning permission for a block of flats covering the entire piece of land.

It was Theo who found the door leading down to the basement. It was behind a heavy padded draught curtain in a gloomy corner of the kitchen. It was a sturdy-looking door, which I unlocked with the mortice key on my bunch, and again the police went in ahead of me. But after another minute or so, they called me down the steep wooden staircase.

It was a medium-sized cellar, stretching under the entire house, and properly dug out so that the ceiling was at normal height. The light came from a single bulb hanging from a flex in the middle of the room, but there was also some light coming from a sort of skylight at the back of the house, beneath the back wall of the kitchen. The floor was concrete. There was also a black coal stove down there, with its chimney disappearing up through the ceiling approximately where I estimated the kitchen stove would be.

'Look at the walls,' Theo said. 'That's modern brickwork, nineteen-sixties or 'seventies, I'd say.'

'Probably some kind of workroom,'

muttered Harrison.

When we went back upstairs, there were some technicians dusting here and there for fingerprints, but without an obvious enthusiasm. Someone else was bagging little samples of dust from each room.

After a few minutes the two who had been sent round the outside of the house reported that they had found nothing at all of any interest, and then the two scouts who had been sent to talk to neighbours returned.

'Most of 'em didn't know anything at all, guv,' one of them reported to Harrison. 'Couple of people knew this Mrs Baker woman slightly. Said she lived 'ere on her own for donkey's years. Never seemed to go out much, never caused any trouble. You know, nothing really. Woman over there—' he pointed across the road—'said the doctor used to come and see her every now and then. That's it.'

After that the police quickly lost interest and left. I hung around for another fifteen minutes or so, poking around and trying to absorb the atmosphere of the place, hoping that the reason Murdoch Finnegan had bought the house—and then left it to me—might permeate through to me. But nothing happened. The longer I stayed, the more depressing I found it.

And besides, there was a strange and rather unpleasant musty smell about the cellar which reminded me of something, except that I couldn't put my finger on exactly what it was.

# CHAPTER 8

I got back to the office at about five o'clock, and I went straight in to see Arnie. I told him that I thought something extremely odd was going on.

'Yes, I know,' he said. 'There's reporters around there who mess about in taxis all day and never write anything.'

I ignored that, and told him about Arnold Mo, the bequest and what we had found or, rather, not found, at the house. That shut him up. Or maybe it was the chocolate chip cookie in his mouth. Either way, he did not reply, so I continued.

'I think I had better spend some time on all this, Arnie.'

He sighed, swallowed most of the

biscuit, and looked at me with a kind of weary expression. 'OK, Parker, spend some time on it, which of course means that we are not going to see you for days on end, but just make sure we get something good out of it in the end.'

'Arnie, have I ever let you down?'

'Yes.'

I could have asked, 'When?' but I decided to quit while I was vaguely ahead, and I went back to my office, where there was a message on my desk to telephone Alex. That was code for Ambrose Pendleton, lest anyone in the office should become suspicious that I was in communication with the man who appeared to run Golden Daffodils Limited, which owned the *Explorer*.

I rang his private line.

'You just caught me,' he said. 'I have heard from Miss McDuff.'

'Miss McWho?'

'McDuff, the hotel expert I told you about. You wanted her to spend a night at the Chalk Farm Hotel and report on it, remember? It seems she went there last night, and she is ready to report. How do you want me to handle this?'

'I'll handle it. Just give me her telephone number.'

The number he gave me was for a mobile phone and, there being no time like the present for doing things, I dialled it. A woman answered.

'Is that Ms McDuff?'

'Who wants to know?' She had one of those throaty voices with a slightly breathy sound, as if she was leaking air a little, and its effect on me was vaguely disconcerting for reasons I could not instantly pin down. She did not sound like Eartha Kitt exactly, but it was in that sort of direction.

'Do you smoke?' I asked. Well, I had intended just to think that, but apparently I actually said it. The answer was that distinctive peeeeeeeeeep that one hears when someone presses the 'end' button on a mobile phone, the modern equivalent of slamming the phone down. I sighed, called myself an idiot, and dialled the number again. This time the answer was hostile.

'Yes?'

'Ms McDuff, please forgive me, let's start again. My name is Parker, and it is I who asked Ambrose Pendleton to commission a report from you on the Chalk Farm Hotel.'

'Aah, why didn't you say so?'

'I'm an idiot.'

'So it would seem. Well, what can I do for you?'

'You can send me your report.'

'No, I can't.'

'Why not?'

'There isn't one to send.'

'Aah. Well, how about giving me a verbal report, then?'

'Not now.'

'Not now?'

'No, I'm in the bath.' I had nothing to say to that, although I thought some things, and after a few seconds, she continued: 'You could buy me dinner, though, I'm not doing anything tonight. Bring your wife.'

'I don't have a wife. And why should I buy you dinner?'

'I would have thought that someone contemplating buying a hotel should be able to afford the odd dinner,' she replied. There was some logic in that.

'OK, how about the Bluebell?' I suggested. If I was going to have to pay for an expensive dinner, the least I could do was ensure that the profits went to the deserving poor.

'Now you're talking. How about we

meet at eight in that pub in Mayfair called the Slug and Lettuce?'

'How will I recognize you?' I asked.

'Well, I'm about five eleven, with lots of blonde hair, and I have the sort of figure people describe as 'statuesque'. And I'll have a rose clenched in my teeth.' The image was an intriguing one. She went on: 'And you? How will I know you?'

'I'm about a foot shorter than you, rather plain and very pale, a bit pasty even, and I have the sort of body that makes people want to kick sand at me on beaches. Oh, and I've got acne. And one leg shorter than the other.' That was ever such a small lie. Actually I'm five eleven tall, quite nicely built, and there have been women who quite liked the classic ruggedness of my profile.

'I think I might just spot you in the crowd,' she said.

I telephoned Hazel at the Bluebell to make a reservation, and I got Frankie to drive me home. It was nearly six o'clock when we got there, and since I would need him to drive me to Mayfair, I asked him to put on the meter while I showered and changed. He would note the fare in a little red book he kept in the cab, add a fifteen per cent tip, and present me with a bill for extras as the end of each month. No wonder he could afford to have both his kids at private school.

I had never heard of the Slug and Lettuce, but Frankie knew where it was, of course, and we got there just before eight. I immediately wondered whether the name was as clever as it sounded, since there were hardly any customers in the place, and no one I could see was eating salad.

I looked around for a tall, statuesque blonde with a rose clenched between her teeth, and was immediately disappointed. There were two or three couples, a handful of single men at the bar, and a small, pretty woman with dark hair on her own at a table. I parked myself at the bar, ordered a mineral water and swivelled on the stool to face the door, eyes peeled for roses in teeth.

After a few minutes one of the men at the bar, who had clearly been celebrating the end of his working day for some time, drifted over to the pretty brunette, leaned over her table, and asked her something. I couldn't hear what he said, but I assumed he had offered to buy her a drink, because she smiled politely and shook her head.

'Waiting for somebody?' he asked, obviously irritated by the rebuff.

'I'm waiting for you to leave my table,' she replied firmly.

'Hey, I was just trying to be friendly,' he said in that hurt voice that drunks have when they are trying to sound sober and reasonable. But then he made a big mistake. He put his hand on her arm.

Her reaction was unhurried but decisive. She reached over with her right hand, removed his hand from her arm, and then both her hands closed round his wrist. He gasped with sudden pain and dropped to his knees, spluttering. She let go.

'Please go away now,' she said sweetly. The man stumbled to his feet, massaging his wrist, and walked out of the pub, leaving his drink half finished at the bar.

I was impressed. I was also a little puzzled, since there was no mistaking the sound of that slightly husky voice. I went over to her table.

'At the risk of having my arm broken, might I venture to inquire whether you are Ms McDuff?' I asked.

'That's me,' she said. 'And you must be the pasty-faced midget with serious acne and one leg shorter than the other. Sit down,' she invited.

The barman, who had tensed visibly when he saw me approach her table, relaxed and shook his head in that way barmen have of showing that they will never understand women as long as they live.

'Uh, you seem to be a bit short on roses,' I said.

'Sorry about that. It's just that I like to be able to see who I'm dealing with when I arrange to meet strange men in pubs. It gives me a few minutes to size them up, and if I don't like what I see, I can make my escape undetected. What's your excuse?'

'When I arrange to meet tall, beautiful blonde women in pubs, I like to lower their expectations a little so that they are more likely to be impressed by the real me,' I said.

'Well, I can see how that might be necessary,' she said, rather unkindly, I thought.

'Well, now that we have found each other, can I buy you a drink?'

'I already have one, thank you, and if you are going to buy me an expensive wine at the restaurant, I want to be sober enough to enjoy it properly.' Her thinking was logical, if presumptuous.

'So what should I call you?'

'My first name is Samantha.'

'Samantha McDuff. Wow,' I said.

Her reply was a little chilly. 'I don't think that someone with the names Horatio Thorpe should say "wow" about anyone else's names. Ever.'

'You have a point. But how did you find out my first names?'

'I told you, I like to know who I'm dealing with, so I made it my business to find out who you were.'

'Samantha, tell me what you did to that poor man's arm.'

'I pinched a nerve.'

'Show me,' I said bravely, holding out my arm.

'Are you sure?' She had an evil glint in her eye. I nodded and pushed back my cuff.

She put her right hand with her thumb running up the inside of my wrist. Her left hand went round the other side, and I was just thinking that she had lovely hands and a deliciously smooth touch when an indescribable shock of agony shot up my arm. She let go instantly, but my fingers were tingling and I was still a little shaken.

'Ow!' I said weakly. 'Where did you learn to do that?'

'Oh, here and there. I grew up in Glasgow on the wrong side of the tracks, and it is frequently necessary to be able to deal with obstreperous people in the hotel business. And since I am not very large, I decided to learn karate. I'm a black belt.'

'Let's go and eat,' I said, 'I'm terrified of what you might do to me if you get too hungry.'

The Bluebell was only a few blocks away, and we walked there. On the way she took my arm in a very casual and relaxed way, and I was rather surprised at how pleased I was. I found myself looking haughtily at the men we passed, who were flashing admiring but surreptitious glances in Samantha's direction.

At the restaurant I introduced her to Hazel. 'But don't shake her hand,' I warned. 'She'll break your arm.'

'OK, marathon man,' said Hazel quietly as she led us to the best table in the house. I blushed and hoped Ms McDuff had not heard. She gave no sign of having heard, anyway.

I waited until she had put away a delicate and delicious hors d'oeuvre, a terrine of smoked chicken strips, asparagus and truffles in aspic, before I turned to business.

'Tell me about the hotel,' I said.

'It's a mess,' she said.

'So I shouldn't buy it?'

'I didn't say that. I said it was a mess. Messes can be cleaned up.'

'Go on.'

'I'm not a surveyor, but the fabric of the building seems to be in good condition, basically. But it's suffering from neglect. Repairs are not being done, maintenance is not being carried out. The facilities are basically also good, but again there is a problem with maintenance and repair. In the room I stayed in, for example, the air-conditioning was not working correctly, two window-catches were broken, there were cracked tiles in the bathroom, bad stains on the carpet, no hangers in the cupboard and one of the bedside lamps was broken.

'The service was inefficient and disorganized. Room service took nearly half an hour to bring me a cup of tea and the cleaning left a lot to be desired. From speaking to the maid this morning, I learned that she has too many rooms to clean for her to do it properly.

'The restaurant is a disaster. Apparently the chef they had walked out after a row with the manager, and the food is currently being prepared by semi-trained kitchen workers. There appear to be no plans to recruit a new chef.

'Overall the problem is one of poor, even non-existent, management, lack of direction, understaffing, low pay and resulting poor staff morale.

'On the plus side, I would say that the place has great potential. Its position is excellent since Camden Lock nearby has become a major tourist attraction, and the occupancy rate is respectable if not spectacular. The prices, while slightly on the high side for what you actually get, are not outrageous. But it needs someone to turn it around, and quickly, before it gets a bad reputation.'

She paused when the main course arrived. She had ordered turbot in an exotic sauce of some kind, while I was having salmon. And I had indeed ordered an expensive bottle of wine, a vintage Montrachet.

'I made other inquiries this morning,' she continued. 'It seems that the hotel is owned by a group of investors, dentists I believe, people who know nothing and care even less about the business. My contacts tell me that they would probably sell to anyone who makes a reasonable offer.'

'How would you like to take it on. Turning the place around, that is?'

'I'd love it,' she said, her eyes shining.

'What would you do first?'

'I'd send in an army of builders and workmen to go through the place with a fine-tooth comb to get it back into shape. I would re-train existing staff and recruit new people. I would rip out the appalling New Orleans dining-room and turn it into a proper restaurant, probably simple French/Continental food, for which hotel guests would have to book tables like non-residents—if you want to attract people to a restaurant, they should not feel that they are coming to a hotel dining-room. And before all of that, I would sack the present manager, a snotty little American turd who actually had the nerve to suggest that I might want him to visit me in my room.'

'What did you tell him?'

'I said I would prefer a visit from a cockroach, and that if he even came near my room I would dislocate several of his vertebrae.'

There was another little silence while we ate some food.

'My plan is as follows,' I said eventually. 'I am going to ask Pendleton, with the assistance of Rothschilds, to negotiate to buy the place as quickly as possible. When that is done, I would like to appoint you as managing director of the company—the other board members being me, Pendleton and Douglas from the merchant bank—at a salary which you should sort out with Pendleton. I don't even want to know what it is. You will have carte blanche to run the place as you see fit—with the exception of one or two special requirements which I will make known to you now.'

'What sort of special requirements? I couldn't run the place if there was a pasty-faced midget with acne and a limp constantly bugging me.' She looked belligerent for a moment.

'They are very simple. Room and restaurant prices are to be lowered by twenty per cent, staff salaries are to be increased by a third, there will be a meaningful profit-sharing scheme with staff and when there are vacant rooms, these are to be made available to homeless people, free of charge.'

She was silent for a moment while she finished the last of the Montrachet. Then she said: 'I like the sound of it, except for the very last bit. Homeless people might be a bit of a problem.'

'Nevertheless, that's the package I'm offering.'

She hesitated for about three seconds. 'OK, you're on.'

Neither of us wanted dessert, so I paid the bill and asked Hazel to order a cab.

'Don't worry about a taxi,' Samantha said, 'I'll run you home. I parked my car in a garage nearby.' It turned out to be a rare MGB sports car, one of the few they had built with a V6 engine, and it looked as if it had been cared for lovingly. She drove it lovingly, too, firmly and confidently, without being tempted to participate in take-off competitions at traffic lights.

When we got to Estelle Road she slipped the car expertly into a parking space. I asked if she wanted some coffee. 'Just coffee,' I added, fingering my wrist.

'Thanks, but I've got a long way to go,' she answered.

'How long?'

'Northampton. That's where I live. Well, anyway that's where I live at the moment. I'm doing a locum as stand-in manager in a country hotel.'

'There's no one waiting for you?'

'Not at the moment.'

'Well, then it's ridiculous that you should drive all that way. Why don't you sleep here? I've got lots of rooms.' Her eyes narrowed slightly, and I continued: 'I'm talking about rooms with single beds, and if I come anywhere near you, you can rearrange some of my vertebrae.'

She looked at me suspiciously, but then reached forward and switched off the engine. The resulting silence was pleasant. 'There's something about you that I like. You're strange and full of bull at times, and you haven't told me a single thing about yourself, but for some weird reason I find myself trusting you. I hope you've got a spare toothbrush.'

'Lots,' I said. 'I have statuesque blondes to stay almost every night.'

I ground up some fresh kibo chagger

coffee and we drank it sitting round the heavy wooden table in the kitchen/dining-room.

'There's just you in this whole house?' she asked.

'I bought it with my former and unlamented wife Julia, with the idea that at least three of the rooms would eventually resound to the patter of little feet,' I explained. 'When she ran off with a Welsh mechanic, I initially intended to sell it and buy something smaller, but in the end I never got round to it. Then I got used to it and I like the space. I use every room for a different purpose. There's a study, TV room, secondary TV room with an exercise bicycle, guest room, formal sitting-room with the hi-fi in it, store room for junk and a top room that I think I might one day use as a sculpture studio.'

'Are you rich?' she asked. I must say I liked the way her fingers curled round the coffee cup.

'Very,' I said.

'How very?'

'Very, very.'

'Ah.'

'Which brings me to something im-portant,' I added. She put down the cup

and raised one lovely eyebrow a fraction.
'Yes?'

'I want your word that you will maintain total confidentiality about the ownership of the hotel. In any circumstances.'

'Otherwise?'

'Otherwise the whole arrangement is off. I wave a polite goodbye to you after breakfast tomorrow and you go back to running your hotel in Northamptonshire.'

'Would you trust me if I agreed?'

'Yes.'

'Why?'

'Firstly, I trust anyone recommended to me by Ambrose Pendleton, and, secondly, I like the cut of your jib and the way you hold roses in your teeth. Also because you said you seem to trust me, and one good trust deserves another.'

'You are totally full of shit, and I don't know why you want to be such a retiring flower, but you've got a deal, Horatio Parker.' She put a warm and smooth, but firm, hand out, and I shook it.

'Just call me Parker,' I begged.

Later, lying wide-eyed in bed, I cursed myself for drinking two cups of freshly ground coffee so late at night. I found myself thinking of all kinds of things, but my mind kept coming back to the thought of Samantha McDuff asleep in the guest room downstairs. Would she really rearrange my vertebrae if I went to visit her? I was much too scared to find out.

## CHAPTER 9

I woke up that Friday morning to the sound of blustery rain hitting the window-panes and I could feel that the temperature had dropped significantly. The early summer had turned bad-tempered.

My house guest and I had breakfast together and I found to my surprise that I was more interested in looking at Samantha McDuff than at the *Independent* and *Hampstead Explorer* which had been delivered through the door—even though my story about poor Murdoch Finnegan was the front page lead.

There was only one bad moment and that came when I finished my toast and coffee and remarked that it was time to go to work.

'Which is what, exactly?' she asked.

'I'm a reporter on a local newspaper.'

'Oh yeah.'

'It's true,' I protested.

'Then you probably own the damn thing.'

She caught me unawares, and there was no way I could avoid the stricken look which flashed across my face. And she was too sharp to miss it. She grinned.

'Wow, bingo! Got it in one. And you've probably sworn them all to secrecy as well, right?'

'No,' I said quietly, 'none of them know.' My face was very serious, and she didn't miss that either. There was a moment's silence.

'You are a very strange man, Parker. This confidentiality is very important to you, isn't it?' I nodded. 'Well, I don't understand it, but I'll respect it.' I didn't say anything. I was looking at her face and wondering what it was about her that made me want to tell her everything.

'I mean that,' she said, and then her face softened. 'On one condition.'

'Which is?'

'That you promise never ever, in any circumstances whatsoever, to use the phrase, "Lay on, McDuff." '

'What?'

'You know, that line from *Macbeth*, when he's fighting McDuff at the end of the play.'

'It hadn't even occurred to me,' I said.

'It would have, eventually. Sooner or later everyone gets round to saying that to me, and it gets on my nerves.'

'I won't,' I promised.

'Also, *never* call me Sam. That's a man's name.'

'Fine.'

'Then we have a deal, Parker.'

Even though he was parked fifty yards away I could see Frankie's eyebrows reach up almost to his hairline when I came out of the house with Samantha, and they didn't drop until she had got into her MGB and driven away.

'Oi, oi, oi,' he said as I got into the cab, shaking the rain off my umbrella.

'And what does "oi, oi, oi" mean, pray?' I replied rather tetchily, although secretly I was pleased. The sexist bastard usually uttered only two 'ois' when he saw an attractive woman.

'It means, if you don't mind me saying so, guv, that it's about time you had lady friends to stay again.'

'She's not a lady friend. She's a business acquaintance. And she wasn't staying, she merely slept here because she... Never mind, Frankie. Look here, I employ you to drive me around, not to comment on my social life or lack of it, OK?' I tried to sound angry, but I could see that he was still grinning broadly.

'OK, guv. Where to this morning? The *Explorer?*'

'No, St Pancras Coroner's Court.'

On the way there I telephoned Ambrose Pendleton, told him about my discussion with Samantha and asked him to liaise with her and Douglas of Rothschilds to put in an offer to buy the hotel. He sighed in a long-suffering sort of way and asked whether I was sure that I wanted to go into the hotel business. I said I wasn't sure at all but that we were going to do it anyway.

The coroner's court is a depressing building. Actually it's quite a cheerful-looking place, as courtrooms go, but the depression comes with the knowledge that the only matter ever under discussion there is death.

There had been so many times when I had sat there and listened to pathologists, police, firemen and ambulance staff giving dispassionate evidence about sudden, tragic horrific, painful, lingering, unnecessary, lonely and deliberate deaths. The details were often nauseating, and the distress of relatives and friends of the deceased was always difficult to witness.

On this occasion there were no grisly details given, however. This was merely a formal opening of the inquest, to hear evidence of identification of Murdoch Finnegan's body, so that it could be released for burial. The proceedings would then be adjourned pending the completion of the police investigation.

Theo was there, along with one or two people I vaguely recognized as coroner's officers or police. And there were a couple of other journalists at the press table. One was from a local news agency, and the other was Kippy Kypriades from the *Kentish Town Courier*.

'Did you see my story?' he whispered when I sat down.

'No.' I hadn't even seen my own yet. He pulled a creased copy of the give-away newspaper out of his pocket and handed it to me. The headline across the top of the first page was:

## P.I MURDER 'NOT
## A MAFIA HIT'
## SAY BAFFLED POLICE

Hampstead police denied this week that the brutal slaying of an American private detective in a flat in Belsize Park was the result of a mob contract.

And they refused to comment on whether the 45-year-old detective, Murdoch Finnegan, had been tortured or mutilated before being shot to death at close range with a shotgun.

I had read enough, and I handed the paper back to him with an encouraging grin. 'Great stuff!' I whispered.

A few more people had come into the court, including Arnold Mo, who sat down next to Theo. He waved at me. I also noticed a group of three men sitting in the public seats, where families and friends of the deceased usually sit, but I didn't recognize them. The reason I noticed them was that they were obviously together and yet they were such a mismatched trio. The one in the middle was tall and distinguished, about sixty years old, with a very sober and serious look about his face and a full beard of silvery hair. He was wearing an expensive-looking dark suit, and a top coat with a velvet collar. I looked for a bowler hat but I didn't see one. The other two, in contrast, were both fairly short, bald, slightly overweight and anything but distinguished. They were both wearing light-coloured suits which looked baggy in the pockets, creased round the collars and long overdue for a visit to the cleaners. They looked so similar that I decided that they were brothers, possibly twins, even.

I didn't pay them too much attention, however. There were a number of cases on the list that morning, and since I didn't recognize them I assumed that they were connected with some other unfortunate deceased.

Murdoch's case, because it was just an opening, was called first, and lasted precisely six minutes. Evidence of identification was given by Arnold Mo after the coroner had been told that the victim had no relatives in this country, and that was it. I followed Theo and Arnold out into the foyer.

'What about his parents?' I asked them.

'Are they coming here for the funeral, or is the body to be flown to America?'

'Neither,' Arnold said. 'His father is very old and infirm and cannot travel, and his mother said she would not come alone.'

'You've spoken to them?'

'Of course. I am handling his affairs, after all. They want him buried here. They said that he would want that since he had made England his home.'

That sounded a bit odd to me, but my attention was diverted by the sight of the three strange men emerging from the court. They must have been there for Murdoch's inquest after all, since the next case hadn't started yet. Without catching anyone's eye, the threesome walked through the foyer and out through the glass doors into the rain. The three of us watched in silence as a chauffeur leaped with an umbrella from a metallic silver Jaguar to escort them to the car. All four then got in, and the car slid away.

'Anyone know who they were?' I asked.

Arnold looked puzzled. 'Yes, indeed. I know the elderly man. That's Mr Justice Leonard Rose, a High Court judge. What the hell was he doing here?'

'And the other two?' I asked.

113

'Morris and Mervyn Jacobson,' said Theo with a distasteful sound in his voice, 'sometimes known as the Jacobson twins. They're extremely dodgy private investigators, with an office in Holloway Road. Not the classiest of gentlemen; in fact they work for some of the most unpleasant people around.'

'Are they really twins?' I asked.

'It certainly looks like it. They always do everything together, even when they are giving evidence in court, both of them come,' Theo said. 'You would not be surprised to hear that they are not the most popular firm of private operators at local police stations.'

'What are they doing knocking around with a High Court judge?' I asked, but no one could answer that one.

Theo was about to take his leave when I reminded him that he owed me a favour. He looked at me blankly.

'Murdoch's flat, remember? You said I could see it.'

'Now?'

'Why not?'

'I don't have the keys on me.'

'I have a taxi waiting outside. We can go past the police station and pick them up.'

There was nothing he could say to that, so he gave a resigned shrug. 'Do you want to come?' I said to Arnold Mo.

'Sure, why not, I haven't been there since the murder.'

Frankie, as usual, gave no sign of recognition as he drew up outside the door when we emerged, and I was irritated to see him turn on the meter. That was our arrangement, designed to mask the nature of our association, but the trouble was that every time he turned on the meter, the total went into his little red book, even if it was just for show.

In the taxi Arnold said to Theo: 'I hope you guys catch the bastard who murdered him.'

'So do I,' Theo replied. 'The trouble is, even if we do, what happens then? Whoever it is will just get life imprisonment—assuming we manage to get the charge to stick, that is—and that can mean as little as seven or eight years in prison nowadays. Sometimes I wonder why I'm not a supporter of capital punishment.'

'What does the Talmud say about justice and mercy?' I asked.

Theo thought for a moment. 'One of the teachings declares that for three hours each day God sits and judges the world. But, just when he sees that the world is deserving of being destroyed because of the prevalence of evil, He gets up from the throne of justice and sits on the throne of mercy.

'The Talmud even tells us that God prays to himself that in the time of His anger He should remember mercy, and that His compassion should overcome his wrath.

'And when He is compelled by justice to inflict punishment on evil doers, He does so with regret and pain.'

Murdoch Finnegan's flat was even more depressing than the coroner's court. For one thing the coroner's court didn't have the lingering smell of dead bodies.

The police had removed the bloodstained bedclothes, but there was still a horrifying caked brown stain on the bare mattress where Murdoch had bled and then lain dead for days until he was discovererd by his cleaning lady.

Theo and Arnold stood talking in the living-room while I kind of mooched around the flat, looking in cupboards and opening drawers. Each time I looked in a drawer, I found the things one expected people to put away in drawers. Socks, shirts, underwear, personal effects. The cupboards contained clothes. Everything felt lonely, neglected, forgotten. I felt like a sneak. In the bathroom there were bathroom things. In the kitchen there were kitchen things.

And in the living-room there was a desk and filing cabinet.

As I moved towards them, Theo put his hand out to stop me.

'What?' I said.

'There's nothing in the desk. And the filing cabinet is out of bounds. I said you could look round the flat, not go through private papers.'

'Oh, for Christ's sake, Theo!' I exclaimed, my frustration bursting through.

'Forget it, Parker. Look, that filing cabinet contains notes on all the cases Finnegan worked on. How do you think his former clients would feel if a journalist was allowed to rummage through them

'In any case, this is not police property. His papers belong to his estate, and to look at them you would have to get permission from his heirs, or at least his lawyer. So try the lawyer, he's standing here.' I looked at Arnold, who looked a little uncomfortable.

'I think he may have a point,' Arnold said. 'Strictly speaking, all this stuff belongs to Murdoch's parents, and I would need their permission to allow you to look through them. That's apart from the issue of whether these files contain sensitive confidential information.'

'But I'm a benefactor in his will,' I tried.

'He only left you the house. All other effects go to his parents,' Arnold said.

'In any case,' Theo added, 'I can tell you that there's nothing of interest in the files. The CID have been through them, and there's nothing there that would relate in any way to his murder. There's just case notes on jobs he did, a few personal papers, letters and things. Nothing even remotely suspicious.'

I wasn't convinced, but I could see that further argument, as they say, was going to get me nowhere. I asked Arnold for Murdoch's parents' address. He pulled out a slim address book from his pocket and read it to me. I wrote it down in my notebook.

I think they both thought I was going to write a letter. But I had another idea.

# CHAPTER 10

I dropped Theo at Hampstead nick and Arnold at a tube station and I got back to the office just before lunch-time. For the first time that day, I had a chance to look at that morning's *Explorer*. Unlike the *Kentish Town Courier*'s, my report was factual and straightforward, and had a lot more background about Murdoch, thanks to my own acquaintance with him.

'Nice of you to look in,' Arnie Bloch muttered when he saw me.

'I've been working, Arnie. I was at the Finnegan inquest opening this morning, and then I went to have a look at the scene of the crime.'

'And what did you get out of that?' He was eating a Mars Bar.

'Not a lot,' I admitted.

'Fat lot of good that was then, wasn't it?' Then he drifted off to make someone else's life a misery. What irritated me was that he was right; I hadn't picked up a word of usable copy the whole day.

At about three o'clock a thought struck me and I dialled Samantha McDuff's mobile telephone. When she answered there was a roaring sound in the background.

'Hi, it's your employer, where are you?'

'I'm on the M1, on the way home,' she said.

'What's been happening?' I asked.

'I was on the 'phone most of the morning with Pendleton, the Rothschilds' bloke and some of the hotel owners. They sound very interested. We've arranged a meeting for Monday afternoon at Rothschilds' where we'll make them an offer they won't refuse.'

'Why won't they refuse it?'

'Because we'll be offering them lots of your money.'

'Oh,' I said. A familiar air of unreality came over me. I had been mega-rich for a year, but I still couldn't get used to the scale of financial transaction I was now constantly involved in. It still felt like someone else's money.

'You getting cold feet?' she said.

'No, I just don't want to hear the figures involved. Listen, what are you doing this weekend?'

'Nothing. I'm on the way to Northampton to pack my stuff. I've resigned my temporary job.'

'Why don't you come away with me for the weekend?' There was a silence filled only with the sound of the MG roaring past noisy juggernauts. 'Strictly separate bedrooms, of course,' I added. There was another pause.

'Where to?' she asked.

'America.'

'Say that again, there's a lot of noise here.'

'America. New York, Boston and New Hampshire.'

'That's what I thought you said. For the weekend?'

'Yes.'

'To do what?'

'I want to visit the parents of a late friend of mine. Why don't you turn around at the next junction and meet me at Heathrow at six o'clock.'

'I don't have enough things with me.' But her voice was softening.

'We'll buy stuff in Boston,' I promised.

'Separate bedrooms?'

'I promise, on the health of my vertebrae.' She laughed. A lovely throaty

121

giggle which made me wonder whether the bones of my back didn't in fact need a little realignment.

'OK, which terminal?' she asked.

'Number four, I'll meet you at the Concorde check-in.'

'Wow, you really *are* rich, aren't you?'

'Yes.'

Samantha was dead on time, as was Concorde's departure, as always. She was delighted and fascinated by the supersonic jet and didn't pretend she wasn't. We were plied with champagne and good food, and we spent the time finding out about each other.

She had been brought up in a rather culturally sterile home in Glasgow, where eating out meant a meal in a fish and chip shop, and holidays meant a fortnight in a rented caravan on the coast of Lancashire near Blackpool. The high point of her childhood had been when she was twelve, when her mother had won a competition in the *Daily Express* for a family weekend at the Grand Hotel in Brighton.

From the moment they had crossed the threshold Samantha had been entranced by the artificial world inside, the carefully constructed luxury and the lovingly re-hearsed obsequiousness of the staff. Her parents had spent most of the weekend on the beach and on the seafront, but Samantha hardly set foot outside the hotel. She explored the lounges and lobbies, befriended the staff and inspected the secret places guests never see. She was shown the kitchens and the stores, the staff quarters and the booking office, and from that moment there was never any doubt in her mind about the career she wanted to pursue.

During school holidays she found herself chambermaid jobs in hotels. Later, when at university in Bristol studying languages, she worked part-time as waitress, room-maid, barmaid and receptionist in any hotel that would have her. After that she had spent a year at catering college, followed by two years at a top hotel in Geneva, and three years in the training scheme of one of the big British hotel groups.

For my part, having had more champagne than I should have on an empty stomach, I told her my own remarkable story, about Edwina Llewellyn, about buying the *Hampstead Explorer*, and about the incredible investigation into the death of Monique Karabekian, the film star wife of former Hampstead Tory MP, Malcolm Halifax. At one stage I noticed that Samantha and I were holding hands, although I could not remember how that had come about.

Concorde delivered us to New York in the usual three hours, enabling us to arrive before we set off, as far as local time was concerned. From there we took a shuttle to Boston where we checked in at the Hyatt Hotel. We were both exhausted by this time, and after a light snack in the cocktail bar we retired to our rooms.

On the Saturday morning we went shopping in downtown Boston for the things Samantha needed, although she refused to let me pay for anything. Next on the agenda was Hertz, where I recognized the warm weather and hired the largest convertible they had—a huge red Cadillac. Then we hit the road.

Samantha navigated expertly with the detailed road map we got from Hertz, taking me faultlessly through the maze of freeways and turnpikes until we were safely heading north on Interstate 93. I set the cruise control at the 55-mile-an-hour speed limit, and we sat back for a couple of hours and watched the scenery change from the rolling hills of western Massachusettes to the more mountainous terrain of New Hampshire. At some stage during the morning, Samantha had the temerity to ask where the hell we were going. I told her who Murdoch had been, what had happened to him, and that we were on our way to see his parents. But what exactly I hoped to learn was not yet clear. It was just that things just didn't sit right. She shrugged.

After about 150 miles we turned on to route 104 which eventually took us into the town of Meredith where we had a light lunch.

From there we drove to Center Harbor, at the northern end of the vast Lake Winnipesaukee, the largest lake in the state, about 60 miles long with 185 miles of shoreline, and covering a total of about 72 square miles. It is just south of the famous Squam Lake where the film *On Golden Pond* was made, but the scenery looked identical.

The address I had for the Finnegan home just said Marlborough Neck, Center

Harbor, so I did what everyone does when you are looking for someone in small town America, I pulled in at the town's main petrol station.

The man who came out to fill the tank was about thirty years old, wearing his baseball cap the wrong way round—that is, with the peak sticking out at the front. He seemed totally unimpressed by the gleaming red Cadillac convertible.

'Uh, do you by any chance know where the Finnegans' house is, on Marlborough Neck?' I asked him.

'Yup,' he said, and he went on pumping, a dreamy look in his eye. I looked at his face in an attempt to glean whether he was, perhaps, taking the piss. But nothing was forthcoming. I had asked him if he knew where the house was, and he had said yes, he did. I saw that I would have to get subtle.

'Uh, would you tell us how to get there?

'Sure.' But he just went on pumping.

'Uh, today?' But he didn't answer. When the tank was full (it seemed to have absorbed about 200 gallons) I went with him into the office to pay with my credit card, and only when the transaction was

126

complete did he beckon to me. We walked back out on to the forecourt and he took my elbow while he pointed down the road.

'Carry on in that direction for about two miles and you'll see a sign pointing to Marlborough Neck Road. Take that, and after about four or five miles you'll see another road down to the left posted Buzzard Cove. You got that?' I nodded. 'Ok, now the Finnegan place is off that road. You can't miss it if you keep a sharp eye out for the signs.'

I thanked him, but he didn't let go of my elbow.

'You don't upset them, hear. Their son was killed last week. In England.'

'I know,' I said. 'He was a friend of mine.' He didn't answer, but just turned on his heel and disappeared into the workshop.

The directions were precise and accurate, and led us into a thickly wooded road. We found the Buzzard Cove road easily; there was a big fluorescent sign hanging on it which said NO SNOWMOBILES! A mile after that we found a sign that said: FINNEGAN. We followed the track through the trees and round a bend, and quite suddenly we were at the house. It was a large double-storey house, made of wood, of course, with a screened-in 'deck' or porch facing out over a small cove of the lake. It was an idyllic setting. There was a large lawn which sloped down to the water's edge where there was a private landing dock and a boathouse.

I parked at the end of the drive and we got out. We walked through the screen door on to the porch and I knocked on the front door. It took about a minute before the door opened to reveal an elderly woman, and the instant I saw her, the words 'tired' and 'beaten' flashed into my mind. She didn't really look that old, but it was the way she stood, as if holding up the world, that emphasized the years she had passed through.

'Mrs Finnegan?'

'You must be the people who asked for us at Jed's. Come in.'

Baseball cap must have telephoned to warn of our impending arrival. She led us through a hall and into a large sitting-room, one wall of which was made of stone, with a huge fireplace and a long mantelpiece above it, full of framed photographs. 'Jed said you were a friend of Murdoch's, is that right?' Her voice was thin and weary.

'That's right, Mrs Finnegan. My name is Parker, Horatio Parker, and this is a friend of mine, Samantha McDuff. I was a friend of Murdoch's for some years. Please accept our condolences for your loss. It has been a terrible business.'

'He never mentioned you in his letters,' she said. That surprised me. Murdoch had always said that his parents had virtually disowned him for evading the Vietnam draft by going to England, and he certainly never gave the impression that he was in correspondence with them.

'Well, I can't claim that I was a very close friend. But I knew him professionally. I'm a reporter on a newspaper in the area where he lived in London, and we came across each other quite often.' I showed her my press card.

'Sit down, I'll make some coffee,' Without waiting for a reply, she shuffled out of the room. She hadn't given Samantha more than a cursory glance.

I walked immediately to the mantelpiece and started looking at the photographs. Most of them were of a tall, well-built man, usually pictured in a hard hat and often wearing overalls, in front of various oil wells, rigs, pumping stations and similar installations, and in locations apparently all over the world. Mr Finnegan senior, I presumed. Murdoch had said he had been an executive with Exxon before he retired. The pictures of him took up nearly the whole mantelpiece.

There were a few family photographs towards the other end. One or two pictures of Mrs, looking younger, considerably more attractive and infinitely more vivacious than the woman who had opened the door to us. My eye was caught by a picture of Murdoch, around sixteen years old, standing on the boatdock. In the background was another boy sitting with his legs hanging off the boards, his back to the camera. The next picture was of two boys in a canoe in the cove. One was clearly Murdoch, but I didn't recognize the other. Murdoch had certainly never mentioned having a brother. In fact he had once told me that he was an only child.

The next photograph gave me a shock. It was of Murdoch in uniform, standing next to the boy from the other photographs, also in uniform. They were slightly older looking, about eighteen and nineteen respectively. There was a typed strip across the bottom which read: Saigon, 1970.

That left me flummoxed. For years I had known Murdoch as the Vietnam draft dodger, and for the life of me I couldn't understand why he had denied his army service. I looked closer at the photograph. The older boy had sergeant's stripes, but Murdoch's collar showed a captain's silver bars. I was astonished.

There were two other pictures. One was Murdoch, looking slightly older still. There was a maturity and toughness in his face that wasn't there in the previous photographs, and I assumed it had been taken after his return from Vietnam. The last was of the other boy, also older and tougher; but in this picture there was something wild and disturbed about him. His hair was very long and unkempt, and he had not shaved. It was not a beard, but more what they would call 'designer stubble' today. The eyes were in sharp focus, but they were looking elsewhere, not at the camera, as if looking into another life.

Before I could look at anything else in the room, Mrs Finnegan returned pushing a trolley carrying a coffee jug, milk, three cups and a small plate of biscuits. She poured three cups, asked about milk and sugar and offered us a biscuit.

'Is Mr Finnegan here?' I asked her. She shot me a funny look.

'Of course he's here. He doesn't go anywhere.'

'Could I speak to him?'

There was a wry smile. 'You could speak to him, but he wouldn't speak to you.'

'I know he's not well, but I really wouldn't take up a lot of his time...'

'Doesn't matter how much of his time you take up,' she interrupted. 'He won't speak to you. Won't speak to me either, for that matter. You want to see him? C'mon.' Without waiting for an answer, she got up and walked out of the room. I followed her through the hall and into another room, on the lake side of the house. It had obviously been a den or study of some kind. The walls were lined with books, and there were some framed certificates on the walls. Next to the window, facing the lake, was a large black leather chair containing an emaciated husk of a man. Murdoch's father. He looked to be asleep, with his head lolled to the side, but then

I noticed that his eyes were half open.

'He had a stroke, eight years ago, and he's been like that ever since. Nurse comes twice a day. Gets him up, washes him, feeds him, puts him in the chair. Comes back in the evening, washes him, feeds him again, puts him to bed. Doctor says he can't see, hear or understand anything. Doctor also says he should be in an institution, but I won't have that.'

'I'm sorry, I didn't know,' I said. She didn't answer, but just led the way back to the living room where Samantha was waiting.

'So what did you come all this way for, Mr Parker?' she asked when we sat down.

'Well, it's hard to explain really. It's just that some things are just very puzzling, and I wondered if you could help me understand them.'

'Like what?'

'Well, I know you had your differences with him, but I—'

'What?' she said sharply.

'You didn't always see eye to eye with him—'

'What on earth are you talking about?' she demanded.

I took a deep breath. 'Mrs Finnegan, Murdoch told me that you and his father had, well, virtually disowned him. That you wouldn't speak to him because he had evaded the Vietnam draft by going to England.'

She was looking at me with incredulity written all over her face. 'That's the most absurd thing I have ever heard in my life. I cannot believe Murdoch told you that! Anyone who knew him well would know that he volunteered for service in Vietnam. He was a captain in the Intelligence Corps. We were very proud of him, and we were very close to him after he went to England. He wrote home and telephoned every couple of weeks, and he came over to see us two or three times a year!'

'Then why did he go to live in England?' I asked. I was very confused.

'You don't know that?' She could see I didn't. 'Then you were not a close friend of his.'

'Why aren't you bringing him back for burial here, if you don't mind my asking?'

'What other questions do you have?' she asked. There was an unpleasant edge to her voice now.

134

'Well, I wanted to ask whether you knew anything about a house Murdoch had bought in London, and about where he might have got the money for it. I would also want to ask you whether you knew if he had any enemies, or whether he ever said anything to you which might explain why he was murdered.' Then something occurred to me. 'Oh, and perhaps you could tell me who the other boy in those photographs is.' I pointed to the framed pictures.

There was dead silence. Mrs Finnegan sat with her hands pressed tightly in her lap, her face a mask of white. And when she finally spoke, there was anger and unconcealed hostility in every word.

'I don't know what kind of smear you're trying to put together, Mr Reporter!' I tried to protest but she just raised her voice and went on. 'But what I do know is that you were not a friend of Murdoch's. It is clear that you hardly knew him, if at all, and you are trying to stir up who knows what scandal in your newspaper.

'You have misrepresented yourself, and come here asking deeply personal questions that touch on private family matters that have no interest to other people. I want

135

you to leave right away. Now. And you too, miss, you should be ashamed of yourself!'

'Please, Mrs Finnegan! I assure you—' But I didn't get a chance to get any further.

She was shouting now. 'Get out! Go on! Get out! Now! Get into your fancy red car and rake your muck somewhere else. I won't have you here another minute!'

I was stunned by her reaction, but did not need to have it explained to me that our welcome had expired. Samantha was pale and embarrassed, and we left as quickly as we could. Certainly it was obvious that any attempt to reason with her would merely increase her anger and distress.

We were quiet in the car for a few minutes. When we hit the main road back to Center Harbor, Samantha said: 'It's just as well you're very rich.'

'Why do you say that?'

'You're not much of an interrogator.'

I had to admit she had a point. Tact and interrogation had never been among my strong points. And my performance that afternoon had marked the low water mark of my career. I felt awful.

# CHAPTER 11

It was about five o'clock in the afternoon when we passed through Center Harbor. We didn't stop at Jed's petrol station on this occasion, just in case Mrs F had phoned ahead and asked him to get his shotgun out of the pick-up.

But there was no way I was going to drive all the way back to Boston that night, so I pulled into the first decent-looking motel that I saw. The Lakeview Motel, about a mile out of town, turned out to be a charming establishment with a row of pleasant little semi-detached chalets actually overhanging the water's edge. Samantha and I had rooms next door to each other and, we discovered, a common balcony in front on which we could sit in the last of the afternoon's warm sun and gaze out over the remarkable, it must be said, lake view.

The restaurant, called the coffee shop, was just about empty when we arrived for dinner at about half past seven. I had forgotten that New England ate dinner at around half five or six at the latest.

The waitress, with a charming smile and the name tag 'Carol' on her left breast smiled happily and showed us to a table.

'We're not too late?' I asked.

'Nope! All paying customers welcome.' She grinned.

'The cook won't complain?' Samantha asked.

'He better not, he's my husband! We own this place.'

Carol brought us steak, French fries and salad of the kind you somehow just cannot get in England. And, remembering the sleepless night I had the last time I drank coffee in the evening, I ordered a vanilla milkshake. Why not go the whole hog, I thought.

When she cleared away the plates half an hour later, Carol suddenly said, 'You're the folks from England went to visit the Finnegans, huh?'

I looked up at her sharply, alarmed that word about the nature of our departure from Buzzard Cove might have got around the village. But Carol, a buxom woman on the wrong side of forty, was smiling benignly.

'It's a small town, mister,' she laughed. 'Not much that happens around here out of season that we don't all get to hear of pretty quickly. Jed was in here for coffee late afternoon. Told us you'd gone down there. You friends of the family?'

I was still cautious. 'I knew their son in London,' I said.

'Yeah, terrible business. Anyhow, how's old Mrs Finnegan holding up? I haven't seen her in town for a few days.'

I wasn't sure how to answer. 'She, ah, seems to have a lot of problems to deal with,' I said carefully.

Her face went sombre. 'Yeah, well, they've had far more than their share of heartache. They've just had one tough break after the other. And it all started all that time ago when Michael went to live in England.'

'Murdoch, you mean,' I said.

She looked at me. 'No, Michael, the older one.'

My pulse quickened. 'There were two boys?'

'Of course.'

'Did you know him? Michael, I mean.'

'Know him? Mister, I was the one who waited for him for five years till it was clear he wasn't never coming back. I would'a stuck by him no matter what; I never believed all that stuff they said he did. But he never did come back. So after a while I married Cliff, in there.' She cocked her head in the direction of the kitchen.

'Carol,' I said as pleasantly as I could, 'could you maybe join us with a cup of coffee and tell us about those boys? If you're not too busy, that is.'

'Why, sure. Seeing as you're friends of the family and all. Glad to be of help.' She went off, poured herself a cup from the pot on the warmer and sat down at the table. She didn't need any prompting, and just launched into the story.

'We were all at school together, of course, it being a small town and all, and everyone knew those two kids. They were like two peas in a pod, you know. Not that they looked that much like each other, but in the sense that they did everything together. Michael was only about a year and a half older than Murdoch, and they seemed to prefer to be with each other instead of with other people of their own age.

'They weren't the same kind of people though. Murdoch was the quiet sort who kinda worked at what he wanted to do. Michael, on the other hand, was a wild one.' Carol laughed suddenly.

'Hoo boy! Was he wild? He was always getting into scrapes in one way or another, and Murdoch was usually dragged into it somehow. Nothing serious, though. I'm talking about kids' stuff; you know, stealing fruit, playing practical jokes, letting down car tyres, playing hooky from school. That kind of thing.

'I fell heavily for Michael at high school. I thought he was the handsomest darned guy in the whole world, and he was such fun! We were gonna get married and run a water-ski school for tourists out on the lake in the summer and snow-skiing in the winter. Yeah, we had it all planned out. Then the war came.'

'The war?' I said.

'Vietnam. Michael was drafted. He didn't wanna go, but he had to, and he went. Murdoch signed up the next year, as soon as he graduated from school. I think he wanted to go there because that's where Michael was. Anyway, he went to officer school and did pretty good for himself, and I think he tried to take care of Michael, but it was never the same after that.'

'How do you mean?'

'Well, they both came back from 'Nam all right, but Michael was a different guy.'

She had stopped talking and was gazing intently into the past. I nudged her gently with a question: 'Different in what way, Carol?'

'He was a very unhappy guy. He never spoke about it, but everyone said he'd had a hard time over there, you know, like some of the boys did, but somehow he never got over it and he didn't talk about it. We heard later that he had been wounded and got a Purple Heart and another award for bravery, but he never told us about it. He did a lot of drinking, but he wasn't talking about water-skiing any more, and he was very bitter about things. He also got into trouble a lot. Worse trouble than before. He was using some drugs, and he stole a car once to pay for some dope. He got probation, though, because it was a first offence. Then he went to Boston, and that was the last I saw of him.

'Still heard about him though. Next thing we knew he was arrested in Brookline, accused of raping some young girl. I knew he never did. He just wasn't the raping kind of guy, you know? Anyway, it turned out that it was a case of mistaken identity, and they let him go in the end. But not before he had spent three or four months in state prison.

'After that he went to England, and he had that trouble there.'

'What trouble?' I prompted.

'You don't know?'

'No. I only knew Murdoch.'

'And he never spoke about it?' It was clear that she thought that was pretty odd. Come to think of it, so did I.

'No, Murdoch never said anything about it.'

'Well, I don't know the details, but he was arrested there in London for something or other, until they decided they had got the wrong guy again and let him go. This must have been around nineteen-seventy-two. And then he disappeared.'

'Disappeared?'

'Never was seen again. That's why Murdoch went to England. He went to find Michael. His mother told us that he had vowed never to come back unless he found his brother. The whole thing was just too much for the old man. He went downhill fast after that, and then he had his stroke some years back. Been a vegetable ever since.'

She got up. 'Hey, I got a mess of work to do back there in the kitchen. I'll see you folks at breakfast. In the meantime, you want something in the night just call. Just dial room twenty-six for room service anytime until midnight.'

She drifted off, unaware of the confusion, in which she had left me. I had thought I had such a clear picture of Murdoch Finnegan, the lovable, bungling private detective buying drinks for his mates in the pub and regaling us with stories about his disasters. Suddenly I had discovered a new character entirely, a captain in the intelligence services who served in Vietnam and was adept at pulling the wool over people's eyes. He certainly fooled me for all those years.

We went back to the chalet where we sat on the balcony drinking whisky from the mini-bar in the rooms and watching the moon rise over the lake. By nine-thirty it seemed as if we were the only people awake in the whole world, and we decided to go to bed. I said good night to Samantha, considered again the prospect of having my vertebrae rearranged, but thought better of it, and went to have a shower instead.

A few minutes later I was lying in bed, wide-eyed and far from sleep, thinking about Murdoch and Michael Finnegan—did he have a beard which the wind blew in again?—and listening to the sound of the lake lapping at the supports of the chalet, when I suddenly heard a sound which made my hair stand on end.

It was a long, echoing cry which drifted in over the water, somewhere between the angry shriek of a locomotive in the night and the anguish of a howling wolf. It was at once hauntingly beautiful and utterly terrifying. I lay there rigid, thinking to myself: What the fuck was that?

A few seconds later there was a tap at my balcony door. I wrapped a towel round me and found it was Samantha, dressed deliciously only in a nightie, looking pale and very beautiful in the moonlight. 'What the fuck was that?' she said.

'I don't know,' I said. 'Come in, and I'll ring Carol and ask.' I got back into bed and dialled the room service number. Samantha was sitting on the edge of my bed. When Carol answered I said: 'It's Mr Parker in room sixteen. Sorry to disturb you, but can you tell me what that sound was that we just heard come in off the lake?'

She burst out laughing. 'That was a loon, a kind of duck. That's the call they make at night. They do it all the time. We think it's beautiful.'

'It is, when you know what the hell it is,' I said. I thanked her and hung up. I told Samantha about the loons, and we laughed nervously. Then I noticed that she was shivering. The temperature had plummeted since the sun had gone down.

'You're cold,' I said.

'Yes.' But she didn't move.

'Why don't you come here and warm up?' I suggested, heedless of my backbone.

She didn't say anything. She just slipped into bed next to me, and I put my arms around her. She felt cold and she was trembling slightly. I must have been too, because my heart was making a determined escape bid from behind the prison bars of my ribs.

After a little while she turned her face towards mine, and I kissed her. She kissed me back, and then we weren't cold any more.

She had a small firm body, which held me fiercely and which shuddered when I touched her. And at just the right moment I'm damned if there wasn't another haunting call which came sliding in off the lake to add an uncanny touch of eerie to the ecstasy. The lake moved.

'Thank you, loon,' I whispered as I felt sleep creeping inexorably up on me a few minutes later. Samantha was already asleep, small in my arms. And then I was.

## CHAPTER 12

Sunday morning sun streamed in early off the lake and woke me up about six o'clock. For one very small moment I did not know where I was. And then a little movement in the bed next to me brought me back up to date. I turned to look at Samantha and found her eyes open in a kind of mock surprise.

'What are you doing in my bed?' Her

voice was husky with sleep.

'I think you will find, upon investigation, that this is my bed,' I remarked.

'You know what happens to men who attack me?'

'Yes, but my defence is that you attacked me.'

'I think I'll do it again,' she said. And she did. And my back felt fine.

Later we had breakfast on our little terrace, eggs sunny side up and hash browns, pancakes, maple syrup, toast and good coffee, while watching the loons fishing in the lake.

They were large birds, with extraordinary speckled plumage, which would suddenly up-end themselves and disappear beneath the water for minutes on end, surfacing suddenly up to a hundred yards away without warning. Remarkable birds, to whom I had taken a decisive liking.

On the way back we took a lazy detour including a westward loop through the Berkshires, eating lunch in Tanglewood before returning to Boston.

The shuttle to New York and the Concorde flight home was uneventful, except that I think we held hands like teenager lovers all the way. I told her all I knew about Murdoch Finnegan and about the house in Golders Green. I told her again about Moniqe Karabekian and about Edwina Llewellyln. After a few glasses of champagne, I even told her about my ex-wife, Julia, but by then Samantha was, mercifully, asleep.

We picked up her car at the airport and got back to Estelle Road late at night. This time there was no discussion about where she would spend the night.

In the morning we were slightly jet-lagged and exhausted but there were things to do and people to see. Samantha had a meeting in the afternoon with the hotel owners, and I had specific plans of my own, so we were out bright and eager at nine o'clock.

Knowing that it would please Frankie, I kissed Samantha goodbye at the front gate.

'I've just thought of something,' she said. 'I'm homeless.'

'Poor little waif,' I replied. 'Why don't you move in here until the hotel deal goes through, or until such time as you decide otherwise? You can use any room you want.'

She looked at me quizzically. 'I'm not sure whether you don't want to crowd me, or whether you don't want me to crowd you. But either way, it's a generous offer, and I appreciate it. See you later.' With a little squeeze of my hand that left my fingers numb, she was off.

Frankie was so delighted by the scene he had witnessed that he managed to say nothing at all about it. But he had a huge grin on his cheeky mug as he razored his usual swathe through the traffic. On the way to the office I thought about what she had said about crowding, and concluded that I too didn't know. What I did know, however, was that it was a good feeling to know that I would be seeing her again that evening.

At the office I decided to bring Arnie Bloch up to date with my latest information about the Finnegans. He had the temper of a bull and the social graces of a yak, but Arnie was a superb editor with an instinct for news that I had never seen bettered.

He listened carefully to my story, asked some intelligent questions, and then lapsed into a kind of repose. Nothing moved except his jaw, which was chewing mercilessly on a defenceless toffee.

'Stick with it," he said eventually. 'There's something bleddy strange going on."

That, I knew, was a free pass for two or three days. He wouldn't be expecting me to be in the office producing copy until the end of the week at least.

I went back to my office where I found a telephone message to ring Mohan Mistry. I did so right away.

'I've cracked your con man's secret,' he said.

'You're amazing, Mohan. How did he do it?'

'Why don't you come round when you've got a minute and I'll show you.'

I said I would, and would have gone right away had not the telephone rung again. It was Arnold Mo, of Mo, Murphy and Forbes, who didn't beat about the bush.

'Can you come to my office at two o'clock this afternoon?' he asked.

'Of course. What's up?' I replied.

'Judge Rose is coming here to see me, with his assistants, as he described them, the Jacobson twins.'

'What's it about?' I asked.

'I'm not entirely sure. He rang me first thing this morning to ask for the meeting, and when I asked what it was about he would only say that it concerned the status of the late Murdoch Finnegan's house in Golders Green. So I thought that you, as the prospective owner of the place, should be there.'

'Very odd,' I said.

'Indeed,' said Arnold.

'Well, I suppose we'll find out soon enough. I'll be there at two.'

I went downstairs to find Frankie parked at his usual spot on double yellow lines and deeply engrossed in something. He was tapping away at his laptop computer, and the front of the cab was a mess of papers and books. When I opened the door and got in, he looked up at me in irritation.

'Sorry to intrude,' I said sarcastically. He had the grace to grin apologetically. It took him a minute or two to clear up and stow all the papers in his briefcase. I told him where I wanted to go.

'Sorry, Mr P. It's just that I thought you might do some work this morning and leave me in peace for a couple of hours.'

'Cheeky bugger,' I said. 'What are you doing that's so important, anyhow.'

'An essay. It's got to be in by the end of the week.'

'Well, maybe if you went home in the evening now and then, instead of frantically looking for fares, you would have some time to work properly.'

'The family's got to eat, guv.'

'Balls!' I retorted. 'I pay you a princely sum. The family can eat fillet steak every night.'

'Do you know what the fees are now for one term at University College School where Peter goes?' he challenged me. I had to confess I did not. 'Then there's Lucy's school fees at Channing in Highgate, not to mention the ballet classes, the tennis lessons, the extra French tuition, the skiing trips, the educational school visits to Florence. Also I've got a crippling mortgage, a wife who doesn't work and a brother-in-law who thinks that the only reason I was put on this earth was to lend him money...'

He went on in this vein for a few minutes, but I was unmoved. Frankie was more than well paid. I made sure of that.

When we got to Mohan's shop he was busy selling someone a dinky little mobile telephone about six inches long, the first one I had seen which would really fit unobtrusively into a jacket pocket. I instantly wanted one.

While I was waiting he pointed to a display of blank audio-cassette tapes behind the counter. 'Choose one of those at random and open it,' he said. 'I won't be long here.' I did so.

The customer left a few minutes later and Mohan reached under the counter and brought out a portable radio-cassette player.

'Here, put that cassette into the machine and press the play button,' he said.

For a few seconds there was just the hissing of the tape, and then I heard a click followed by voices. It was a recording of the telephone conversation he and I had had half an hour before. I was suitably impressed.

'How the hell is it done?'

'Very simply,' he said with a smug look on his face. 'It took me about half an hour to work out the principle, and only a day or so to iron out the electronic problems posed. It's an ingenious idea, but once you've thought it up, any competent electronics man can put together the equipment. Look, I'll show you.'

He took a screwdriver and quickly

unscrewed the back of the ghetto blaster. He turned it round to show me the innards. None of it made much sense to me; it was the usual jumble of electronic components, circuit boards and wiring—until I saw the little micro-cassette recorder taped into one of the cavities in the machine. It was one of those little black machines with a tiny cassette which people use for dictating notes, I whistled.

'It took me a while to get the system straight. I had to reverse some of the wiring and solve a few problems a bit too complicated for you to understand. But essentially what happens is that when you put a blank cassette—or any cassette, for that matter—into the main machine and press the play button, the command activates the small recorder, and what you actually hear is what is recorded on the micro-cassette.' He was beaming proudly.

'And, at the same time, the message is recorded on to the big cassette, so you can re-wind it or take it out and play it on any other machine and still hear the same thing. What's more, it will only do this process once, and after that it will operate as a normal ghetto blaster until you reset it. What do you think of that?'

'Brilliant, maestro! You've got to sell this one to me. How much?' He mentioned a figure which, although high, was reasonable given the amount of time he had spent on it. Mohan spent a few minutes showing me how to take the small recorder out, record on to it and reset the ghetto blaster into trick mode.

I also bought one of the dinky little mobile telephones. Mohan telephoned the cellular line company which opened an account and issued a mobile telephone number for me on the spot.

Back in the taxi with my purchases I tried out my new toy. I dialled directory inquiries first to get the number, and then I telephone Wheezy Wallis. I knew he would be at home, since Wheezy only worked nights.

'I've got some news for you,' I said when he answered. 'I know how that scam was worked,' and I explained it to him.

'That's great, Parker, but it isn't going to get our cash back, is it?'

'Probably not,' I admitted. 'But listen, Wheezy, I've got a job for you. The pay's good.'

'What sort of job?' He sounded distinctly unenthusiastic. Wheezy regarded having a job as being only one step better than being in prison, and he avoided both states of being quite vigorously.

'Don't worry, this is the kind of job you do already, and I'll only need you for a few hours.'

'I don't know what you mean,' he said, a note of innocent nervousness in his voice.

'Come on, Wheezy, we both know what I mean. I want you to meet me at about one o'clock tonight, or rather tomorrow morning, outside Belsize Park tube station. And bring your tools.'

'What tools?' He was distinctly nervous now, but I didn't have time to beat around the bush.

'Your burglar tools, Wheezy. Your lock picks, your jemmy and your glass cutter and whatever else you carry round with you on your nocturnal wanderings.'

'Christ, Mr P, you're talking on a bloody open telephone line! Who knows who could be listening!'

'You mean there could be some retired bank manager with a houseful of scanners recording this call to send to the *News of the World?* It's very unlikely, don't you think.'

'I dunno, Parker. But if there is someone

157

listening, it's me that gets the grief from it.'

'Never mind all that. Just meet me at the tube station at one o'clock.' Then I added: 'Goodbye, Squidgy.'

I was still chuckling to myself when Frankie said over his shoulder: 'What the hell are you up to with Wheezy Wallis, guv?'

'Never you mind, driver.'

'I don't like the sound of this. Something tells me I should be around tonight, whatever it is you are planning. You two are certain to come a cropper otherwise.' Actually, that sounded like a very good idea; having a getaway cab handy would be very useful.

'That's a very good idea, Frankie, and to show my appreciation I will now take you to a hostelry of your choice for lunch.'

'How about a rise as well?' he asked bluntly.

He caught me off guard, and right then, with no warning, I couldn't think of a single reason why I, with a post-tax income in excess of forty-five thousand pounds a week, shouldn't give a little more of it to Frankie. 'How about ten per cent?' I sighed.

'Fine!' he beamed.

We went, as we always did when he was choosing, to Ed's Easy Diner in Hampstead High Street, more because of the 'fifties and 'sixties music on the jukebox than for the hamburgers. Frankie must have played Dion's *Runaround Sue* five times, and was still whistling the cursed tune when he drove me down to Arnold Mo's office, just before two o'clock.

A friendly and efficient black receptionist smiled at me and showed me straight in to Arnold's office, where an icy atmosphere had almost caused frosting to appear on the windows.

Arnold was seated behind his desk looking a little jumpy. And, seated on a couch at the side of the room, was Judge Rose—flanked by the Jacobson twins. The Judge was looking grim and businesslike, and the Jacobson twins just looked grim. Now that I could see them close up I noticed that although they were fairly short, they were both very thickset in a way which suggested lots of muscle and not a lot of fat. Their necks were ominously short and bulged before diving into tight collars, and I also made a mental note about their hands, they were large, but with short stubby fingers, and when closed formed fists like hands. I was introduced briefly, but no one stood up to shake hands. I sat down in a chair next to the desk. The receptionist was hovering.

'Coffee, anyone, before we start?' said Arnold, trying to be cheerful.

'Yes, please,' I said.

'Good idea,' said one of the Jacobson twins.

'So, five coffees, then,' said the receptionist. 'How do you like them?' she asked pleasantly, looking at the visitors.

'Black, please, no sugar,' I said.

'The same,' said the Judge. He did not say please.

'I like my coffee like I like my women. That's white and very sweet,' said the other twin. There was an appalled silence except from the other twin, who wheezed merrily.

To give him the benefit of the doubt, I think the man was actually trying to make a joke. But nobody found it funny, nobody other than his brother, that is.

I flashed a glance at Arnold who was looking aghast. The black receptionist hadn't exactly paled, but there was a thin set to her lips. 'Right,' she said brightly. 'That's three black without, and two white with,' and she withdrew.

There was a very short silence after the door shut behind her, and then the Judge spoke. 'I would appreciate it if we could start now. I have a lot to do this afternoon.'

'By all means, Judge Rose,' Arnold said. 'You asked for this meeting, and I have explained why I thought Mr Parker here should join us. But the floor is yours.'

'I don't think this should take very long.' The Judge's voice had a distinctive quality about it and a quality which, I imagined would cement his authority in his courtroom. 'The simple point is that, however unfortunate it may be, there appears to be a misunderstanding about the will of the late Murdoch Finnegan, which...'

'Well, I have it here,' said Arnold, picking up some papers. 'What is the misunderstanding?'

The Judge looked at him as if to say: In my courtroom I don't get interrupted.

Arnold looked at him levelly. The unspoken reply was: You're not in your courtroom now, you're in my office.

161

'The point is that there was a subsequent will, one which post-dates that one,' the Judge said, his eyes glinting. One of the Jacobsons plunged a ham-like fist into a briefcase and brought out a file. Papers were extracted and placed on Arnold Mo's desk.

The Judge continued. 'You will find that the particulars of this document are identical in every respect to those in the previous will, of which we have seen a copy, except for the one clause regarding the house in Golders Green. And I'm sorry if this is bad news for Mr Parker, but the fact is that Mr Finnegan did not leave this property to him.' He stopped talking.

Arnold broke the silence: 'Well, just who *did* he leave it to, then?'

'To me.'

Arnold, who had not yet picked up the papers from his desk, looked amazed. 'You won't be surprised to hear that I am somewhat flabbergasted by this, Judge Rose. Mr Finnegan was my client for some years, and I was under the impression that I handled all his personal legal affairs. I was in touch with him until shortly before his death and he never mentioned the existence of a subsequent will to me.

162

And I can assure you that our relationship was such that he would certainly have said something to me about this.'

'Nevertheless, there it is,' the Judge said. 'I suggest you inspect it. Oh, and you will also notice that you are replaced as executor of the estate by my own solicitors.'

As Arnold began to read the document, the door opened and the receptionist entered with a tray. She handed out the coffee, placed a tray of biscuits on the desk, and withdrew. We all drank our coffee while Arnold read silently.

I was bewildered. The loss of the house that I never wanted or expected in the first place meant nothing to me, except that I would still have liked to solve the mystery of why he had left it to me in the first place. At least in his first will. But what puzzled me was the fact that Murdoch appeared to have been connected with a High Court judge and two particularly tacky private investigators. Arnold finished reading, and handed the papers to me without a word.

It was dated eight days before he was murdered. And indeed it appeared to be identical to the one Arnold had shown me in the restaurant except that where my name and address had appeared, the Judge's name and address in Northway, Hampstead Garden Suburb, now replaced it. It was signed with what looked to me like Murdoch's distinctive spidery signature, and witnessed by the Jacobson brothers.

'Am I permitted to ask about the circumstances in which Mr Finnegan made his will?' Arnold asked when I had finished reading.

'I can tell you only that Mr Finnegan approached my solicitors on that date, showed them a copy of the earlier will, and requested that they draw up a new one with those changes made to it,' the Judge replied. The twins showed no signs of being interested in joining the conversation, but just sat there with their huge hands in their laps.

'The document was drawn up then and there, signed and witnessed, and then deposited with the firm by Mr Finnegan. I cannot comment on why he did not inform you about the change, nor indeed can I explain why he did not ask you to make the change yourself.'

'May I ask, also, what your relationship was with Mr Finnegan?' Arnold said. He was leaning back in his chair, his hands clasped across his chest. It was apparently a relaxed attitude, but I could sense the tension in him.

For the first time, the Judge looked slightly hesitant. 'You may ask, of course. But I will say only that our relationship, which went back some years, was of a personal nature.'

'He never mentioned you, ever,' Arnold said, almost through his teeth.

'I cannot comment on that either, except to say that perhaps you had misunderstood your own relationship with Mr Finnegan.'

There was silence in the room, but only because Arnold did not bristle audibly. He handed the papers back to the Judge. 'I find this all very unsatisfactory.'

'Be that as it may. The point is that there was apparently a misunderstanding. We had assumed that you knew about the new will, and only realized otherwise a day or two ago. I regret the disappointment it represents to you—' the Judge turned to me—'but there it is. We must respect Mr Finnegan's last wishes.' He sighed and then took a breath. 'Who has the keys to the house?'

I took them out of my pocket, and put

them on Arnold's desk. The Judge got up and picked them up.

Then I spoke for the first time. 'The thing that puzzles me most is why an apparently respectable High Court judge is associating with these two low-life sleazeballs.'

That put some life into the party.

'Who the mighty fuck are you calling low-life sleazeballs?!' roared the twin on the left. I think it was Morris. They had both sprung to their feet and were towering menacingly over me. Well, towering only because I hadn't stood up yet.

I, however, was still looking straight at the Judge, whose face had gone deathly white. 'Are you going to answer me?' I said.

'I most certainly am not!'

'Then it appears that our meeting is over,' Arnold chipped in. 'Good afternoon, gentlemen.' There was but a moment's hesitation before the Jacobsons' threatening tableau broke up and they all three left briskly.

Arnold Mo took a sip of coffee and looked at me ruefully. 'I'm sorry.'

'Don't be, really. I'm not distressed. As you know, I did not expect the bequest, and I really did not need the house. The reason why Murdoch left it to me in the first place is still a total mystery.'

He shook his head. 'Something stinks to high heaven.'

'Is their will valid?' I asked.

'Seemed OK to me,' he said.

'The signature?'

'It was Murdoch's.'

'Signatures can be forged,' I said.

'I know. Do you want to challenge their will?'

'No. Well, not at this stage, anyway. Let me think about it for a day or two, and I'll be in touch. Thanks for all you've done, anyway,' I said, and we shook hands. The more I saw of Arnold Mo, the more I liked him and, even more important, my instinct told me I could trust him.

On the way out I stopped at the receptionist's desk. 'I hope you spat in their white coffees,' I said.

'I did better than that!' she replied, her eyes shining. 'They each got five Dulco-lax tablets.'

'What's the recommended dose?'

'One or two. They'll be lucky if they make it home in time.'

# CHAPTER 13

Samantha and I had dinner together at my place that Monday evening. I cooked a blanquette d'agneau from Patricia Well's marvellous *Bistro Cooking* and watched her eyes open appreciatively wide as she tasted the cubes of lamb which had been gently cooked in white wine, thyme, crème fraîche and lemon juice.

'You appear to be a man of many parts,' she said.

'My parts are spoken of with awe throughout the world,' I noted, pouring her a glass of very good Pomerol.

She gave me one of her hard looks which, I was beginning to notice, were not as hard as I had originally thought they were. Or perhaps it was that I was beginning to forget what she had done to my wrist the first night I met her.

Earlier she had told me about her meeting with the hotel owners, who had turned out to be a consortium of fourteen endodontic specialists—that is, dentists

168

who specialize in digging root canals at six hundred quid a shot—who now realized that they had been very poorly advised and were so delighted to have found a buyer for the hotel in a recession that they accepted an offer significantly below Samantha's anticipated ceiling. They were eager to sign the papers and rid themselves of an administrative headache.

'Looks like you'll be in the hotel business by the end of the week,' Samantha said.

I told her about my own meeting that afternoon, and it was useful to have someone to bounce my puzzlement off. Why, I mused, had the Judge and his henchmen waited four or five days before coming forward with their will? Why, indeed, had the Judge chosen to participate in the meeting in the first place? Presumably his solicitors could just as easily have delivered the message to Arnold Mo. What had Murdoch to do with Judge Rose and the Jacobson twins? Why had he bought the house in Golders Green? Why had he left it to me? And why had he subsequently changed his mind, without telling Arnold Mo? I had answers to none of these questions. Nor did Samantha. But I did know that they were all somehow connected to Murdoch's murder.

At about midnight Samantha kissed me languidly, her soft lips tasting faintly of cognac. 'Coming to bed?' she whispered invitingly in my ear.

'Um, sorry. I have to go somewhere.' My voice was laced with regret.

'Now?'

' 'Fraid so.'

'Should I ask where you're going?'

'It would be easier if you didn't.'

'Then I won't. But you will be coming back tonight?'

'I certainly hope so,' I said, although I was aware of the distinct possibility that I could end the night in a police cell.

'Where should I sleep?' she asked.

'Where you slept last night, although if you want to sleep somewhere else, there's a whole house full of rooms.'

'Ah, I see, this is Parker being non-presumptuous, I suppose.'

'Yes.'

'Well, I'll think about it.'

Frankie arrived at ten to one and we picked up Wheezy a few minutes later.

His eyes boggled when I drew up next to him in the cab.

'Jesus, Mr P, this is the first time I've taken a taxi to a job,' he remarked anxiously. I assured him that Frankie was to be trusted, and explained what we had to do. He listened carefully, and when I was finished he was shaking his head with a worried look on his face. By that stage we had arrived outside Murdoch Finnegan's block of flats.

'I don't like working with amateurs. That's how people get nicked,' he moaned.

'Wheezy, I'm intending to pay you a fortune for this,' I said.

'What kind of fortune?'

'How about five hundred pounds?' His face brightened up significantly. 'Come on,' I said, reaching for the door handle, 'let's get to it.'

'Oi, hang on. Look, if we're going to do this, we'll do it my way.'

He told Frankie to park the taxi in the heavily shadowed vehicle entrance to some offices across the road, and we sat quietly in the darkness for a few minutes.

'What are we doing?' I asked.

'I'm getting the feel of the place. Which one is the flat?' I pointed out the relevant window. He in turn pointed out that some of the windows around it were still showing lights, and we settled down to wait. Frankie put the radio on softly. It was an hour before Wheezy was ready to move.

'OK, you,' he said to Frankie. 'You keep your eyes peeled, and if you see anything funny, give a couple of toots on your 'ooter.'

'I'll do better than that,' Frankie said. 'If I see anything, I'll bell you on Mr P's mobile.'

Wheezy closed his eyes and took a deep breath. 'Oh Gawd, I'm on a job with a couple of bloody yuppies! I hope you can get us a good brief when we're nicked.'

'Stop being such a pessimist. Let's go,' I said.

'Wait. Take off your shoes.'

'Why?' I hissed.

'Because we don't want you clomping along the corridors and in the flat, that's why. Just do what I say.'

'But what if we need to make a run for it?'

A look of pain crossed his face. 'There's no such thing as making a run for it, for Christ's sake! We either get away with it or we get caught. There isn't a PC in 'Ampstead who couldn't run you down. They're all 'alf your age and twice as fit. Just do as I say!' I took my shoes off. He also handed me some white cotton gloves, and I put them on.

Wheezy picked up a small nylon bag and we were off, my heart thumping so loudly in my chest that I thought he would complain about it. It was now about half past two in the morning, and the street was quite deserted. I felt stupid crossing the road in my socks, wearing white gloves.

I must admit that he made short work of the main entrance door downstairs. He had it open in about three seconds flat with a piece of plastic. 'They're always loose, those front doors,' he whispered when we were inside. 'Makes it easy to get a piece of plastic round.'

My confidence in Wheezy grew, and then declined again after we had climbed three flights of stairs to the third floor and he was having obvious trouble opening the door of Murdoch's flat. He tried the piece of plastic but the door was tight against the jamb and he could not get it in. He tried in vain a number of keys he had in his bag. And then he started to pick the lock with what looked like a collection of hairpins. I was appalled at how long it was taking and convinced that, any second now, lights would come on and hordes of people would start demanding to know what we were doing. Then I forced myself to calm down. I realized that Wheezy was making almost no noise at all, and that while it was slow, he did seem to know what he was doing.

Finally, after about five years, the door opened and we were in Murdoch's flat, with that dreadful lingering smell again.

Wheezy shut the door quietly behind us, and then knocked my arm away as I reached for the light switch.

'No lights, dickhead!' he hissed.

'But the curtains are drawn,' I whispered.

'They still let some light through!' He switched on a small torch and moved it around the floor, careful not to let the beam play on the curtains. 'Gawd, it smells like something died in here!'

I carefully said nothing.

We went into the living-room and I pointed to the desk. 'Over there. Can you open it?' Wheezy crossed the floor slowly, putting his feet down tentatively before transferring his weight as he walked, no doubt attempting to avoid squeaky floorboards. But there were none. I followed, my heart still beating fast, and my breathing sounding very loud in the silence.

The drawers of the desk were unlocked. And empty. I pointed to the two-drawer metal filing cabinet. 'Can you open that?' I said, speaking so quietly that I was almost just mouthing the words.

'Piece of cake.' Wheezy took an old-fashioned hand drill out of his bag, fitted a narrow bit, and began carefully and quietly drilling a little hole in the top of the filing cabinet, about one inch in from the front right-hand corner, and just above where the locking button was. It took about two minutes. He put the drill away, and took out a thin screwdriver which he inserted into the hole. He pushed down carefully, and then the lock button popped out with a crash that almost deafened me. I was rigid with shock, until I realized that it had only sounded loud because of the relative quiet, and because of my own tension.

The drawers thankfully slid out noiselessly, and Wheezy held the torch while I began to look through the files.

There were not as many as I had

expected. I counted thirteen in the top drawer. They contained personal papers, tax affairs, bank correspondence, statements and used cheque stubs. There were files with electricity, telephone and gas bills, and even one for television licences. Murdoch had been a lot more organized than I had thought. I quickly scanned the bank statements and the correspondence, and was instantly surprised to find that my image of him as an incompetent and impecunious private eye was not borne out by his financial affairs. He had a healthy bank balance, a share portfolio and more than one equity-based savings plan.

I closed the top drawer and opened the bottom one. These were the case files, and I was sure that I was going to strike gold. Each hanging brown folder had a little plastic clip on it showing the file name, which in most cases was the surname of the client or the name of a company. I looked for 'Parker' and found it immediately. Inside was a typed account of the work he did for me, together with dates and details, although the episode in the tree was alluded to only as 'a misunderstanding with the local police'. Also in the file were the handwritten notes he had made when

I first came to see him and told him what I wanted done.

I found the Mohan Mistry file and again the details were on a typewritten sheet. I started looking through the other files. Some of the names I recognized, and others I knew quite well, but the majority were just names. There were fifty-seven of these files, and when Wheezy saw that I was going to open and peruse them all, he became agitated.

' 'Ow long are we going to be 'ere?' he growled in my ear.

'As long as it takes. You got any more batteries for that thing?' I nodded at the torch, which was beginning to dim.

'Of course!' I had wounded his professional pride. How could I have imagined that he would have gone out burgling without spare batteries for his torch? Unthinkable!

I carried on reading. There were a handful of fairly sordid surveillance cases to collect evidence of adultery, but the majority were much more interesting, sometimes involving quite large companies. After a while I began to realize that Murdoch had become an expert on tracking down the producers and importers of counterfeit goods and pirated films, compact discs and audio-cassettes. Murdoch had never mentioned *these* cases to us when regaling us in the pub with stories about his own incompetence.

He would start by buying a fake Rolex, or illegally copied video, and by a combination of clever paperwork and dedicated surveillance, he would work steadily backwards until he found the people his clients wanted. He was obviously very good at it, and some of the companies had used him time and time again. And these were big companies who would have paid him a great deal of money for the kind of work he did. I began to understand for the first time where he got the money to buy the house in Lemon Grove.

It was all very interesting, fascinating even, but there wasn't anything which I could even remotely connect to his death. I began to work faster, making a little pile of the files I had inspected on the floor next to the cabinet. I had done about half of them and I was reaching for another when something caught my eye.

I grabbed Wheezy's arm and pointed the torch so that the beam fell on the bottom of the drawer. There was a green file folder lying flat there, which would have been completely hidden when the other files were in place. 'Bingo!' I said to myself as I lifted it out.

It had no file name, but printed in ink on the green cardboard was the following: MICHAEL.

Even without opening it, I knew I had found what I had come for. I left it lying on top of the filing cabinet, and quickly went through the remaining files in the drawer, checking that they were just more of Murdoch's cases. I replaced all the other files and then I opened the green file.

It contained newspaper clippings, old and yellowed, and brittle with age. The top one was dated Wednesday November 12, 1972, and was from the *Daily Express*. The headline was: MASSIVE POLICE HUNT FOR GIRL, 9.

I looked at the next cutting. November 13, the next day, also from the *Daily Express:* POLICE DRAG HENDON RE-SERVOIR FOR MISSING GIRL.

I was about to look at the next one when the little telephone in my pocket rang with what seemed like an ear-splitting shriek. I dug frantically in my pocket to get it out, and searched even more frantically in Wheezy's wavering torchlight to find the answer button to stop it ringing. It took me a second, and then the ringing stopped.

'What?' I gasped into the mouthpiece. Then I heard Frankie's voice, low but urgent.

'There's two men on the way up, guv. They came in a Jaguar, the same one I saw at the coroner's court on Friday.'

Jesus! The Jacobson twins. In my mind's eye I saw huge fists.

'OK!' I rasped. I turned off the telephone and turned to Wheezy. 'There's two guys on their way up. We've got to get out of here!'

'No! There's no time. We'll never get out of the corridor before they arrive. Quick, follow me.' Wheezy quietly pushed the file drawer closed, and then pushed the button in to lock it. I grabbed the green file and followed him into the bedroom. He flashed the torch at the bed and said: 'Get under it!'

'Are you mad?'

'No, c'mon, move!'

We both crawled under the valance where it was stuffy and dusty and the smell of poor Murdoch's blood was even more overpowering. My heart was beating so fast it felt like one continuing throb, and a wave of nausea surged through me.

'They'll only look under beds if they've come looking for people,' Wheezy whispered in my ear. 'There's no way they can know we're here, so they can't be looking for us. Just sit tight, Parker, and we'll be OK.'

I tried to breathe deeply and the nausea began to recede. Then I heard a key go into the front door, and the door opening. A light snapped on in the entrance hall, and then one in the living-room. After an hour in the dark it felt like a searchlight had been switched on. From where I was lying I could see through the doorway into the sitting-room. A pair of legs in dark trousers and shiny black shoes appeared. Another similar pair appeared and, behind them, a small two-wheeled trolley. Then I could see nothing.

We listened to some unidentifiable noises, like scrapes and grunts, as if they were lifting something. And then I saw the filing cabinet appear, sitting on the lip of the trolley, as it was wheeled past. Then the lights were switched off, and I heard the front door of the flat being closed quietly. Neither of the men had said a word. I began to move but Wheezy grabbed me.

'Wait!' We listened some more and heard, faintly, the sound of footsteps disappearing down the corridor. 'OK,' he said. We crawled out from under the bed, and Wheezy went straight to the window which overlooked the street. I joined him and we stood there motionless, looking down until, two or three minutes later, the two men emerged from the building, carefully lowering the filing cabinet down the steps on the trolley. One of them opened the boot, and then they both lifted the filing cabinet into the car. The trolley went on to the back seat, and a few seconds later the Jaguar was gone.

My heart was still hammering to get out, and my breathing was ragged, but I had the panic under control. 'Let's get the hell out of here,' I said.

'My pleasure,' Wheezy said grimly.

We met no one in the corridor or on the stairs—it was after three o'clock in the morning, after all—and got back to the taxi without incident. Frankie was looking pale, but grinned when we got in.

'Thanks for the warning,' I said, 'but

the phone bloody nearly gave me a heart attack.'

'Find what you wanted?'

'Yes.' I was holding the green file tightly under my arm. If that's what the Jacobson brothers had come for in the dead of night, I had beaten them to it.

'Right,' I said, 'let's take Wheezy home.'

## CHAPTER 14

It was half past three in the morning when Frankie dropped me outside my home, and I told him not to come back before noon. The adrenalin was still rushing around my body, and I had no intention of going to sleep yet.

I went into the kitchen and put the kettle on. I made a cup of caffeine-free apple cinnamon tea and sat down at the kitchen table with the file I had liberated.

The first cutting from the *Daily Express* was a single column story from an inside page, and read:

A major hunt for a missing nine-year-old

183

schoolgirl was launched by Hendon police yesterday afternoon, after she was last seen talking to a man near the Welsh Harp reservoir.

The search was ordered a few hours after Rebecca Rosenberg, 9, failed to return home from school.

Initial police inquiries revealed that schoolfriends had seen Rebecca walking with a man they did not recognize in the direction of the reservoir.

More than a hundred police, including cadets from the nearby Hendon Police Training College, some using specially trained dogs, were searching the area for the girl.

Hendon police Chief Superintendent Paul Gallacher told journalists that Rebecca usually took the school bus home from the Bet Yisroel Jewish primary school in Maitland Park Avenue, but her absence had not been noticed by the bus driver or the other children until they had seen her, from the windows of the bus, walking with the stranger. At the time they had thought he was her father or a relative.

The description obtained from the children and the bus driver was of a man approximately 5ft 11ins in height, bearded, with long dark hair to his shoulders, wearing an embroidered sheepskin coat (sometimes called an 'Afghan' coat) and blue denim jeans.

'We do not know who this man was, or what he was doing with Rebecca, and at this stage, while we have no evidence that the child has been harmed, we are very worried indeed about her well-being,' the police chief said.

'I would call upon this man, whoever he is, to contact police immediately so that arrangements can be made to return Rebecca to her parents. I can assure him that he will receive all the help we are able to give him.'

Rebecca's parents, Mr and Mrs Julius Rosenberg, who have two other children, were last night said to be under medical care with relatives.

The next day's cutting from the *Express* had a bigger article and a bigger headline, reporting that the hunt for the little girl was continuing unabated, that the Welsh Harp was being dragged and searched by police frogmen, that police were interviewing all her friends, teachers from the school, and calling on local people who may have seen the pair walking near the reservoir, famous for its boating activities, to come forward with information. The chief superintendent was quoted as saying that he was now 'acutely worried' about Rebecca's safety.

This cutting also had a picture of the missing girl, a slightly fuzzy photograph probably taken from a small snapshot, but it was good enough to reveal a pretty, round-faced child with long, dark hair and dark eyes.

I was puzzled by all this. I couldn't remember the case, and I couldn't imagine what this had to do with Murdoch Finnegan who, if I had my dates right, hadn't even arrived in Britain until 1973. I carried on turning over the cuttings.

By the Friday, all the papers were carrying reports of the missing girl and the police search, including the *Hendon Times*, which had a better picture of Rebecca taken from its own files. She had been involved in a school activity which had been covered by the paper, a sponsored spelling competition in aid of charity, which she had won. This one showed her in her school uniform, her hair tied back in a pigtail, receiving her prize from the mayor, her proud parents and relatives standing in the background.

The *Hendon Times* had more information about the family. The father, Julius Rosenberg, was an accountant with a large firm in the City. His wife, Debbie, was a prominent member of the B'nai Brith Jewish women's social and fundraising organization. They lived in a typical semi-detached house in a residential street in Hendon, which was pictured. They had two other children: David, aged seven, and Sasha, four.

By the middle of the following week the coverage in the daily newspapers had reached a crescendo, with large articles about the missing girl. The distraught parents had appeared on television to appeal for the return of their daughter, and the police requests for information were becoming more desperate and more exasperated.

There was an extensive coverage of the exercise, a week after Rebecca's disappearance, when police staged a reconstruction of the known facts, using one of the girl's friends, in an attempt to jog people's memory, but apart from a few futile leads, nothing came out of it. No trace had been found of the girl or the man who was now assumed to have abducted her, and no further witnesses had come forward.

Coverage of the case then began to tail off in the press. The articles became shorter and less frequent, until it was just the *Hendon Times*, which stuck bravely with the story, as any good local paper should. Each week, on page three, there was a reversed block next to a picture of the girl, stating the number of days she had been missing and reporting on the continuing police inquiry. I could imagine the desperation of the reporter assigned to the story, having to find something new to write about each week in a situation where the police had virtually exhausted all avenues of investigation.

Then all hell broke loose again in mid-January 1973, when Rebecca's body was found in the large and overgrown back garden of a condemned house half a mile from the Welsh Harp.

One of the squatters who lived in a 'commune' in the house had seen crows squabbling over something in the dense undergrowth, and had gone to investigate.

The discovery brought hordes of police into the area who, apart from a minute search of the garden and extensive door-to-door inquiries over a wide radius, also virtually tore the squatters' home to pieces. For that matter, they also appeared to have torn the squatters to pieces. Half of them had been arrested following the discovery of marijuana and LSD in saleable quantities.

There were more sensational headlines when it was revealed that the post-mortem on the body had found evidence of rape and what the police would only describe as 'other horrific injuries'.

And then, a day later, most of the daily papers led on the fact that one of the squatters, said to be an American Vietnam veteran, was being questioned about the murder itself. As I read the cutting my scalp began to prickle, and shudders ran through me.

When, in the next day's clippings, the man's name was revealed after his short court appearance, I knew before I actually got to the name, that it would be Michael Finnegan. He had been charged with abducting, raping and murdering Rebecca Rosenberg, and had pleaded not guilty.

Coverage of the case then eased abruptly, as it has to under British law after someone has been charged with a crime. Nothing further happened until three months later when, at the committal proceedings, the defence made the unusual request that reporting restrictions should be lifted, and the magistrates agreed.

The police case was that Michael Finnegan precisely fitted the description given by the children and the bus driver of the man seen with Rebecca, down to the long hair and beard, and the Afghan coat and blue jeans which had been found among his possessions. Secondly, Rebecca's body had been found in the garden of the house where he was squatting. Thirdly, the accused had been unable to account for his movements on the day of the child's disappearance, had admitted frequent use of mind-altering drugs and heavy alcohol abuse, and had also admitted to having bouts of severe depression and periods during which he could not remember anything. Finally, and most conclusively, the prosecution revealed that a small pencil box which had belonged to Rebecca and would have been in her school satchel, had also been found in Finnegan's room in the squat.

A Home Office pathologist had given harrowing evidence of the injuries Rebecca had suffered and of the cause of her death. The child had been raped vaginally and anally, being severely injured in the process. And, if that wasn't bad enough, he also described 'shallow mutilations in the area of the chest and buttocks' which had apparently been inflicted by a sharp knife. His conclusion had been that the girl had bled to death. All the papers had run sensational stories, under huge headlines.

On the second day of the committal the defence presented its case. A young barrister by the name of Kenneth Gilbert had angrily attacked the police evidence, describing it as vague, sloppy and 'shamefully unjustifiable'.

He admitted that his client roughly fitted the original description of the abductor, but noted that there were thousands of hirsute young men of around the same height, wearing the immensely popular embroidered sheepskin coats. He revealed that the police had held an identity parade at which not one of the children nor the bus driver had been able to identify his client.

Gilbert recalled police witnesses and, in cross-examination, established that the police had not been able to bring forward a shred of forensic evidence linking his client with the crime, and despite the evidence by the pathologist that the victim would have bled profusely, no trace of blood of any description had been found on Finnegan's clothes and possessions which had been confiscated by the police.

He demonstrated that the squat had had a constantly changing population, with none of the more permanent members of the so-called 'commune' able to remember who precisely was in residence on the day of the abduction. A number of the squatters had admitted using and possessing hallucinogenic drugs, and would no doubt be prosecuted for that, but that did not constitute any evidence of guilt of murder and torture by his client.

He called as a witness a psychiatric registrar from the local hospital, who confirmed that he had been treating Michael Finnegan for severe depression. He was not surprised that Mr Finnegan could not remember what he had been doing on a particular day, months before the police questioned him. The psychiatrist said that his patient had been suffering from serious psychological traumas which were a direct result of his experiences in Vietnam, where he had been captured by the Viet Cong and tortured for four days before being liberated by American troops, after which he had been decorated by the army. He said his patient was depressed and traumatized, but had never shown any indication that he might be sexually perverted or violent.

In fact, the psychiatrist said, one of his patient's problems stemmed from the fact that he had been completely impotent—for physical reasons—since his experiences in Vietnam, and would thus have been incapable of committing the act of rape.

Kenneth Gilbert asked the magistrates to consider why, if his client had indeed committed the terrible crime, he had been content to go on living a matter of a hundred yards from the body which was sure to have been discovered sooner or later.

Michael Finnegan himself gave evidence on two points. He said he had found the pencil box during one of his daily walks around the Welsh Harp, but had never dreamed it had belonged to Rebeecca Rosenberg. Gilbert then made the point that police had never traced the school satchel itself.

Finnegan told the court that he had even

shown the pencil box to a teacher from a local school—not Rebecca's—and asked her in any of the children had reported losing it. The teacher was subsequently called and confirmed Finnegan's evidence. She said that she had told him that children were always losing their pencil boxes, and that he should probably keep it and not worry about it.

Then Finnegan had told the court that he had been assaulted by the police who arrested and then questioned him. Gilbert called a doctor who gave evidence about unexplained bruises, a broken finger, cracked rib and two chipped teeth, which Finnegan claimed was the result of the beating at the hands of his interrogators.

Finally Gilbert, in a brilliant cross-examination of the police concerned, had established that Finnegan had never been cautioned on his arrest, a number of the officers all having assumed that someone else had cautioned the prisoner.

In his summing up, Gilbert described the police case as a 'disgraceful example of a police force under enormous pressure to produce a culprit, violating both the rules of natural justice and my client's civil rights'.

He added: 'There is not, and there never was, enough evidence to arrest my client, let alone charge him and send him for trial. An obviously innocent man, who is also a vulnerable person, has been arrested, assaulted, and subjected to a terrifying ordeal for the simple reason that he was an unauthorized occupant of the house near to where the victim's body was found.'

The magistrates retired for a mere seven minutes before returning to dismiss the charge. And in so doing, they also made a point of castigating the actions of the police in bringing a charge based on such flimsy evidence.

Some of the papers had then interviewed a stubbornly unrepentant Chief Superintendent Paul Gallacher who had, despite the magistrates' criticism, truculently stated that as far as he was concerned, the case was closed, and he was 'not looking for anyone else in connection with this terrible crime'. The police would, however, continue to search for evidence. The clear implication of the interview was that Gallacher thought Finnegan had got off on a technicality and that they would not abandon their pursuit of him.

There were some follow-up stories for a few days, but then the matter appears to have finished its run in the press. There were no more clippings.

I sat in my kitchen, and became aware that dawn was beginning to break and that daylight was coming in the windows. Thoughts were churning in my head, but simple fatigue kept me from concentrating.

I went upstairs and found Samantha fast asleep in my bed and I managed to get in without disturbing her. I lay there reviewing the events of the day, and trying to empty my mind of images of little Rebecca Rosenberg, when I suddenly realized why the Jacobson brothers had only come looking for that filing cabinet in the middle of the night.

Dulco-lax tablets work quickly, and had kept the boys uncomfortably near a toilet for around eight hours. My helpless giggling woke Samantha.

'What's the matter?' she grumbled sleepily.

'Nothing, go back to sleep,' I whispered softly.

Just before I fell asleep with a huge grin on my face, I made a mental note to send Arnold Mo's secretary a huge bouquet of flowers.

# CHAPTER 15

I may have dropped off with a grin on my face, but that didn't stop the nightmares from invading my slumbers and making my sleep fitful and unpleasant. In one of the dreams I found myself walking on a residential street, about fifty yards behind a man who was dragging a little girl along with him by the hand. I ran to catch up with them but they kept disappearing around corners.

When I woke up, at about eleven o'clock that Tuesday morning, Samantha had left, leaving a note saying that she had gone to the hotel and would ring later. My mouth felt like a sandpit, and my head ached.

I ran a bath and then using my new telephone, I made some calls while lying in the hot water. The first was to Arnie at the office, to check that he wasn't getting ready to fire me again. He agreed, sullenly, that I should continue my 'researches' but he would expect me in the office on Wednesday morning to write an update on the murder inquiry. The hot water was beginning to make me feel human again.

Then I rang Theo at Hampstead police station. I did not feel it necessary to tell him about my nocturnal pursuits, and therefore could hardly raise the matter of the Rebecca Rosenberg file with him. I would have liked to ask him how the CID people who were supposed to have looked through the filing cabinet had missed it or, if they hadn't missed it, what they had made of it.

But I did tell him about Murdoch's new will, and about the meeting with Judge Rose and the Jacobson twins. There was silence on the line.

'Theo?'

'I find this connection between a High Court judge and the Jacobson brothers very distasteful,' he said eventually. 'The Talmud tells us: "The associate of a thief is like a thief," and those two are definitely bent.'

'Do you know anything about Judge Rose?' I asked.

'No, but I will make some inquiries.'

'How about checking to see if either of the Jacobsons has a shotgun licence?' I suggested.

'Hmmm,' he said.

After some prodding, Theo almost admitted that the police were getting nowhere on the murder inquiry. There were no clues, no motive and no suspects. The official answer was: 'Police inquiries are continuing.'

I got out of the bath, dressed and made myself some breakfast: strips of bacon with avocado on toast with expresso coffee from my little machine. There's no reason why a disturbed night's sleep should interfere with the important things in life. The newspapers were boring, or perhaps it was that I couldn't concentrate on them, and after about three minutes I found myself looking through that file again.

I realized, as I turned over the brittle pieces of newspaper, that the events they described had taken place twenty years ago and, had she lived, little Rebecca would now have been twenty-nine years old, probably married and possibly with a nine-year-old child of her own. That made me wonder about her family, who would also all be twenty years older. Little David would be twenty-seven, and Sasha twenty-four.

I turned to the picture of them all in the

*Hendon Times* article, but before I could look at the children, something else caught my eye. I was looking at a man in the background of the family photograph and I nearly spilled my coffee when I realized who it was. Judge Rose.

It took me a few seconds. Rosenberg; Rosen; Rose. Many Jews, along with so many other immigrants from Europe, had Anglicized their names—particularly those in professions where they felt they would be handicapped by a foreign name.

I looked at the caption, which I had skipped the night before, and there it was.

'Mr and Mrs Julius Rosenberg, pictured this week with their children David, 7, and Sasha, 4, and Mr Rosenberg's brother, Leonard Rose, QC.'

My heart was racing now. I didn't know what it all meant, but here was the connection which closed the circle. It had been obvious that Mr Justice Rose was connected in some way with Murdoch and the house in Golders Green. But here was a link which bound him to Rebecca Rosenberg and the file I had found in Murdoch's filing cabinet which also associated him with Michael Finnegan.

A horrible thought wormed its way into my mind. Had he been the mysterious stranger seen with Rebecca on the afternoon she disappeared? That would explain why the child might have gone with him in the first place. And had Murdoch somehow been able to establish that?

I reached for the telephone and dialled Ambrose Pendleton's direct line. There wasn't a prominent person in the legal profession that he didn't know.

'What do you know about Judge Leonard Rose?' I asked him.

'He's a High Court judge.'

'No, I mean his character, personality, that kind of thing.'

'I'm not sure what you mean. As far as I know, he's a well-thought-of judge. Very sound, knowledgeable and rarely overturned on appeal. Impeccable character.'

'Has he ever been involved in any controversy?' I asked.

'Not that I'm aware of. I used him once or twice when he was a QC; he came highly recommended and he did a very good job.'

'What sort of case?'

'A criminal case. He defended a client

201

on a manslaughter charge.'

'What sort of cases does he hear now?

'Criminal cases. That's his field, you see. As I said, he's very sound on the law.'

'Would you happen to know who his solicitors are? I mean the people he uses for his personal affairs?' Ambrose hesitated for a moment, no doubt wondering why I was asking these questions, but he was much too circumspect to inquire.

'I'll make discreet inquiries and call you back,' he said.

While I was waiting I dialled the *Observer* and asked to speak to Andrea Ferris. 'How would you like to have an expensive lunch with an ex-lover?' I asked her.

'How expensive?' Her voice gave me a tingle down my spine. I had been devastated when she walked out of my life, but I had recognized the impossible pressures she had experienced in our relationship, and I knew too that she would always associate me with the dreadful events surrounding the killing of Monique Karabekian, some of which she had witnessed herself.

'As expensive as you like.'

'Well, there's an *extremely* expensive

place just opened near here, except that it's full of foreign exchange dealers and stockbrokers, but it will do.'

'Sounds fine,' I said. 'I'll pick you up at one o'clock. You make the reservation.'

A minute or so later Ambrose called back. 'Judge Rose, I am told, uses a firm of solicitors by the name of Cohen, Hertz and Mandelstam. I gather there's a family connection with a senior partner.'

'Which one?'

'Mandelstam. Elliot Mandelstam is the brother of one of his sisters-in-law.'

'Do you happen to know which sister-in-law?' I held my breath, and with good reason.

'Debbie Rosenberg, I believe, she's married—'

I finished the sentence for him:—'to Julius Rosenberg, the Judge's brother.'

'Yes.'

'Did anyone mention the Jacobson brothers?'

'The who brothers?'

'Jacobson, Morris and Mervyn, they're private investigators with an office in Holloway Road.'

'Good Lord, no!' There was not a little horror in Ambrose's voice. 'I've heard about those two, and I'm sure no one reputable would associate with them.'

The connections of the circle were strengthening, but all they were doing was, well, leading me in circles. I sat for a few minutes, trying to figure it all out, but all that happened was that my head started to spin.

Frankie was waiting outside, and I was perversely pleased to discover him curled up on the back seat of the cab, fast asleep. He unfurled a bleary eye when I opened the door, and groaned pathetically.

'Gawd, I only got to bed at four o'clock, Mr P.'

'Come on, lowly employee, we have places to go to and people to see.'

'Oh,' he said with a faked look of innocence, 'no breaking and entering today, then?'

'Not today. We're going to the offices of the *Observer* in SW8, know it?' His face brightened considerably. He knew who I was going to see, and he drove to Chelsea Bridge House like a maniac.

He and Andy greeted each other like long lost siblings, and I felt quite put out until finally she smiled at me, pecked me on the cheek and said 'Hi!' I had forgotten how beautiful she was. Well, almost forgotten.

'So, Parker, what am I going to have to do for my free lunch?' she said as she got into the taxi. 'I think I'll be able to enjoy the food more if I know in advance.'

'Ah, so young and yet so cynical,' I lamented.

'Am I wrong, then?' she said sweetly. I knew when I was beaten. So did she.

'I just thought that, after lunch, you might spare me a few minutes and look up a few people in the *Observer's* files.'

'Why of course, Parker.' She smiled and those famous green eyes bored through me. 'On one condition.'

'Oh Lord, is an expensive lunch not enough?' She shook her head. 'OK then, what is it?'

'That I get an exclusive, with all the information you have, the Sunday after the *Hampstead Explorer* publishes whatever scoop it is you are working on.' It reminded me that Andy was probably a better journalist than I was.

'It's a deal,' I sighed.

Lunch was at a trendy little restaurant called L'Ecu and, as Andy had said, it was full of foreign exchange currency dealer types drinking champagne like it was Perrier and behaving as if they were on a fourth-form outing. They were almost throwing bread rolls.

Our table in the non-smoking section was relatively quiet and secluded, and although the pretensions of the menu were way beyond the talent of the chef, the meal was pleasant enough.

We brought each other up to date on our lives. She was seeing one of the senior Parliamentary lobby correspondents and doing very well as the paper's education correspondent. I stifled a pang of jealousy when she told me that she was very happy. For my part, I told her about the Bluebell Restaurant, the Chalk Farm Hotel and Samantha McDuff. I could have no secrets from Andy.

Finally I paid an outrageously high bill and we went back to the *Observer* where she led me into the library. 'What are the names?'

'Rebecca Rosenberg, a little girl who was murdered in 1972.' Andy shuddered, but she wrote down the name. 'And Leonard Rose. He's a High Court judge.' Her eyebrows went up.

Andy disappeared for a few minutes

and came back with two files which she put down on a table. 'Give me a buzz when you're finished and I'll come down and photocopy anything you want to take away.' She gave me her extension number, and pointed to a phone on the wall.

I opened the Judge's file first. It was marked LEGAL: *Personalities*. Then the name: Leonard Rose, barrister. The word barrister had been crossed out and replaced by the initials QC. Then the whole lot had been crossed out and replaced by: Mr Justice Leonard Rose, High Court, Strand.

There were about thirty-five cuttings inside, the first being a passing reference to him as the defence counsel in a Crown Court case in the early 'fifties. The subsequent clippings charted his career as a sought-after criminal lawyer, the cases becoming more and more prominent as the years went by. There was his name in the list of people who had taken silk, and the cases continued to increase in importance. He had defended politicians, films stars and sportsmen on a range of charges from shoplifting to attempted murder. When he had been appointed a judge, some of the papers had run short profiles of him, which could be summarized as: very competent and very reliable, but not eager to attract personal limelight. There was one cutting which mentioned his name in relation to the Rebecca Rosenberg case, quoting him as a 'spokesman for the family', but without revealing his relationship with the victim's father.

I made some notes, and I scanned through the case again, looking for some pattern. But there was nothing. I looked at the list of people he had defended, but again there was no pattern and nothing leaped out at me.

I turned to the Rebecca Rosenberg file and found, as I had expected, that there were more clippings here than Murdoch had been able to collect. But again I was disappointed, because it was all the same information. I noticed that one of the articles in the *Daily Telegraph* in 1972 had focused briefly on the fact that the family was Jewish, members of an Orthodox family, and that the children had been sent to private Jewish schools.

For some reason that made me look again at the cuttings from the *Jewish Chronicle* which I had glanced at a few moments before. One carried a picture of the Rosenbergs' house which, I now realized, had been quite a large mansion with wrought-iron gates and a driveway leading past the front of the building. There was a rather stout woman walking up the driveway, away from the camera, who appeared to be wearing some kind of nurse's uniform. I looked at the caption, which had been folded under the clipping.

It read: *Housekeeper Maureen Baker returning to the Rosenbergs' house...* I didn't read any further because suddenly bells were clanging in my head.

Maureen Baker. Who the hell was Maureen Baker? I closed my eyes and concentrated hard, and after a minute it came to me. The name had been mentioned by Arnold Mo during our lunch together the previous week. Maureen Baker was the former owner of Murdoch Finnegan's house.

I buzzed Andy, thanked her and told her I did not need any photocopies, and I headed for the taxi. The first thing I did was telephone Arnold Mo.

'You mentioned Maureen Baker the other day, the previous owner of that house,' I said to him when he came on the line.

'Yes, what about her?'

'That's what I want to know. Do you know any more about her?'

'No, nothing more than what I told you. She was a retired housekeeper or governess or something like that. Her will stipulated that the proceeds of the house should go to a children's charity.'

'Who drew up the will?' I asked.

'A solicitor in Palmers Green that I have never heard of. I actually asked him about the woman, but he knew nothing either. Apparently she walked in off the street one day and got him to do the will, and he never saw her again. Why do you ask?'

'It's hard to explain, Arnold. It's just that her name has cropped up in another context, and I need to find out more about her.'

'Oh well, if I can be of any help at any stage...'

'Thanks.' I hung up, feeling very frustrated. I needed to talk to Maureen Baker, but she was very dead and not talking to anyone.

My headache was coming back, and I tried massaging my temples. Frankie saw me in his mirror.

'You OK, guv? Want me to take you to the doctor?'

Doctor. Doctor. Doctor. More clanging inside my head as loud bells rang again. But in the end they chased the headache away, because I knew what they were reminding me of.

'Frankie, you're a genius.'

'Yeh.'

# CHAPTER 16

I asked Frankie to head for the house in Golders Green. It may not have been my house any more, but there was no reason why I couldn't talk to the neighbours, especially the one who had told one of the policemen that she had seen 'the doctor' visiting Maureen Baker every now and then.

If the policeman who had interviewed her that afternoon was to be believed, she had said 'the doctor' not 'a doctor', so presumably she knew which doctor it was. I wanted to know too.

It was around four o'clock by then,

and the traffic was awful. It got even worse as we approached the dreaded North Circular Road and Lemon Grove. For the thousandth time I wondered why Murdoch had bought the house, with its constant sound of traffic in the background and its entirely uninspired architecture. And for the thousandth time I wondered why he left it to me in his will. And then changed his mind and left it to Judge Rose. Or did he?

Seeing it for the second time, it was even more unprepossessing than I had remembered, with its garden choked with tall weeds and vicious brambles that looked as if they had been growing there untended for years, and the high dense hedge which grew round the perimeter of the plot.

I stood at the gate and tried to remember where the constable had been pointing when he referred to the neighbour who had seen the doctor arriving. It could have been any of the three houses across the road, but in the middle one there was a woman in gardening gloves pruning roses in her small front garden. She was doing more looking around than pruning, and I suspected that my search was over. In any case, spring was a little too late for serious pruning.

I put on my fifty-two-million-pound smile, elderly persons for the charming of, and crossed the road. She scowled as I approached, and took a firm grip on her wicked-looking secateurs.

'Good afternoon,' I said winningly.

'You from the council?' she growled.

' 'Fraid not.'

She looked as if she didn't believe me. 'I saw you looking in that house. It's a bloody disgrace is what it is. All them weeds and that bloomin' hedge growing all over the pavement. I been writing to the council for months to come and cut it back. But does anything happen?' She didn't look as if she really wanted an answer, so I stayed silent.

'Nothing!' she informed me triumphantly, with a slight nod of her head to emphasize the word. And then without a pause she went on: 'So who are you, then?'

'I was here the other day, with the police,' I said disingenuously. I was aware of the impression I was putting forward, but it was also the honest truth. A little flicker of respect and what I call 'citizens' guilt' came into her face—that's the little frisson of anxiety all law-abiding burghers experience when they see a police car in their rear-view mirrors or a police officer in the street. Or someone they think is a police officer.

'It's about that murder then, is it?'

'What murder?' I asked in what I hoped was an official voice.

'That Mr Finnegan who bought the house. He was murdered wasn't he?'

'How do you know that?'

'I read about him in the *Hampstead Explorer*.'

'No, I mean how did you know Mr Finnegan owned that house? That wasn't in the papers.'

'Well, he came here a few times, didn't he? And he introduced himself and asked me some questions. Nice man, he was.' She obviously didn't miss a trick. When she wasn't in her front garden pruning the roses and trimming the hedge, she was probably upstairs peeking through her net curtains. Burglars wouldn't have a chance in this street, and I made a mental note to warn Wheezy about Lemon Grove.

'What questions did he ask you, Mrs...

'Healey. Mavis Healey. Mrs Mavis Healey, only my husband died twelve years ago, bless him.' She beamed at me in the way people do when they think they are assisting the police. And she carried on beaming.

'The questions...?'

'Oh yes. I was out here doing some gardening one morning and he came over to introduce himself, he did. Told me he'd bought the house at an auction, and he asked me if I knew old Mrs Baker.'

'And did you?'

'Not really. I spoke to her once or twice, but she wasn't a friendly woman, you know. Kept herself to herself. A bit odd,' she said, tapping the side of her head meaningfully.

'In what way odd?

'Well, I went over there once, you know, to be neighbourly. This was many years ago. I offered to help her with the garden, which was already becoming overgrown even then, and she was downright rude. I mean, she said that if she wanted help with the garden she would hire a gardener. And then she said that she didn't like unannounced visitors. "Unannounced visitors," she said. Bloody cheek! Anyway, after that I never spoke to her again, other than to say good morning or good afternoon if we met in the street.'

'Did she go out much?'

'No. Every few days she would wheel her shopping trolley to the Waitrose supermarket and the other shops in Temple Fortune, but apart from that she didn't seem to go out at all.'

'What about visitors?'

'Oh yes, she had visitors all right. Fancy people in fancy cars who always came at night. I always thought that was funny, you know, because she wasn't posh at all, I mean you could see that, even though she did put on airs.'

'Do you know who these visitors were?'

'No, never saw them before in my life. There was a woman used to come about once a fortnight, sometimes with a man and sometimes on her own, and a gentleman came sometimes, very posh.'

'How do you mean, a gentleman?'

'Well, he was elegant and dignified, like, you know. You could see that he had a bit of class.'

'What about the cars, do you know what kind they were?'

'No, long and shiny is all I know. Never driven a car myself. Don't know much about them.'

'You're very observant, Mrs Healey.'

'Well, I am the Neighbourhood Watch

Co-ordinator for this street, you know. People have to watch out for each other, as you people well know.'

'Do you think you might be able to recognize these people who came to visit her, from photographs I mean?'

'Oh, you mean from their mugshots?' She gave me a conspiratorial, crime-fighting wink. 'I dunno. I could come down to the station and have a look through the books. Which station are you at, anyway? Golders Green?'

'Actually, I'm not attached to a police station at all. I'm on what you might call a special assignment.'

'Ooh, you mean you're Special Br—'

'Shhh!' I interrupted her, tapping the side of my nose and winking. Her eyes widened. 'I do have a few photographs I want you to look at, but I'll bring them to you in the next few days.'

She was beaming proudly now. 'Any time you like, I'm always here.' That was an understatement.

I was about to take my leave when I remembered that I hadn't asked her the question that had brought me here in the first place.

'Mrs Healey, I think you told one of

the constables the other day that you saw a doctor coming to the house.

'Oh yes! I nearly forgot. Dr Kaplan, from the Hampstead Garden Suburb Health Centre in Meadway Close, he used to come every Monday morning, around eight o'clock, like clockwork. I knew it was him because I used to go to the Health Centre years ago, although now I have another doctor. And that I found a bit funny, too. I mean someone would have to be pretty sick to warrant a visit from a doctor every week like that, and she didn't look sick to me. Used to walk pretty sprightly, I thought.

'And what was also funny was that when she did begin to look poorly, and walk with a stick and all that, the doctor had stopped coming.'

'Can you remember when he stopped coming?'

'Not exactly. But it was a good few years ago.'

'And the other visitors, did they stop coming too?'

'Come to think of it, they did! Around about the same time, too. Goodness, I hadn't really thought about it. Is this all very important?'

'Yes, it is. When did she die?'

'About six or seven months ago. She was dead for a week or more before they found her. The police broke in when the postman reported that he could see letters on the mat inside the door.'

'No meals on wheels or anything like that?'

'Not that I saw.'

'Well, Mrs Healey, you've been a very great help, and I'm very grateful.' Then I gave her a stern look. 'But I think it would be wise if you spoke to no one about our little chat.'

'Of course not!' She gave me a look as if to say: What do you think I am? The neighbourhood gossip?

I told her I would return at some stage with the photographs I wanted her to look at, and then I went back to Frankie's cab.

' 'Ullo,' he said as I got in.

'Hello,' I answered, slightly puzzled. He didn't usually greet me every time I got in.

'No, I meant 'ullo, here's a funny thing, look at that car.' I looked up and saw a familiar green Jaguar driving towards us. I immediately dropped down below the window-ledge.

'Tell me where it stops and who's in it,'
I said to Frankie.

'It's stopped outside your house. I mean
what used to be your house.' Then a
pause. 'And it's them two geezers that
came for the filing cabinet last night.
Nasty-looking buggers an' all.'

'Did they see me?'

'Nah, don't think so. They're not looking
over here at all. They've gone inside.'

'OK, do a U-turn and pull up next to
that woman I was speaking to if she's still
there.'

Of course she was still there. I peeked
cautiously through the window, and the
Jacobson brothers were nowhere to be
seen.

'Did you see those two men?' I called to
Mrs Healey. She nodded. 'Have you seen
them before?' She came through the gate
to the taxi.

'I don't think so, but I think that's one
of the cars that used to come here,' she
said, her eyes shining.

'Which one?'

'The one the distinguished gentleman
came in.'

Rose. It had to be the Judge who had
visited Maureen Baker regularly in the

evenings. The Jaguar must be his car. But why? I wondered briefly, if they had been having an affair, but dismissed the thought instantly. She was a retired governess, an elderly woman at least twenty or thirty years older than he was. What could they have possibly had in common? And who was the woman who came every week, sometimes with a man?

'Look,' I said to the Neighbourhood Watch Co-ordinator, 'please make a note of how long those two stay in there, and I particularly want to know if they are carrying anything when they come out, even if its a bunch of papers or a file or something like that. Can you do that?' It was a silly question. The woman had been practising doing that all her life.

'Of course!'

'OK, give me your telephone number and I'll call you later to see what happened.'

I wrote her number on a piece of paper, and we left. I asked Frankie to head for Meadway Close, and the Garden Suburb Health Centre.

It was the usual sort of set-up for a large doctors' practice, with a big waiting area strewn with toys and magazines, and two harassed receptionists answering the telephone, dealing with patients, responding to the doctors and trying to stop hyperactive children from wrecking the joint. I waited my turn politely and finally a young woman with strands of hair straying over her face asked me if she could help me.

'Sorry to bother you at such a busy time, but I've come for Mrs Baker's prescription from Dr Kaplan,' I said to her.

'No bother.' She smiled and rifled through a box under the counter. The smile turned into a slight frown. 'I'm afraid it doesn't seem to be here. When did she ask for it?'

'I'm not sure, she just asked me to pick it up for her.'

'Wait a minute, I'll see if there's anything on the computer.' She began tapping keys on a keyboard. 'Baker, you said. What's the initial?'

'M for Maureen, in Lemon Grove, NW11,' I said.

She frowned again. 'She's not listed.'

'That's very strange. I could have sworn she said she was a patient of Dr Kaplan's.'

'Well, that doesn't seem to be the case. She's not registered here at all, and never has been, according to these records. Do you want me to check with Dr Kaplan?'

'No, don't bother him. I'm sure the mistake is on our part. You know, come to think of it, she could have said "Dr Copeland". Is there another health centre around here?'

'Yes, there's the Golders Green Health Centre, near the tube station. They might have a Dr Copeland there.'

'That must be it. Silly me. Sorry to have wasted your time.'

'Not at all,' she said, and turned to the next person waiting.

I walked back to where Frankie had parked, hoping that my inquiry had been low key enough to pass swiftly from the busy receptionist's mind. I was also hoping that my surprise hadn't been too obvious. I had expected the woman to tell me that Mrs Baker was deceased, not that she had never been registered with the practice in the first place.

And why, I wondered, had Dr Kaplan spent so much time on regular visits to someone who apparently wasn't ill, wasn't registered with him, and was obviously not a relative?

All this was pushed from my mind when my little telephone rang. It was Samantha.

'Congratulations,' she said.

'For what, exactly?'

'Well, you are the proud new owner of the Chalk Farm Hotel, and I am your proud new manager. All the papers were signed this afternoon, and I've never seen a bunch of dentists more eager to take their money and run. Come for a drink.'

'Now?'

'Why not, the bar is open, and the beer is cold. Furthermore, there are a number of bedrooms which seem to be empty at the moment...'

Her logic was faultless. How could the new owner of a hotel fail to inspect the bedrooms as soon as possible?

## CHAPTER 17

When I walked into the hotel that Tuesday evening there was already a tangible difference in the atmosphere. A passing waiter smiled at me, and the young woman behind the reception desk beamed at me with all teeth showing. I noticed, too, that although it was now after six o'clock in the evening, there was a man washing the steps in the entrance hall.

'Ms McDuff, please,' I said politely.

'Of course, sir. Can I take your name?'

'Parker.'

She smiled again, dialled on a house telephone and murmured discreetly. 'The manager will be here in a minute, won't you take a seat, Mr Parker?'

'What happened here?' I asked her innocently. 'It's like you've all won the pools or something.'

She laughed. 'Well, something like that. It's just that the hotel has been taken over by new owners today and most of the staff are delighted.'

'Most of the staff?'

'Yes.' And then she leaned forward conspiratorially. I could see that she knew that she shouldn't be talking like this with a complete stranger, but she was also dying to tell someone what had happened. 'The previous manager was sacked on the spot, together with the restaurant manager—but apart from them, everyone is very happy,' she whispered.

Neither of us heard Samantha arrive. 'Not divulging confidential information, I hope, Shirley,' she said sternly, but I could see she was faking the harsh tone. The receptionist gave me a sharp, panicky look and I stepped in to save her.

'No, Shirley was just telling me discreetly where the gentlemen's loo was,' I said.

'I see. Well, Shirley, this is Mr Parker, a famous journalist with the *Hampstead Explorer,* who I hope is going to be coming to the hotel frequently. And when he does, please ensure that all his bills are sent to me personally. I would be obliged if you would let the rest of the staff know that as well.'

'Yes, Miss McDuff.' She looked at me with new respect.

'Ms,' Samantha said sharply.

'Sorry, Ms McDuff.'

We went into the bar and sat down at a table at a big window overlooking Chalk Farm Road and the Round House theatre. A waitress arrived in about half a second flat, and brought a bottle of champagne in record time.

'To your new venture,' Samantha said, raising her glass.

'And to your new job,' I said, touching hers with mine. 'The staff all look happy about it, I must say. What have you told them.'

'Well, just firing the previous senior management went a long way to cheering them up, but when they heard about the pay rises and the profit-sharing deal, they were ecstatic—after I managed to persuade them that it wasn't all a joke in poor taste, that is.

'I also gave them a pep talk about service, quality, cleanliness, customer care, efficiency, honesty and discretion, and it looks like they have taken it all to heart. The porter immediately started cleaning the entrance hall and stairs outside.'

'I noticed,' I said. 'Any other staff changes in mind?'

'Not at the moment. I want to see how they all respond before I decide whether we need to bring in anyone else. I've told the chef he'll be out on his ear unless he can prepare a first-class meal for me and a guest tonight, and I've made the head waitress acting restaurant manager on a trial basis. I think she'll be fine.'

After chatting about this and that and one thing and another for about half an hour, Samantha took me into the restaurant and introduced me to the acting manager.

It was Pam, the woman who had served

me and Frankie the week before, and I could see that she recognized me.

'Did you have something to do with all this?' she said, waving her hand so as to take in the whole hotel.

'Me?' I protested. 'I am a mere scribbler of words. I have nothing to do with hotels.' Alas, I could see that she was not entirely convinced, but she said nothing.

The meal, much to the relief of the chef who kept peeking anxiously round the door to the kitchen while we ate, was excellent, comprising an interesting terrine of salmon as a starter, and an unusual Lebanese main course of baked tongue in a lemon and garlic yoghurt sauce.

During dinner I told Samantha about the baffling connections I had uncovered between Murdoch and his brother and the family of the tragically murdered little girl, and about Maureen Baker and her visits from the doctor and the Judge. She was equally baffled.

'It's like a thick porridge that keeps bubbling in the most unexpected places. You can look down on it, but you can't see what's really cooking inside,' I said.

'Very poetic,' she remarked. 'What are you going to do?'

'I am going to stir things up.'

'Meaning?'

'Turn up the heat.'

'Aah, you mean bring things to the boil?'

'Indeed, I am going to disturb the hornets' nest and rattle their cages.'

'Kick a little ass? And put a cat among the pigeons?' Samantha grinned.

'Knock over the first domino.'

'Break some eggs?'

'Precisely. I am going to run a flag up the flagpole and see who salutes. And definitely no more mister nice guy.'

We were both laughing, and I sounded very confident, but I also knew that the whole thing was not funny. One man had been murdered, and there was an undertone of old murders, missing people, strange relationships and nocturnal skulking. In some ways it should all have been rather alarming, especially for a confirmed coward, but I was too personally involved in the mystery, and too committed to the chase to back off now. Another problem was that since I had obtained much of my information illegally, I couldn't turn to my usual source of protection, advice and support in the form of Theo Bernstein of Hampstead police. He was not the sort to regard a little breaking and entering with intent to snoop and steal as a kind of forgivable reporter's prank.

I suddenly realized that Samantha had said something which I had missed. 'Pardon?'

'I said, if I can drag you away from your mystery for just a moment, that it is time to inspect the bedrooms.' She had a kind of gleam in her eye. A wicked kind of gleam.

'Right,' I said decisively, getting up, 'where should we start?'

'Oh, I think we'll start with my suite and see how far we get.'

I have to report that we didn't manage to get any further.

Some time later something occurred to me and I whispered in her ear: 'I'll have to sleep here tonight, you know. I don't have any transport to get home. Is that OK?'

'Shut up, you idiot. You own this place, remember?'

'Aah yes.'

'You can do anything you want.'

'Anything?'

She turned her head to look at me, and I noticed there was still a bit of that wicked gleam left. 'Yes, anything.'

I knew then that I was going to do well in the hotel business.

In the morning we had breakfast together beneath the approving looks of sundry waitresses and hotel staff who appeared pleased to discover that their new manager was human. Little did they know that I, on the other hand, had been superhuman.

I telephoned Frankie, who was outside my house, and asked him to come and fetch me from the hotel. While I was waiting, I took a blank audio cassette from my briefcase and went into Samantha's office where I wound about half a roll of sticky tape around it. I put it in a large brown envelope, folded it, and then wound more tape around that. Then I typed a note, addressed to Elliot Mandelstam, Judge Rose's solicitor (and Mrs Rosenberg's brother), which said:

Elliot,

When you receive this tape, sign and date the envelope and put it in your safe unopened. For security reasons, do not discuss this matter with me or anyone else until required by me to do so.

L.R.

I put the little parcel and the note into another envelope, and addressed it to Mandelstam at the offices of Cohen, Hertz and Mandelstam in Seymore Place, Marylebone.

I was waiting outside when Frankie arrived a few minutes later. 'Not burglarising hotel rooms now, I hope, Mr P,' he said as I got in. I gave him a warning look and told him to take me to the office. I then sent him off to deliver the parcel, anonymously, at Mandelstam's office, and I went upstairs.

Although I was early, Arnie Bloch scowled at me. One of my ambitions was to get to the office before he did, but I had never managed it yet.

'Nice of you to look in,' he grumbled, a bacon and egg roll from the Greasy Spoon around the corner in his hand.

'You should eat more honey and sweet things, Arnie,' I told him.

'Why?'

'They improveth the humour and restoreth light to the eyes. That's from the Talmud, Theo tells me.'

'That's all very well for Theo; he doesn't have to produce a newspaper with a bunch of half-wits and layabouts,' said Arnie, as he lumbered off back to his office.

I made a cup of coffee and sat down at my computer terminal and began to write.

Murder victim Murdoch Finnegan who was found dead in his flat in Primrose Gardens, Belsize Park, last week, had mysterious links with the family of a little girl who was raped and killed 20 years ago.

The *Explorer* has discoverd an extraordinary connection between Mr Finnegan and a High Court Judge, Mr Justice Leonard Rose, the uncle of little Rebecca Rosenberg who was murdered in 1972 when she was nine years old.

Mr Finnegan, 45, who was shot to death in what police believe was a professional assassination, owned a small house in Lemon Grove, Golders Green—which he left to Judge Rose in his will.

The Judge, who attended the formal opening of Mr Finnegan's inquest with controversial private investigators Morris and Mervyn Jacobson, had refused to comment on the nature of his relationship with the murdered man, or to explain why he was bequeathed the house.

The Jacobsons, who are twin brothers, were also seen unlawfully removing a filing cabinet from the deceased's flat early on Tuesday morning.

But, in an even more bizarre twist, it has been discovered that Mr Finnegan's brother, Michael Finnegan, was once accused of the murder of Rebecca Rosenberg although he was later cleared of having been involved in the crime.

Shortly after the committal hearing in 1973 at which charges against him were thrown out, Michael Finnegan disappeared and was never seen again. It is thought that Murdoch Finnegan, a former intelligence officer in the US Army, had spent much of the twenty years he lived in London, searching for his missing brother.

My article went on to give details about the murder of Rebecca Rosenberg, biographical details of Judge Rose, a short report on the opening of the inquest and a paragraph on the faltering police investigation into Murdoch's murder. If that didn't stir things up, nothing would, I thought.

When I had finished, I reached for the telephone and dialled Ambrose Pendleton's direct line.

'You may get an urgent telephone call from Arnie Bloch soon, who will be worried that a piece I have written for this week's paper is highly libellous of a High Court judge,' I explained.

'Is it?' asked Ambrose.

'I'm not sure. I don't think so, but the point is that I don't care. I want you to assure Arnie that it is perfectly safe, and encourage him to run it.'

'Libelling a High Court judge could cost you a very great deal of money,' he warned.

'I have a very great deal of money,' I reminded him, although I don't think he had forgotten.

'Well,' he sighed, 'you're the boss.'

'So I am,' I said happily.

I printed out a copy of the article, put it on Arnie's desk, and went back to my office to await the eruption. It took about twelve seconds.

'PARKER!' he bellowed. It sounded more like 'Porker', but the volume caused a deathly hush throughout the newsroom, and most of my colleagues must have been convinced that I was about to be fired. Again.

When I went into his office, Arnie was

red in the face and staring incredulously at the sheaf of papers I had given him.

'What the fuck do you call this?' he demanded.

'I call that the best splash story we've had for many months,' I said coolly.

'Do you know what I call it?' Arnie didn't wait for my answer. 'I call it a blank cheque, on which Mr bloody Justice Rose can write his own name and amount of libel damages!'

'Which bit is libellous?'

'Which bit isn't? The whole thing suggests that Judge Rose is mixed up in some way with Murdoch Finnegan's murder and that he is a shady and mysterious character, when we haven't got one shred of evidence that he isn't a fine and upstanding citizen and a respected High Court judge to boot.'

'Every fact is true,' I protested.

'Every fact may well be true, but every adjective is actionable, and the way it's all been put together damages his reputation. And how do we know that there isn't a perfectly feasible and reasonable explanation for all this? Just because he refused to talk to you doesn't mean he's dirty. We are not using this. Finished!'

'Let Ambrose Pendleton have a look at it,' I suggested.

'I don't need Ambrose Pendleton to look at it!' he stormed. 'I am the bloody editor of this bloody newspaper and I say it's libellous and I say it's not going in!' When he had finished pounding his desk and shouting, and the echoes of his voice had stopped bouncing off distant walls, there was another hushed silence in the newsroom.

I spoke quietly. 'Arnie, I bet you fifty quid that Pendleton approves it like it is.'

The prospect of a quick fifty pounds calmed him down remarkably quickly. His eyes glistened. 'OK, smart arse, fax it to Pendleton. And make sure you bring me my fifty quid in cash when you get his reply.'

Ambrose waited a judicious hour and twenty-five minutes, and then faxed through a note to Arnie:

Dear Mr Bloch,

Careful scrutiny of Mr Parker's piece by myself and an experienced libel barrister of my acquaintance has led us to conclude that there is nothing actionable in the article as long as Mr Parker can assure us that the information therein is accurate.

Furthermore I would like to congratulate you and your staff for planning to divulge this information, which I consider to be squarely in the public interest. It is precisely the sort of brave and thrusting journalism which the owners of the newspaper expect from you and which vindicates their decision to make you the editor.

The decision whether you should run the article and in what form, is yours and yours alone. All I can say is that if you decide to use it in its present form, the owners will be prepared to underwrite any legal costs that may be incurred as a result.

From then on it was like the whole thing had been Arnie's idea in the first place. He instructed the sub-editors not to change a word, and he devoted page three to a big follow-up display reproducing the headlines and photographs in the old clippings I showed him from Murdoch's file and the stuff I had found in the *Observer's* library.

The front page headline read: JUDGE IN MURDER RIDDLE.

Arnie Bloch never mentioned the fifty pounds he owed me.

# CHAPTER 18

That Thursday, while the newspaper was being typeset and printed, I busied myself with further mischief.

I telephoned the High Court in the Strand and, with some difficulty, finally managed to get put through to Judge Rose's administrative assistant. I left him an 'extremely urgent' message to telephone Dr Kaplan as soon as possible.

I then called the Hampstead Garden Suburb Health Centre and left a similarly urgent message for Dr Kaplan to call Elliot Mandelstam, Judge Rose's solicitor (and the brother of Debbie Rosenberg, the murdered Rebecca's mother). I left a message for Mandelstam to ring Julius Rosenberg (the father), and one for Julius Rosenberg to telephone his brother, Judge Rose.

I also called the Jacobson twins' office and, thankful that they were not in at the moment, left an emergency message with their secretary for them to contact

239

Mrs Maureen Baker on a matter of life and death. Maureen Baker was, of course, already in the second category, but I thought the message might nevertheless intrigue them.

I rang the Rosenberg residence and, finding myself talking to an answering machine, left a message in a strong Indian accent for Mrs Rosenberg to ring Dr Kaplan.

Finally I looked in the telephone directory and found a number for a Paul Gallacher at a Hendon address. A woman answered and, after confirming that her husband was the former chief superintendent of Hendon police, regretted that he was out at the moment. I left a message for him to call Mervyn Jacobson on a matter of the utmost importance.

'He knows the number, doesn't he?' I asked.

'If that's Mr Jacobson the private detective, yes, I think so,' she said obligingly. So, Gallacher was involved, too, although in what I didn't have the faintest idea.

Considering that my stock with Arnie Bloch was still high after my little subterfuge of the day before, I slunk out of the office without him seeing me, feeling relatively safe from the threat of being fired.

I got Frankie to take me to a little florist's shop in Temple Fortune where I became instantly popular when I ordered eight huge bouquets of flowers for priority delivery to Judge Rose, Julius Rosenberg at work, Debbie Rosenberg at home, Dr Kaplan at the health centre, Elliot Mandelstam at his office, Morris and Mervyn Jacobson at their office and former Chief Superintendent Paul Gallacher.

In each case, I specified with a conspiratorial wink, the flowers should be accompanied by a card bearing the message:

IN MEMORY OF MURDOCH AND
MICHAEL FINNEGAN,
WHOM THE WIND BLEW IN AGAIN.
FROM THE MASKED AVENGER.

'What does it mean?' the young woman asked.

'I don't know,' I said truthfully. 'But I think they'll understand it. It's a kind of family joke.'

She appeared perfectly satisfied with the

explanation, particularly since I paid in cash, and she didn't even get round to asking me my name. I felt no twinge of guilt. Any of the recipients not involved in something dirty would be merely puzzled by the bouquets. Only the guilty would be alarmed, and alarm is what I was looking for.

Next stop was Mrs Mavis Healey, the all-seeing eye of Lemon Grove, to whom I showed the newspaper photographs of Judge Rose from my collection of clippings.

'That's the man. He's the posh one used to come and visit Mrs Baker every couple of months of so,' she confirmed.

I showed her the pictures of Julius and Debbie Rosenberg, parents of the murdered Rebecca.

'That woman used to come often, at least every second week, and always at night. I saw her often. And sometimes she came with that man, but I can't be sure about him. He didn't come all that often.' Her face was glowing with the pride citizens feel when they do their civic duty and play their part in ensuring that wrongdoers are brought to book and the glorious system of jurisprudence is strengthened by just that little bit.

She also reported that after we had left the other day, the two men who had gone into the house had spent about two hours there, but had emerged carrying nothing. 'Well, nothing I could see, at any rate.'

'You've been a great help,' I told her.

'I'm delighted to have been able assist the Special—'

'Shhhhhhhhh!' I interrupted her, my finger on my lips. 'The very hedges have ears around here. As far as you are concerned, I am just another private citizen, OK?' She winked at me, and nodded. I wondered how furious she would be if she knew that was the truth.

'Is there anything else I can do?' she whispered, turning her back on the nearest hedge.

'As a matter of fact, yes. You can go on keeping an eye on that house, and if you see anything strange going on, no matter what time of day or night, you ring me.' I gave her the numbers of my mobile telephone and the phone in the taxi, on a piece of paper.

'Just ask for Parker, or, if I'm not there, speak to a Mr Frankie. No one else.'

'No, of course not.' She looked hard at

the piece of paper, obviously memorizing the numbers, and then crumpled it up. I thought for a second that she was going to eat it, but then she put the little ball in the pocket of her gardening smock. 'I'll burn it later,' she assured me.

I decided it was time to visit Theo Bernstein to bring him up to date with the tangled web of intrigue and mystery I had stumbled on, and I had also thought up some simple lies which would enable me to omit the bit about me and Wheezy breaking into Murdoch's flat.

I knew that nothing would irritate Theo more than discovering that I had pertinent information that I was withholding from him or, even worse, reading about it first in the *Hampstead Explorer*. And an irritated Theo, particularly if he were irritated with me, was not a pleasant prospect. He was a rather big chap, with a mighty temper on a short fuse. He also had a fantastic memory for a whole list of misdemeanours and activities for which journalists could be prosecuted or just merely harassed.

'Where the hell did you come across this stuff?' he asked when I showed him my file of clippings and he had spent twenty minutes skimming through them.

'The *Observer* cuttings library,' I partly lied.

'What led you to them?' Theo's voice was strangely muted, and he was being far less aggressive than I had expected.

'I took a leap in the dark,' I lied. 'I looked up 'Finnegan', hoping to find something on Murdoch, but I found the cuttings about his brother. When I read those I looked also at the cuttings about the Rosenberg murder.' I also told Theo what I had found out in America about the two brothers, and what Murdoch had really done for a living.

'I remember that case,' he said softly. Aah, so that was it. 'Lovely little girl, she was. I was a relatively new PC on the beat, stationed in Hendon. We spent weeks looking for that kid in the undergrowth and in the Welsh Harp.

'I even vaguely remember Michael Finnegan being arrested and later released, although I had completely forgotten his name. I had no idea of this connection between the Finnegan brothers and the Rosenberg case.' He paused, and then: 'You think he spent all those years here in England looking for his brother?'

'Yes and no,' I said. 'I think he probably looked very hard at the beginning, and in the end he just got used to living here. It became his home, I suppose. What does it all mean, Theo?'

'I haven't a clue.'

'Any assistance from the Talmud?'

He thought for a minute, and then said: 'The rabbis tell us that each person has two portions, one of which lives in the Garden of Eden, and the other in Gehinnom—which is our version of hell. The exact proportion only becomes apparent during scrutiny on the Day of Judgement. I suppose the message is that there is no way we can tell what is in the hearts of our fellow men.' We were both silent for a few moments.

'Oh, by the way,' he said suddenly, 'your hunch was right. Both Jacobson brothers are registered as owning shotguns. They go grouse-shooting in Scotland, apparently.'

'Have the guns been inspected?'

'However, quite by chance, both these gentlemen reported their shotguns stolen in a burglary at their home last year.'

'No more grouse-shooting,' I said.

I left Theo in a sombre mood and went home. Samantha was busy with a training evening for staff, and would not be coming by later, so after making myself dinner, I decided to cheer myself up.

I got out the Yellow Pages telephone directory and spent an interesting hour making urgent calls to a whole series of twenty-four-hour plumbers, electricians and locksmiths from all eight of the players in my mystery, requesting immediate attention to burst pipes, faulty wiring and jammed locks. In each case I told the company to ask for Mr Finnegan at the address I gave them.

Within an hour or two there were going to be a whole lot of angry workmen demanding to know who was going to pay their call-out fees. Something told me that the fees would be quietly paid.

I also rang the Gas Board and told them there was an urgent gas leak in the basement of Judge Rose's home, and the Thames Water Authority to report effluent flooding from the toilets at Dr Kaplan's house.

Finally I telephoned Scotland Yard Drug Squad's Citizen's Line, on which people are encouraged to divulge anonymous information about drug dealers. I told them that I bought most of my heroin, cocaine, crack and marijuana from a Mr Finnegan at Morris and Mervyn Jacobson's address, and that he was usually heavily armed.

Having ensured a busy and interesting evening for a number of my fellow Londoners, I went to bed and slept soundly.

# CHAPTER 19

Mr Justice Leonard Rose telephoned me at the office at about twenty past nine on the Friday morning, publication day, which was about twenty minutes later than I had anticipated given that the *Hampstead Explorer* had been on the streets since dawn and our switchboard opened at nine.

'Do you know who this is, speaking?' he hissed. I could hear the rage bursting through all the seams in his speech.

'Of course,' I said, 'this is Camden Council's refuse contractors. Do you mind telling me why my bins haven't been emptied for a week?' There was a satisfying silence on the line.

'This is Leonard Rose.' The words were squeezed out, as through a mincer.

'Aah, the mysterious High Court judge. Sorry, you sounded exactly like a garbage collector just then. How are your close friends, the Jacobson twins?'

'Are you out of your mind, printing that sort of rubbish about me?'

'Aha! I knew refuse came into it somewhere. But the simple fact is that it's not garbage, since every word is true.'

'It's the most defamatory hotch-potch of innuendo, allegation and distortion that I have ever seen, and I demand a full retraction and apology in your next issue.'

'There is no question of that,' I said calmly.

'I will speak to your editor.'

'Feel free, but he'll tell you the same thing.'

'Then I am going to sue you and your newspaper for exemplary punitive damages. As far as I am concerned, this is the most deliberate and aggravated case of libel I have ever come across. It's inexcusable harassment, and if you thought that I wouldn't sue because I am a member of the judiciary, you have made a terrible mistake.' His voice was shaking with anger.

'I look forward to your writ,' I said. 'And I look forward even more to your cross-examination, under oath, when the case finally gets to court. Maybe then we'll find out about your relationship with Murdoch Finnegan, and why he left you the house.'

'These are private matters which concern no one but me,' he spluttered. 'I regard your intrusion as a gross invasion of privacy, and I am going to take decisive action against you. I warn you again, I will sue you and ruin you unless you print a retraction and prominent apology next week.'

'You can take a flying fuck at a rolling doughnut,' I said.

'What?'

'It's a phrase I borrow from one of my favourite authors, Kurt Vonnegut Jr,' I explained. 'I like it because it is such a graphic expletive, and so much more imaginative than merely saying fuck off.'

There was a deep silence on the line but eventually he spoke, and he sounded calmer now. 'Was it you responsible for all the nonsense that went on yesterday?'

'I regret that I haven't the faintest idea what you're talking about. What nonsense?'

'The telephone messages, the flowers, the tradesmen coming round late at night, not to mention the Gas Board insisting that I had reported a leak. Some other members of my family were subjected to similar abuse.'

'Sounds like you had an interesting evening.'

'Parker, you're walking on very thin ice.'

'Is that a threat, Mr Rose?'

'You will be hearing from my legal representatives.' And he put the telephone down.

There was also a great deal of interest expressed in our front page story about Judge Rose by a number of journalists from national newspapers, television news and radio reporters, but somehow I knew nothing would be appearing in their papers and on their programmes. Their lawyers would not be as supportive as ours were.

There was a more concrete reaction that evening, however. Samantha and I had been to the Screen on the Hill cinema in Belsize Park, and we were walking down the hill towards the hotel, arm in arm and in animated conversation about the film we had just seen. The spring weather had brought people out of doors and the wide pavement, with its restaurants, bars and coffee shops was bustling with Friday night crowds.

There was nothing special about the two men walking in the opposite direction, except perhaps that they appeared to be on a slight collision course with us. But then that sort of thing happens on crowded pavements, and what usually happens is that both parties then take automatic evasive action without even noticing. We didn't pay them any attention until, when we took our few steps to the left, they moved in the wrong direction, towards intercepting us again.

Samantha sensed the danger a moment before I did. Her reactions were fast and she began to pull me sideways, but she was not quick enough. Out of the blue, as far as I was concerned, a large and heavy fist plunged into abdomen, rattled around in my solar plexus, and drove a week's supply of air from my lungs.

I was bent double in agony, whooping desperately for breath, and aware through rather unfocused eyes that the fist was being drawn back in a leisurely fashion and would no doubt be travelling back in my direction shortly, perhaps with the object of restructuring my face. I remember wondering whether it would hurt, but there was certainly nothing I could do about it.

'Hey!' Samantha's voice rang out sharply. The fist, which had started its descent, hesitated and stopped. I managed to look past the fist and up the arm until I reached the face, which was not very reassuring. The man had short spiky hair, and the sort of puffiness of the features that one associates with professional boxers. His ears were scarred and misshapen, his nose was flattened and his mouth was fixed in a rather unpleasant grin, all the more alarming given that he wasn't looking at me, but at Samantha.

She was standing there, all five feet four inches of her, with her hand out, for all the world as if they had just been introduced at a garden party. Man number two, a little taller and slimmer, also with a face full of crude features, was standing a few feet off to the left, apparently happy to let his partner conduct the business for the time being.

'Well, hello, little lady!' said the man

who had hit me, and he put out his hand to shake hers.

It was, of course, a dreadful mistake. For him, that is. I saw Samantha's grip tighten instantly, and her left hand came over like a streak of light to settle on his wrist. His gasp of agony made me feel a lot better, and gave me new heart in my struggle to persuade my lungs to re-open for business. It was fascinating to see what total control she had over this enormous man. Samantha was holding his hand and wrist while he danced on the tips of his toes, desperately trying to reduce the pressure on the poor pinched nerve in his wrist, his left hand flailing helplessly in an attempt to keep his balance. This enabled Samantha to wield him as a kind of shield against man number two, who had suddenly come to life and was trying to lunge at her. But she simply kept her victim dancing in the way, and all the time he was making these staccato whimpering noises as the pain in his arm shot up into his brain.

She chose her moment carefully and then, with perfect poise and the most exquisite flowing movement, she delivered the most decisive kick in the balls ever seen in Haverstock Hill. I mean, just the sound of her shoe disappearing into his groin—impossible to describe really, but something like unripe plums being trod underfoot—brought sympathetic tears to my eyes. The recipient of the blow retired instantly to contemplate the meaning of life and the possibilities of future love, and played no further part in the proceedings.

Man number two was now treating Samantha with a lot more respect, and was being particularly careful not to shake hands with her. He was facing her in a kind of crouch, the two of them half circling each other before a fast-growing and utterly transfixed crowd of people.

'They're filming a movie,' I heard someone explain.

The two of them continued this wary dance for about twenty to thirty seconds before Samantha stopped moving, straightened up and said to me: 'Do you want to kill him, or should I?'

I, now able to breathe again, replied: 'Let me kill him. You always do the killing. It's my turn for once.'

Our prey had a glint of panic in his eyes but, to give him credit, he stood his ground. I for my part, was preparing to punch him in the face so hard that his nose would in future be at the back of his head. I wrapped five of my fingers together on my right hand, drew back my arm, and then, using all the weight of my body, delivered the human projectile at lightning speed. I missed his head by about eighteen inches, but in taking the necessary evasive action, the man had taken his eyes off Samantha McDuff for a fraction of a second. Another terrible mistake for their team.

I can't really describe what she did, because it all happened so fast that I didn't see it all. But what appeared to happen was that she dived into a kind of half handstand, the result of which was that her legs swung round in an arc and scythed his from under him. He landed heavily on his front with Samantha astride his back (how she got there so fast, I cannot say). She took a handful of his hair and sharply introduced his face to the pavement, just once, and the whole performance seemed to be over.

Someone in the crowd actually started clapping, and a few people began asking questions, but it wasn't long before a tall and very skinny young policeman shouldered his way through the gallery and demanded to know what on earth was going on.

Samantha pointed to the two men—one still writhing in a pool of vomit, his hands searching for life in his groin, and the other lying very still—and said: 'These two men attacked us!' She wasn't even breathing hard.

I had been punched brutally in the stomach, and was still feeling extremely tender in the region of the abdomen, but no injury could have stemmed the hysterical laughter that welled up in me and emerged in a long wheezing giggle which was probably the final straw which convinced the constable that we were lying, or taking the piss, or both. When Samantha started giggling too, he called the reinforcements.

It took a couple of hours at Hampstead police station before everything was sorted out. They called Theo Bernstein at home to vouch for me, and one of the nice people from the ringside seats had accompanied us to make a statement to the effect that he had seen me attacked, without the slightest provocation, by the big man with the broken nose. Our statements were taken and we were told that charges would probably be laid against the two men the following day. The trouble was, the police explained, they had both been taken directly to hospital, and no one even knew what their names were yet.

Samantha and I finally completed our walk down the hill at about one o'clock in the morning. When we arrived at the hotel, word of what had happened had somehow found its way there ahead of us, and there was an avenue of cheering staff to applaud us all the way to the lifts.

A few minutes later I was lying in a hot bath, trying to soak out the soreness in my midriff. Samantha was sitting on the edge of the bath, looking down scornfully.

'Just tell me one thing,' she said. 'Why didn't you hit that man back?' I closed my eyes and waited patiently for the humiliation to pass. She went on: 'You should have socked him in the jaw.' I considered putting my head under the surface and inhaling water. End it all right there.

'Just as well I was around to take care of you,' she said tenderly, taking a bar of soap and beginning to massage the bruised part of me with soapy movements.

Perhaps that's all she had in mind, but of course other matters reared their heads.

'Hullo,' Samantha said, widening her massage, 'seems like you are good for something, after all.'

## CHAPTER 20

Saturday is shopping day, even for multi-millionaires. I spent the morning playing dodgems with my supermarket trolley against the aggressive old ladies at Waitrose in Finchley Road. Many of them are refugees from brutal regimes in central and eastern Europe, and a mild-mannered English journalist is not even regarded as serious opposition by most of them, especially since my ego had already been severely bruised on the way in.

A squat elderly lady with a curly ginger wig, her arms full of parcels, had appeared to be having trouble pushing open the side door of the supermarket. In my usual gallant way I had leaned past her and opened it for her, my chest lightly coming into contact with her shoulder.

'Don' push!' she snapped at me irritably.

'I was just trying to help,' I explained, somewhat taken aback.

'Vell, pushink is not helpink!' she retorted angrily and bustled into the store. I stood there nonplussed, feeling like a member of the Gestapo.

When I came out there was a young man sitting on the pavement with a haversack and a small grey dog with a bushy face like a lavatory brush. The dog, that is, not the young man. He was holding up a notice which read:

I GENUINELY CANNOT FIND A JOB; I CANNOT GET BENEFITS, AND I HAVE NOWHERE TO LIVE. PLEASE HELP ME TO AVOID BECOMING A VAGRANT. MONEY WOULD HELP, BUT WORK WOULD BE BETTER.

I immediately felt guilty with my trolley piled high with goodies. I had been passing the fruit juice section when I remembered that my after-tax income was forty-five thousand pounds a week, and I had bought the two-litre container of freshly squeezed orange juice. Unbelievable extravagance.

'Is that true?' I said to him, nodding at the notice. He looked at me with slightly glazed eyes, and I wondered for a moment whether he was on drugs. Then I decided that this was the glaze of boredom, of desperation and of receding hope.

'If you don't believe it, just pass on,' he said. The voice was neutral, the accent Birmingham.

'I didn't say I didn't believe it,' I said. But he clearly didn't care what I believed or didn't believe. He wasn't even looking at me now. 'What would you prefer, fifty pounds now or a job on Monday?' I asked.

He squinted up at me. 'The job.'

'What do you do?' I said.

'Anything.'

'I mean, do you have any training?'

'I'm a graduate.'

'In what?'

'What does it matter?'

'I want to know.'

'Why?'

'Because I'm interested.'

'Nuclear physics.' He wasn't smiling. 'Bombs are out of fashion. Reactors are bad news, and research facilities have been clobbered by the government.'

'What degree have you got?'

'Ph.D. I was going to leave when I had my M.Sc, but there were no jobs. So I stayed on to do my doctorate. New varieties of fast breeder reactors. Even fewer jobs.' He snorted. 'Great career advice I got!'

'What's your name?'

'What's yours?'

'Parker.'

'Parker what?'

'Just Parker, don't push it.' People have been known to laugh when I say Horatio.

'Jerome, Martin Jerome.'

'What's the dog's name, and what kind of dog is it anyway? It's got a face like a lavatory brush.' He smiled for the first time.

'She's a miniature schnauzer. Sadie.'

I squatted down and said: 'Hello, Sadie!' She barked at me and backed away.

'Come on, Martin, I've got a job for you. And you can stay at my place.'

'Hang on, I don't even know who you are.' He paused, and then added: 'I'm not gay.'

'Nor am I.' I showed him my press card. 'I've got a big house with just me in it, and a friend who manages a hotel. Ever worked in a hotel?'

'No.'

'Want to try?'

'I'll do anything.'

I wheeled the trolley to the taxi-rank (Frankie didn't work at weekends—or, rather, Frankie didn't work for *me* at weekends) and I took Martin Jerome home with me. And his dog.

The first thing he did was have a bath. Then he changed into clean jeans and a T-shirt and came downstairs to watch me as I made lunch. I was tossing some fresh tagliatelle in a carbonara sauce and he told me his short life story.

He was a victim of his own qualifications, unable to find even menial labour from employers terrified of his accomplishments. And when he had tried to omit his university degrees, they had smelled a rat because of the long gaps in his CV and his total lack of previous employment. Many had assumed he had been in jail. At the age of 27 he had never had more than a part-time holiday job, and his housing situation had become suddenly acute when he had fallen out with his girlfriend and had to move out of the flat they had shared. His benefits had run out, he had been sleeping rough for eight days and had been on the point of, as he put it, losing the desire to keep clean.

After lunch I telephoned Samantha at the hotel, told her about Martin and asked her if she had a job for him.

'Do you want me to have a job for him?'

'Yes.'

'Then he starts on Monday.'

'As what?'

'We could do with another barman in the cocktail lounge.'

When I told Martin he was delighted, then he paused. 'What about Sadie?' I hadn't thought about that, and I said we would speak to Samantha about it, but I wondered what he would say if she said he had to get rid of the dog. I mean, after all, what was more important, a job or a dog? I was to feel somewhat differently about the dog the next day.

After lunch I got a call from Theo to say that our two assailants had been treated overnight in hospital, charged with assault and released on bail at the magistrates' court that morning.

'Released?'

'Yes. We opposed bail, of course, particularly since we suspect that they gave us false names, but the magistrates felt that the charge was a minor one, especially in view of the fact that the victims were apparently unharmed and the perpetrators appeared to have been beaten to a pulp.'

I bridled slightly at the suggestion that I had been unharmed. My abdomen still felt severely bruised, to say nothing of my ego, which was still on a life-support system. But I let that pass. 'What names did they give?'

'Gerald Mooney and Patrick McCarthy. We've never heard of them, which makes me think that they don't exist. The address they gave was a single men's hostel in Kings Cross.'

'Which was which?'

'McCarthy is the impotent one. Or will be for some weeks.'

'Oh.'

Samantha came round for dinner and met Martin and Sadie. I must admit I held my breath when they shook hands, but he escaped with just a friendly squeeze. Later Samantha asked me if I wanted a job in the hotel kitchen. (I had served quails with polenta, the breasty little birds lightly browned first in the pan, and then cooked gently with shallots.) I declined the job offer politely. Martin offered to wash up, and I congratulated myself on my choice of house guests.

We watched some awful Saturday night television and then retired. Martin couldn't wait to get into a real bed, and we were still exhausted from our very late visit to the police station the night before. Besides, my poor bruised belly was still very sore, and was crying out for another massage...

I was in a satisfying and well-deserved deep sleep when I dreamed that dogs were barking. I opened one eye, saw the glowing red figures on the radio alarm clock which read 4.22 a.m, and was about to close the eye again when I realized the dog was still barking. We had put Martin and Sadie in the spare room above my bedroom in the roof space at the top of the house. I grumbled to myself, wondering whether my homeless person and his barking dog was such a good idea after all. Furthermore, I realized he was smoking up there.

Then, with a chill of understanding which turned my bowels to ice, I realized that I was not smelling cigarette smoke. It was far too bitter and acrid. I thumped Samantha who came instantly awake.

'Get up and put something on, I think we've got a fire!' I said urgently, aware of the necessity not to panic. There was a tracksuit hanging over a chair and I put it on in five seconds. Then I flew up the stairs and pounded on Martin's door. Out in the passage the smell of smoke was intense, and getting worse, and Sadie was now barking furiously. Martin opened the door wearing green stripe pyjamas, looking shocked.

'There's a fire downstairs, come with me.' He made to go back into the room, but I grabbed his arm. 'Leave everything! Come on, now!' He picked up the dog and followed me down to the third-floor landing, where Samantha was standing in her dressing-gown.

Like most people, I had worked out a vague plan of escape in the event of a fire. My plan was to go out through the doors to the flat roof patio on the second floor and then simply jump over the low parapet wall to the neighbour's property. But now the smoke had become thick and swirling, and I could hear, although still couldn't see, any flames. It was a dull, crackling sound of intense ferocity, and I couldn't believe how quickly it became difficult to breathe without choking. But I knew we had to go down one flight of stairs to escape.

Coughing and wheezing, I explained what we had to do, and they both nodded. Martin holding tightly on to the struggling little dog. 'Come!' I shouted and I started down into the thick smoke, holding my breath.

It should have taken two or three seconds to open that door. The keys were on a hook to the right of the door and even in the pitch dark there should have been no trouble. I pulled back the bolt, put the key into the mortice deadlock and turned it. Then I pushed the door. It should have opened easily. But it didn't. I pushed harder, thinking it was just stuck, but there was no give at all. Panic began to well up in me, and I spent vital seconds cursing myself for having thick burglar-proof bars fitted over the glass. The other two, seeing me struggling, came to help, and the three of us heaved against the door. Without the slightest effect.

That's when a sheet of orange flame

came shooing up the stairs towards us, and we ran coughing and gasping back up the stairs. The heat was instantly furnace-like, as if someone had played a blowtorch on our backs. I could feel and hear my hair and clothing beginning to singe. I knew that there was no refuge in our bedroom on the third floor, and we pounded up to the top room.

I came into the room last, and slammed the door. Samantha was already stripping blankets from the bed and she threw them at the bottom of the door in an attempt to stop the smoke that was flooding in and poisoning us.

From here there was only one way out. The only windows in the room were three Velux roof lights, set into the thirty-degree angle of the roof and they were about eight feet from the floor. I dragged a chair over, climbed up on it and opened the window closest to the house next door, my heart sinking at the prospect of somehow climbing out on to the sloping roof and crawling along the tiles, with nothing else to hold on to. But there was no time for panic. The room was filling steadily with smoke, and I knew it was only a matter of a minute or so before we all succumbed to the cyanide in the fumes. Nobody gets burned to death in house fires; the smoke gets you long before the flames arrive.

I was about to haul myself up when Martin pulled me down off the chair. 'Let me! I know how to do it!' he shouted.

For one terrible second I thought he was panicking and desperate just to get out first, but when I saw the way he pulled himself up to the window ledge, first to his chin and then his elbows, I could see the training of a gymnast there. He leaned forward, did a kind of forward somersault and disappeared. There was another terrible long moment when I thought he had plummeted four storeys to the ground, but then his head reappeared.

'Give Samantha a hand up and I'll help her out.' I grabbed her around the knees, and lifted her up so that she was high enough to grab hold of the window-ledge. She pulled herself up so that her head was through the window. Martin reached down with his right hand, grabbed hold of the cord of her dressing-gown at the back and heaved her upwards. A second later her legs were through the window.

'There's a flat strip of roof on the top. I'll get her up there and I'll come back for you. Hang on!' and he disappeared again.

I looked back towards the door and was horrified to see a rim of angry red around its edges. I could hear the flames roaring behind it, and I could see the door blistering and the panels actually beginning to warp and buckle in the heat. The smoke appeared to be coming in from everywhere now, even the floorboards, and I realised that if I wasn't out of there in the next few seconds I would not survive. I climbed up on to the chair again and waited for Martin. It felt like an hour, although it was probably just ten or fifteen seconds before his face was there again. I put my hands up and prepared to pull myself up.

'Sadie,' he said. 'Sadie first.'

His face was about three feet from mine, and I was looking directly into his eyes. They were bright and unwavering, and there was no arguing with them. 'If you don't get her, I'm coming in myself!'

There was, literally, no time to argue. I jumped down from the chair and looked around for the dog, but couldn't see her.

That's when the lights went out. 'She must be under the bed!' he shouted.

I crossed the room and felt blindly under the bed. Nothing. No, not nothing. There she was, huddled terrified into a scorched fluffy ball in the furthest corner. I dived under, grabbed a handful of dog coat, and dragged her out. She didn't struggle at all.

I took hold of the loose skin around her neck and handed her up to Martin. He took her from me and disappeared again. By this stage I was coughing seriously, every breath an agony of fire as the acrid smoke burned its way into my lungs. My eyes were streaming and all I could see was the dull outline of the open window through the dense clouds of smoke. And then suddenly there was brilliant light in the room. A tongue of flame licked through a gap at the top of the buckling door, and, like a wave of water, flowed across the ceiling.

Time to go, Martin or no. I pulled myself up so that my chin was at the level of my hands, but was shocked to find that I had no strength left. I couldn't breathe properly and I was hanging there, aware that I could not push myself further out, and that it was only a matter of seconds before I fell back into the room, to certain death.

I felt the flames begin to explore around me with a surge of heat, and I knew the strength was going from my fingers. Then a hand clamped itself on the fabric of my tracksuit and began to haul. I pulled upwards on my screaming arms and then somehow I was half across the window-ledge, my torso hanging down alarmingly towards the gutter and forty-foot sheer drop to the ground.

'Come on! Push down with your arms to get your legs out. You won't fall, I've got you!' I looked up to see Martin lying full length on the tiles facing down the pitch of the roof. Hanging on to his ankles for dear life was Samantha.

That hand clamped on the back of my tracksuit gave me the confidence to heave myself through. It was the hand that stopped me rolling down the roof while I was convulsed by a paroxysm of coughing. The tiles were becoming burning hot and there were wisps of smoke curling up between each one. Another minute or two and we would begin to fry. I began inching myself up the pitch of the roof, half under my own steam and partly dragged by Martin and Samantha, and then, after a burning age, I was on the flat part. I couldn't breathe and I couldn't see any more, but hands seized me under the arms, and we half crawled over the parapet wall on to my neighbour's roof. As we went over I looked back and through the thick red mist of my weeping eyes I saw flames roaring upwards through the open window with the intensity of blazing gas from a bunsen burner.

I lay on the cool asphalt roof, for the second night in a row whooping and fighting for breath. This time, though, it was a losing battle. I could feel the darkness gathering around me like an oppressive cloud and everything seemed to be moving further and further away.

I remember three things from those moments. One was Samantha's hands pushing down rhythmically on my back, helping me to breathe. The other was the distant sound of sirens yelping and blaring in what seemed to be the very far distance. Then there was the wet lick on my cheek from a little pink tongue as my nostrils filled with the smell of scorched miniature schnauzer.

# CHAPTER 21

Heroes in novels wake up in hospital and don't know where they are. In my case, I woke up a minute or so before I opened my eyes, and I prayed that I was in hospital. There was a pounding in my head, rushing noises in my ears, my lungs seemed to be filled with hot coals and there were burning sensations in various parts of my body. I don't think I would have been too surprised had there been a red geezer with horns and a pitchfork standing by my bed.

In fact, what I saw was an angel. Samantha was smiling at me.

'Lazy bastard. Just like you to go to sleep when the rest of us had to do all the work.'

'How am I?' I asked. I urgently needed to know if any importants bits had been burned off me. Except that the words came out like 'Howama?' and I discovered that I had an oxygen mask over my mouth. I pulled the mask away.

'Howama?' I asked. The old throat felt a bit rough.

'Not too bad. A few superficial burns, a little scorching. You've lost a few tufts of hair and you look pretty funny. Your main problem was breathing. For a while you weren't doing a lot of that, but you seem to have got the hang of it now. Personally, I always make a point of continuing breathing, no matter what. Even in the most exceptional circumstances, I tell myself: Samantha old girl, the thing is to keep breathing...'

Her voice tailed off because although she was trying to be funny, and succeeding what's more, the pressure of her hand on mine was just too tight to hide the emotion in her. The tear that rolled down her cheek was a bit alarming, too.

'Whereama?' I rasped.

'St Columba's. It's a private hospital in St John's Wood. Ambrose Pendleton took charge and had us all whisked out of Casualty at the Royal Free and brought here. At your expense, I presume.'

'You OK?'

She smiled. 'Fine, really. Just a bit shocked for a while, and a bit sore in the chest.'

'Nothing wrong with your chest,' I croaked, 'that a little massage wouldn't put right. Rub in a little goose fat, my grannie used to say.'

'Sounds as if you are going to live after all,' she noted, holding firmly on to my hand that was about to demonstrate what I meant.

'Martin Jerome? Sadie?'

'They're OK. The dog is a little scorched and subdued, and Martin has some burns on his hands, but he's fine. Seems the dog was less affected by the smoke because she's closer to the ground.'

Slowly but surely I managed to get the story out of her. The fire brigade had indeed arrived just as I was losing consciousness and it hadn't been long before we were rescued from the rooftop by beefy firemen who had come sailing up on a hydraulic platform. The firemen had taken over the artificial respiration and also fed me oxygen before an ambulance had arrived and taken us all to hospital.

Apparently, there had been a bit of a fuss in Casualty when Martin refused to be separated from his dog, and hospital security men had been on the point of taking drastic action when Ambrose

Pendleton had arrived on the scene.

'I didn't know who else to call,' Samantha explained.

At St Columba's I was apparently paying for a special room for Sadie, the promise of much money having smoothed the path of inter-specie hospital harmony. A vet had even been called from Cricklewood to treat her. His bill would probably be the biggest, I suspected.

The other two had been treated for shock and, like me, for the effects of toxic smoke inhalation. Except that I had been in the house for a good few minutes longer than they had. I had been unconscious and sedated, but at least breathing on my own, for the rest of the night and all the morning. I had woken up at the three o'clock on Sunday afternoon.

'The house?' I asked.

'Yes, well, the thing is, there isn't one. It burned right out. It was all the firemen could do to stop it spreading to the house next door.'

I thought of all the years I had spent in the house, and all the possessions which had gone up in flames, and I felt curiously unmoved. I had bought the house with my ex-wife Julia, with the intention of filling its many rooms with miniature Parkers. But when the marriage failed, and she motored off with her Welsh car mechanic, I had never really enjoyed living in such a big place on my own. There were some books, and some records that I would miss, but not much else.

'Martin was terrific,' I said. 'I don't think I could have made it on my own. I suggest we give him an increase in salary.'

'Can't do that. He's resigned.'

'Before he started? That was quick.'

'He's decided he wants to be a fireman. And when the firemen heard about what he'd done, they said that would be a jolly good idea. They are going to recommend him for the fire service training school or whatever it's called. They also want Sadie as a station mascot, so that seems to be working out well.'

'I hope he hasn't told them that he's a nuclear physicist. Not yet, anyway. Tell him he can live free at the hotel until he's organized.'

We chattered away for a few minutes, and then I asked Samantha where my clothes were. 'You don't have any,' she said.

'How on earth am I going to get out of here if I haven't got any clothes?' I protested. A steely look came into her face.

'Parker, if you so much as attempt to get out of that bed, I am going to rearrange your vertebrae, and that will be after we shake hands,' she said meaningfully. I knew an effective threat when I heard one, so I decided to keep very still. I could always make a break for freedom later.

A doctor came in soon after that, beamed warmly at me, listened to my chest, said I was doing nicely, inspected a few minor burns, the worst being on my legs, and then injected me with sedative and antibiotics using a needle and syringe the size of a bicycle pump.

The next thing I knew it was Monday morning. Samantha had gone, but Theo Bernstein was sitting next to my bed. He didn't look like an angel at all.

'How are you?' he asked.

'Starving,' I said. 'Do you know how to call room service in this place?'

Theo sighed and went out. Two minutes later he was back with a nurse.

'Would it be possible to get a full

English breakfast, with coffee, toast, baked beans, sausage, the works?' I was expecting a snappy put-down, to be followed by a bowl of thin gruel, and I was amazed when she said she'd see what she could do. That's why people go to private hospitals; not for the medical care, but for the waitress service.

'My visit is not entirely a social one, Parker,' Theo said. 'I've just been down to talk with the fire investigation people in Kentish Town.'

'What caused the fire?' I asked. 'Bad wiring?'

'No, what we have here is arson and attempted murder.'

Suddenly I didn't feel like a lot of breakfast.

'Explain, please,' I said.

'The investigators found clear evidence of the introduction of highly inflammable accelerant to the property. In layman's terms, they believe a good few gallons of petrol were poured into the basement through the coal hole, and followed by a lighted match.'

'No doubt about that? No mistake?'

'No doubt at all. That is, of course, arson, and could also constitute attempted murder given that the person or persons involved must have known, or at least suspected, that the house was occupied at the time. But there's something else.'

'What?'

'The doors to the second-floor rear patio roof were wedged shut with two stout pieces of six by four. Whoever started the fire ensured that there was no way out.'

I remembered the panic as we had heaved in vain against those patio doors, and I felt a new kind of heat flow through my body. A seething anger which quickened the heartbeat and the breath. Friday night had been a clumsy warning. Saturday night had been a professional sortie. War had been declared unilaterally, and it was time for me to muster an army and mount my own campaign.

'Who do you know who hates you so much?' he said eventually. 'No, I'll rephrase that. Which of the many people who hate you would have gone to such lengths to get rid of you?'

'The same person, or persons, to use your phrase, who killed Murdoch Finnegan,' I said without hesitation.

'And who might that be?'

'I don't know. Well, not exactly, anyway, but I'd bet you a million pounds it has something to do with Judge Rose, the Rosenberg family and the Jacobson twins.'

'All that is very mysterious, I agree, and worthy of investigation, which we are doing. But there is no evidence whatever that any of them were involved in the Finnegan killing or in this attempt on your life. Try and bear that in mind, Parker, or you could find yourself in some serious trouble.'

'What about those two goons who attacked us on Friday? Couldn't you get out of them who put them up to it?'

'Those two gentlemen were as tight-lipped as could be. And as far as attacking you is concerned, they claim it was the other way round. An unprovoked attack, they said, and they are considering a cross-summons.'

There was a short silence.

'Theo,' I said, 'I urgently need to be deceased.'

'You very nearly were, from what I hear.'

'No, I mean now. I need to be deceased now.'

'What are you talking about? You sound delirious.'

'No, listen, Theo. How much publicity has there been about the fire? Who knows that I survived?'

'There hasn't been a lot of publicity. Some of the Sundays and the radio bulletins reported that three people and a dog had been rescued from a fire and taken to hospital, but none of them used any names. But I don't understand what you're getting at.'

'I want you to announce that I died last night. After valiant efforts to treat me for toxic smoke inhalation, etcetera, etectera.'

He gaped at me. 'Impossible.'

'Why?'

'Don't be stupid. It's absolutely impossible! It would involve the whole Metropolitan Police force in deliberate mendacity. Something like that would probably have to be authorized by the Commissioner, or even the Home Secretary himself, and there isn't a hope in hell of that happening. Forget it right now.'

I thought for a minute. 'How about

a mistake, then? An inadvertent misrepresentation because of a computer error, which could be corrected after a couple of days? Look, Theo, the police wouldn't even have to say anything. All you would have to do is refuse to comment and refer any inquiries to the hospital. Just for a few days.'

'Tell me why.'

'Don't you read detective novels, for heaven's sake? Because if your person or persons think they got me they'll, firstly, not bother to try again and, secondly, they'll carry on with whatever they were doing, thinking that I'm not around to bug them. It'll make it easier for us to crack this case.'

'Us?'

'Come on, Theo, I'm already heavily involved and you know it.'

'What about your friends and the handful of other people who know you? They'll be very upset.'

'It'll only be for a day or two. They'll hardly have started grieving yet.'

He looked thoughtful. 'I'll speak to the Chief Superintendent. But don't think you're going off on one of your solo flights, Parker. This is a police investigation remember, and you won't take a step without our say-so.'

'Of course, Theo,' I lied.

'And you'll have to sort out the hospital side of things. I'm not having the police involved in putting pressure on them to make this 'mistake'.'

'Leave that to me,' I said.

When the nurse brought me my breakfast (orange juice, poached eggs, bacon, sausage, beans, fried tomato, brown toast, marmalade, filter coffee) and a newspaper, I asked her for a telephone, and she wheeled one in from the corridor. I also asked her to marry me, but she refused.

I telephoned Ambrose Pendleton and asked him to try and set up a top level meeting with the hospital bosses as soon as possible. I telephoned Samantha at the hotel to tell her that I was still in the land of the living, no matter what she might hear later in the day, but that she should say nothing to anyone else. I also rang Frankie in the cab to warn him to be ready to pick me up at the hospital's service entrance after lunch. My last call was to Mr Douglas, the keeper of my funds at Rothschild's, to ask if he could use his influence in getting me a new credit card, since my previous ones had been burned to a crisp.

'I wouldn't be surprised if American Express sent one round by courier within the hour,' he replied.

Ambrose called back half an hour later. 'We're meeting in the hospital boardroom at noon,' he said.

'How did you manage that so quickly?'

'I mentioned money.'

When he arrived, Ambrose and I managed to have about ten minutes alone to discuss tactics before we went in to meet the hospital directors, me still in my ward pyjamas and dressing-gown.

They listened in polite bewilderment while I outlined the plan and then looked extremely dubious, even though I assured them that Hampstead police would be cooperating in the subterfuge. That's when Ambrose chipped in, wondering whether there was, perhaps, some rather expensive item of essential equipment that the hospital urgently needed, because, if there was, he just happened to know of a wealthy mystery benefactor who might be willing to provide just such a machine.

It turned out, as it happened, that the

hospital was actually quite keen at that particular moment to come by a magnetic resonance imaging scanner, and Ambrose said he felt sure that his benefactor friend would be delighted to oblige.

'But on one condition.' Their directorial eyebrows went up. 'The scanner is to be made available three days a week, free of charge, to general practitioners, and national health service hospitals in the area.'

They didn't like that very much, but went for the deal anyway. From one o'clock, callers would be told, tactfully and mournfully, that poor Mr Horatio Parker had shuffled off his mortal coil. And if the shit hit the fan at any stage, they would apologize in consternation, claiming that a computer had confused two patients by the name of Parker.

When Frankie picked me up surreptitiously from the hospital's rear loading bay I was still in pyjamas, and the only thing I owned was a brand new American Express gold card. But not for long. I asked to be taken to Knightsbridge, where I had a little shopping to do.

When I walked into the menswear department at Harrods, a little knot of salesmen looked at me in horror. I stood there patently in my dressing gown, a pleasant smile on my face, until finally an obviously junior member of staff was elbowed in the ribs and pushed my way. His name tag said: 'Mike Harris, trainee.'

'Can I help you?' he said nervously.

'I think so,' I said.

It turned out to be the most exciting afternoon of Mike Harris's young life.

When it became clear what was going on, that I was about to replace an entire gentleman's wardrobe virtually without regard to cost, the senior staff tried to muscle in on the act. But I rejected their advances firmly, and focused my attention only on Mike Harris. Once or twice I even had the floor manager carrying large parcels for me.

It went on for four hours, and resulted in suits, jackets, trousers, jeans, shirts, underwear, ties, handkerchiefs, socks, belts, shoes, coats, gloves and a whole array of leisure wear in a buying spree of dreamlike proportions. I took some essentials with me, and the rest was to be delivered to the Chalk Farm Hotel. When I left, they lined up to say goodbye like I was departing royalty, and said that they hoped I would come back soon.

On the way back to the hotel I stopped in at Mohan's shop to get another of those dinky little mobile phones. I had become used to the luxury of having a instant Dick Tracy communicator in my pocket. Then I slipped into the hotel the back way and took the staff lift to Samantha's suite.

I dialled her ground floor office, and when she answered I said: 'Is that room service?'

She recognized my voice. 'Yes, sir, what can I get you?'

'Well, let's start with champagne, Veuve Clicquot Gold Label '82 if you have it, with some caviar and toast.'

'Will that be all?'

'No. I also want you to send me up a woman. Not too tall, mind you, and very beautiful. She should have dark hair, strong muscles and a complete lack of inhibitions.'

'...lack of inhibitions,' she repeated, as if writing down the order. 'Anything else?'

'Yes. Tell her to make it snappy, because I'm very thirsty.'

# CHAPTER 22

Being dead wasn't nearly as bad as some people make out. I spent much of that Tuesday morning having a leisurely breakfast in my room, trying on different combinations of my new clothes, and thinking. Mostly thinking. In my mind I tried to review all the events and information I had come across in an attempt to make sense of it all, and in the process I came across a name I hadn't followed up yet; Kenneth Gilbert, the young barrister who had defended Michael Finnegan at his committal hearing all those years ago.

I looked in the telephone directory and was rewarded with the information that Mr Gilbert was now a QC, with chambers in Lincoln's Inn. I dialled the number and, to my surprise, was put straight through to him after giving my name. I thought barristers were always with clients or appearing in court or something, not sitting around in their offices taking calls from strangers.

'Hello, Mr Parker, what can I do for you?' said a pleasant voice.

'You don't know me,' I told him, just in case he was mistaking me for someone else.

'I know that, old boy,' he said, just as pleasantly.

'I'm ringing about a Mr Michael Finnegan, someone you defended at a committal hearing on a charge of murder twenty years ago. I was hoping you might remember the case.' There was a lengthy pause.

'Goodness me, you are raking over some very cold coals, but yes, I do seem to remember the case. An American Vietnam war veteran, if I remember correctly, who the police were trying to fit up with the murder of a little girl.'

'That's the one. Could I talk to you about it?'

'By all means, old boy, so long as you first tell me who you are, why you want the information and how you are going to use it.' I spent the next five minutes putting him in the picture.

'A journalist, eh?'

'Yes.'

'How about you take me out for lunch on

292

your expense account, and we'll talk about it then?' I sighed to myself. These lawyers seemed to have a very odd perception of reporters and their finances.

'You mean, today, now?'

'If you're free, why not?'

So I arranged to meet him at the Bluebell in Mayfair at one o'clock, wondering how successful a QC he could be if he was free like that for lunch at a moment's notice. Most other barristers I knew could only give you appointments weeks hence. I mean, you would be wary of any dentist who agreed to see you on the same day, wouldn't you?

The mystery was unravelled soon after my arrival at the restaurant. And after Hazel Cowan, the manager, had pulled me aside in the foyer, told me my guest was already seated, and whispered in my ear: 'He's gorgeous. I want his telephone number.'

'And I thought you only had eyes for me,' I sighed.

But I could see what she meant as soon as I saw him. He was big, in his middle to late forties, with lots of sandy hair, a square jaw, wide mouth and deep blue eyes that twinkled with a mixture of humour and deep knowledge. His hands were delicate, though, with slender lawyer's fingers, some of which were wrapped around a glass of what I noticed was very expensive champagne. He was the kind of man that women instantly find attractive, and men instantly hate. I tried to reserve judgement.

'Hello, old boy. How do you do? Have a glass of this fizz which, incidentally, I am paying for.' That was one point in his favour. He wrapped some of his slender fingers around my hand briefly, and then sat down again.

He was wearing a beige cashmere sports jacket and a light blue cotton roll-neck shirt, not the attire I normally associated with barristers. 'I should have been playing golf today. You were lucky to catch me,' he said.

'So why aren't you?'

'Chap I was going to play with scratched. Bad back or something. But I think he was afraid of losing some money.'

'Golf on a Tuesday? Don't you have to go to court or see clients in the clink on weekdays?'

'Oh dear, civilians have such strange concepts about barristers. No, I hardly ever go to court. I see it as a kind of defeat to have to go to court, and as for seeing clients in the clink, as you quaintly put it, I try to do that on other days of the week. There are times when I do, in fact, have to be in court, but the general approach is that work has to give way to the important things in life.'

'Like golf?'

'Certainly like golf. You know of course that the Lord adds to man's allotted span on earth all time spent playing golf?'

'I didn't know that.'

'Well, now you know, old boy. Now you know.' His speech was a kind of lazy drawl, and liberally sprinkled with 'old boys' and 'chaps'. But there was too much intelligence in his eyes and his demeanour for it to be convincing. I began to think that it was a kind of disguise to distance himself slightly from people he didn't know until he'd had time to suss them out.

My guest ordered snails followed by some complicated dish involving seafood baked in a pastry case. I ordered a large fish soup with lots of garlic *rouille*, and let him prattle on about golf and the ways he had of avoiding working on Tuesdays. A very important day to have as a rest day, he said. Monday was a total shock to the system, and he would never get through to the end of the week without being able to recover from it on Tuesday.

But when the food arrived, it was time for him to sing for his supper. 'So, what can you tell me about Michael Finnegan?' I inquired.

'How much do you know already?'

I told him. It took a few seconds, and he listened carefully. I had the impression that there was a tape-recorder running inside his head, and that he could probably have repeated my words back to me verbatim. And when I had finished he sat thoughtfully for a few moments, gnawing quietly on the shell of some crustacean.

'Yes, you have the bones of it. The reporting of the case in the papers was quite accurate, by and large. I had a look at the file before I came here. It was a strange old case, and I have to admit that at the very beginning I had some sympathy for the police, who were so convinced they had found their man.'

'Sympathy for them? But you flayed them in court.'

'Well, of course, I had to. But if you

look at it from their point of view, there was just so much circumstantial evidence pointing at him, and so much pressure on them, that they simply failed to look at the wider picture. After they arrested him, and particularly when they found out he had been arrested in America on a rape charge, they just stopped investigating the case, they were that convinced they had the right man.'

'But you didn't?'

'No, I suppose I had the benefit of my client cooperating with me wholeheartedly, whereas he was refusing even to talk to the police. I suppose that had we laid it out for them before the committal proceedings they might even have dropped the charge, but I wanted to have it emphatically thrown out of court.'

'Why?' I asked.

'Well, looking back on it after the event, it was probably a tactical error, but the police had been so bloody about it that both Finnegan and I wanted some sort of a hearing so as to clear him formally. We were worried, I suppose, that if they merely dropped the charge, they could continue hounding him and could just as easily have charged him again at some later stage. To have it thrown out at committal would make it a lot harder for them to do that, although, theoretically, he could still have been charged with the same offence again.' Gilbert paused for a moment.

'And I suppose, if I was to be honest, I should also say that there was another agenda.'

'Which was?'

'Chief Superintendent Paul Gallacher, the copper in charge of the case.'

'What do you mean?'

'I mean we took an instant dislike to each other. I felt only contempt for him that he had jumped to so many conclusions about Finnegan. I meant, after he had established that Finnegan had been arrested in connection with a rape charge in Boston, he didn't even bother to get the full details of the case sent over by the Boston police. He actually didn't know until the day of the committal hearing that Finnegan had been the victim of an obvious case of mistaken identity, and had been released without a stain on his character.

'Gallacher blustered at the time that he would have had all the documents by the time of the trial, but it was totally negligent of him. All the other details showed negligence, too. The total lack of forensic evidence, the constantly changing population of the house where the body was found, the inability of witnesses to identify Finnegan as the man they had seen with the child. And then there was Finnegan assessed by a psychiatrist to establish his mental condition.' Gilbert's eyes were flashing with anger now.

'Then there was that business with the pencil box, which Gallacher had thought was the final clincher. Finnegan had told them about the other teacher he had spoken to about the pencil box, but the police had assumed that he was merely lying through his teeth, and hadn't even checked with the woman involved. The whole thing was outrageous. The most shoddy piece of police work I had ever seen. I mean, they didn't even get round to cautioning him properly when he was charged.

'And then they had to try to beat a confession out of the poor chap—a man still traumatized by the treatment he had received at the hands of what he called "Ho Chi Minh's boys" in Vietnam. I was incensed, and determined to expose the police to as much criticism and ridicule as I could, and I succeeded handsomely. And I think, in the end, that was a tragic mistake.'

'Why?'

The words came more slowly now. 'Because it didn't do Michael Finnegan any good at all. The poor fellow was in a terribly bad way to begin with, and all the trauma of being held in prison and subjected to all the publicity could only have made his state of mind that much worse, and I thought he became pretty suicidal. You know he disappeared shortly after the hearing?' I nodded.

'We looked for him for ages. The police looked for him, I hired a private detective, and then his brother, who had come over for the court hearing, came over again from the States and he spent years looking for him. I don't think Murdoch Finnegan ever stopped looking for his brother. And now he's been murdered. Tragic, absolutely tragic. The trouble is, I don't think I ever really believed that Michael would be seen alive again.'

'What do you think happened to him?' I asked.

'I don't know. I just feel that some day

his remains are going to be found at the bottom of a lake or reservoir somewhere, or lying in some dense patch of undergrowth in some forest. My feeling about him was that he was such a terribly damaged person that he just couldn't cope with all that had happened to him, and I think he took a long swim somewhere, or just crawled off into the bushes to be alone for ever. I feel very guilty about it.'

This was a very different Kenneth Gilbert from the one who had jabbered on about golf half an hour before. The façade had dropped completely, and what was exposed was very sensitive indeed.

'Why should you feel so guilty?' I prompted gently. There was no reply. Those clear blue eyes burned fixedly into mine for a long time. I was just taking a breath to ask the question again when he spoke.

'Because I wasn't acting in his best interests. I was gunning for Gallacher, and I was almost blind to everything else. I was too young and too angry to realize that my client was suffering, and would suffer more, as a result. But there was yet another dimension to all this that not even Micahel Finnegan knew about.'

301

'Which was?' I said quickly.

'Gallacher hated me. I mean he *really* detested me. My occupying space on the same planet offended him.'

'Why, for heaven's sake?'

'I'm gay. Homosexual. Queer as a coot. Whatever you want to call it. And Gallacher knew. Don't ask me how, but he knew. Photographs from some student gay rights march perhaps, or from some informer. Remember, this was the early 'seventies, and homosexuality wasn't as common, or as accepted as it is now. The man used to sneer at me, and whisper insults to me as we passed. The bastard! I was fighting him, when I should have been defending my client.' Gilbert's voice was shaking slightly.

There was nothing I could say, so I said nothing, and we drank our coffee in silence. And after a few minutes I could see the composure building again, and the shutters going back up. He'd be calling me 'old boy' any second now. But I had one last question.

'Did Gallacher ever accept that he'd arrested the wrong man?'

'That's an interesting question, and I'm not sure about the answer. On the other hand, he wasn't stupid, and the material I presented was pretty conclusive. But on the other hand, such an admission was quite beyond him. To admit to that serious a catalogue of errors would have destroyed him in his own eyes, and I don't think he allowed himself to believe it all for an instant. After the trial he accused me in private of helping a murderer to go free on legal technicalities. I didn't even bother to argue with him.'

He left a little while later, leaving me with the bill and with Hazel Cowan, who was desolate when I told her the news about my gorgeous lunch guest. She decided that she didn't want his telephone number after all.

I was in a sombre mood on the way back to Hampstead, with thoughts of mystery and death rushing in circles through my mind, and I suppose that's why I started thinking about cemeteries. I put a call through to Theo Bernstein.

'Were you at Rebecca Rosenberg's funeral?' I asked him.

'Yes, a number of us went.'

'Do you remember where it was?'

'Of course. It was the Jewish cemetery in Golders Green. The one off Hoop Lane, opposite the Golders Green Crematorium. Why?' I hung up without answering, and gave Frankie new directions.

Cemeteries are gloomy places at the best of times, and that afternoon was not the best of times. The weather had earlier been mild, full of the promise of spring, but out there among the uniform stones on that largely flat piece of land, what had earlier been a gentle breeze took on a chilly edge.

There were no grandiose monuments in the Jewish cemetery, no huge statues of angels or carvings of animals; just simple graves with modest polished headstones, some of them arranged in pairs for husbands who had been joined by their wives and vice versa.

A very polite man in the cemetery office had looked up Rebecca Rosenberg and directed me to the grave. It too had a simple black stone with letters etched and lined with gold leaf. At the top was a star of David above some Hebrew lettering I did not understand. Underneath, in English, were the words:

# REBECCA LEAH ROSENBERG

*August 22, 1963-November 12, 1972*
*Taken suddenly, and free now from evil.*
*But we do not forget, or forgive.*

The bitterness of the inscription flooded over me in an icy wave. I suddenly had an image of the small coffin buried there and of the child within. But in my mind the body was still perfectly formed, and I pictured the pretty round-faced girl with long dark hair and dark eyes that I had seen in the photographs, resigned to lie there for an eternity until the time finally came for her to tell her terrible story.

I noticed that some of the graves had lines of little stones placed on the base of the headstones, and I jumped to the conclusion that these were placed by mourners visiting; to show they had been. And cared. Something like placing flowers on a grave, but a quiet understatement. I picked up a stone off the path and leaned forward to put it on the grave.

'Who are you?' said a woman's voice behind me.

I was startled, and turned quickly to find myself looking at Debbie Rosenberg, the murdered child's mother. There was no mistaking her distinctive face, but time had wrought terrible damage on the once fine features. And perhaps not just time. Grief too. The woman I had seen photographed in the newspaper cuttings had been elegant and poised, and despite the strain she had been under at the time, her beauty had been evident. She had been in her late twenties when Rebecca was killed, which put her in her late forties now. But I was looking at the countenance of a woman at least ten years older than that.

Her question had not been strident nor accusing, but puzzled. The sort of query anyone might make on coming upon someone placing a stone on their dead child's gravestone.

'I'm sorry. I didn't mean to intrude. Is this a relative? Your daughter perhaps?' I deliberately didn't answer her question, and instead asked two of my own.

'Yes,' she said. 'My daughter.' She was still puzzled, though.

'I was visiting the grave of a friend—' I pointed vaguely in a random direction—'and on the way back I just happened to notice this gravestone, and the wording on it intrigued me.' She didn't answer, and I was relieved to note that she did not appear to know who I was or even to suspect that I was the person who had been sending her family on wild goose chases. 'She was very young,' I added.

'Nine years old,' she said. The voice was clear, and carried no hint of emotion. 'She would have been twenty-nine this August.'

'What happened to her?' I asked gently, knowing that I would get an answer. Those who fear treading on sensitive toes and who avoid asking questions about deceased family members, even children, are wrong. I knew from many years of writing obituaries that the vast majority of the bereaved are willing, even desperate sometimes, to talk about those they have lost.

'She was murdered. And raped.' The voice was still, and with a slightly sharp edge now.

'How absolutely awful!' I commiserated. And of course it was awful. I didn't have to lie about that. 'It must have been terrible.'

'It still is terrible. I still miss her like it was only yesterday.'

'Did they ever find the man?' I asked quietly.

'Oh yes.' There was an icy certainty in the answer.

'And was he punished?'

'Oh yes.'

The cold wind got under my collar and sent a shudder down through my body. Two strangers standing in a cemetery discussing almost unbearable loss. It was now time to go, and I made my soft excuses and left her at the grave.

In the taxi on the way back to Hampstead I said to Frankie: 'Tell me about the psychology of grief.'

'What aspect of grief, guv?'

'Well, specifically, can parents ever really get over the death of a child, particularly if the circumstances are tragic and traumatic?'

He thought for a while. 'Most people can adapt to just about anything life can throw at them, although the death of a kid is particularly difficult to cope with. It's not just a parent or a relative or a partner who has gone, but the child is also seen as being part of themselves, part of their own being, see?' I nodded. I wondered what his taxi-driver mates would make of him in this mode.

'People invest so much in their kids, and so many parents virtually live their own lives through their children. So when one dies the tearing of that particular bond is a real killer. And, if that isn't enough, there is also this feeling that their futures have been robbed. Add the kind of guilt most people will feel about failing to have provided enough protection, or being responsible for an accident, and you have a very dangerous cocktail of traumas to adjust to.

'But having said that, most people do cope with it. I'm not saying that they get over it in quite the same way that they get over the death of an elderly person, but they do reach a means of dealing with the grief and bereavement which enables them to get on with their lives with relative normality.

'The people who suffer most are, funnily enough, those who don't grieve enough; those who never work through the feelings and the loss and the pain. You know the ones I mean, guv. They channel all the hurt and the pain into blaming themselves, or blaming someone else, or campaigning for something or other.

'There was that woman, you may

remember, it was a few years back, whose kid was killed in a climbing accident on one of them adventure weekends. She spent the next six years of her life, and every penny she owned, taking everyone in sight to court. She said she wasn't looking for compensation, but for the truth, so that it could never happen again and that sort of thing.'

I remember the woman he was referring to; angry and hollow-eyed, constantly being interviewed on camera on the steps of the High Court after futile court cases.

'The truth was that no one was really responsible for her kid's death. It was a tragic accident. But by refusing to deal with the real issue—her own bereavement and loss—she dragged out the whole process. Maybe she thought the pain would go away if she could pin the blame on someone. And of course it wouldn't have.'

'What about revenge?' I asked. 'Doesn't that bring some comfort?'

He thought for a little while as he wove his way through the traffic. 'I dunno, guv. That's a bit outside mainstream thinking on the subject of grief, but you want to know what I think personally?'

'Yes.'

'Yeah, well, I figure people *think* they'll feel better if they get their own back, and I suppose they do in a way. Maybe there's some kind of theraputic benefit in obtaining retribution, but I don't think it solves the real problem. I mean, if someone killed a member of your family, and you went and killed them in return, the actual benefits could well be outweighed by the problems, trauma, guilt and, of course, consequences of taking the revenge. And then you would still have to work through your grief on the original loss. Sounds like a losing game to me. I don't think anyone would get any real satisfaction from taking revenge on someone else; it's just another way of displacing the pain and hurt.'

My mind went back a year, to the circumstances surrounding the murder of Monique Karabekian. Someone had come to take revenge, and had been left with such emptiness and despair that he had taken his own life immediately afterwards. A losing game indeed.

It was well after six o'clock by the time we arrived at the *Hampstead Explorer* office. I asked Frankie to wait for me while I went upstairs to check for messages, and he turned on the meter. 'Don't scowl at me like that, guv. You already got a free psychological consultation out of me.'

I let myself in with my key, not expecting to find anyone working late on a Tuesday evening, but of course there was a light on in Arnie Bloch's office. I stuck my head round the door.

'Hi, Arnie,' I said breezily.

He threw a full cup of coffee against the wall, and appeared to regurgitate half a smoked salmon bagel. I looked at him in astonishment, and noticed that he was gaping at me with an altogether unfamiliar expression on an alarmingly white face.

'Holy shit!' he gasped, between bouts of choking.

'Arnie? You OK?' He was shaking like a leaf.

'My God! It is you, isn't it?' he croaked.

'Of course it's...' Then the truth crept in between the sluggish and well-spaced floating brain cells of my mind. I had forgotten to tell Arnie that I wasn't dead. Oops!

I donned an apologetic and sheepish grin. 'I can explain, Arnie.'

By now he was beginning to recover his composure, and his face was going red. 'Explain?' he shouted, 'I should fucking well hope you can explain!' His voice was getting louder and louder.

'I've had a fucking office full of howling journalists all afternoon ever since someone 'phoned the hospital to find out how you were. The bloody story is all over the *Evening Standard,* and I'm sitting here with tears in my eyes writing your fucking obituary, and you waltz in like some fucking ghost! Come here, you twerp!' He was bellowing now, and walking towards me. I was rooted to the spot in terror, but when he reached me he threw bear-like arms around me and tried to crush me to death. Well, that's what it felt like.

After a couple of hours crushing he stepped back, grabbed my shoulders and said: 'Jesus, Parker, if I wasn't so·relieved to see you I'd fire you! What the hell is going on?'

I told him, succinctly and apologetically, and eventually he just shook his head wearily, and let go. I nearly fell. 'Hell, man, you have some bloody strange ideas. I just hope we get a story out of it.'

'Hey,' I said, 'can I read my obituary?'

The glint came back into his eye. 'Get out of here, before I make the news come true!'

# CHAPTER 23

On the way home I picked up a copy of the *Evening Standard* and was impressed to find a picture story about my death on page three. There was a photograph of me from the time of the Karabekian case, and a picture of my poor burned-out house in Estelle Road. Above it was a two-deck headline over two columns which read:

## INVESTIGATIVE REPORTER DIES AFTER HOUSE FIRE

And the copy read:

Horatio Thrope (trust the *Standard* to spell my name wrongly) Parker, the London journalist who last year solved the murder of the film star Monique Karabekian, died early this morning after being caught in a fire in his Hampstead home on Sunday night.

Mr Parker, 35, who was the chief crime reporter of the well-known *Hampstead*

*Explorer* in north London, had been taken to St Columba's Hospital in St John's Wood, suffering from the effects of smoke inhalation. After making initial progress, his condition deteriorated yesterday and a hospital spokesman said this morning: 'Mr Parker passed away peacefully at 5.30 a.m.'

The journalist, together with two other adults and a dog, had earlier been rescued by firemen from the still unexplained blaze at the house in Hampstead.

Mr Parker was the subject of intense publicity last summer when he was closely involved in the sensational events surrounding the death of Monique Karabekian.

Arnold Bloch, editor of the *Explorer*, said this morning: 'British investigative journalism has been deprived of one of its most talented and most extraordinary figures. Horatio Parker was a tenacious sleuth, an inspired problem solver, an excellent writer and a scrupulously honest reporter.

'We will miss him deeply, and his loss is an irreparable one for this newspaper. Mind you, there were times when he was a lazy b—,' Mr Bloch said.

Funeral arrangements are to be announced later.

There were tears in my eyes. Such praise from Arnie. Only a week after he fired me. I wished I had been able to read the obituary notice he had been writing.

It occurred to me, though, that now my death had been announced, I would have to work quickly, before the 'terrible mistake' had to be rectified in a few days' time. When we arrived at the back door of the hotel, I asked Frankie: 'What are you doing at around two o'clock tonight, I mean tomorrow morning?'

'Oh Gawd, don't tell me you're going housebreaking again!'

'Yes.'

He closed his eyes, as if in pain. 'Which one this time?'

'The house in Lemon Grove. There has to be something there that everyone has missed. Will you be the getaway man?'

'Rather me than some incompetent dickhead who'll get you arrested,' he sighed. 'Pick you up here at about half one?'

'Perfect.'

Upstairs in my suite I phoned Wheezy Wallis to give him the good news. It took me a difficult ten minutes to convince him that I was not dead. It also took the offer of one thousand pounds to convince him that he should come along with his skeleton keys, lock picks, jemmies and whatever else self-respecting burglars used for tools. I also suggested a few extra items of equipment. I arranged to pick him up at the same place at a quarter to one.

Then I dialled Samantha's office downstairs. 'Samantha McDuff,' she answered.

'Hello, this is the Devil. You know, he of the nether regions.'

'Oh yes, Mr Lucifer, isn't it? What can I do for you?'

'Well, it's an unusual situation really. You see we had cause to reject someone who was sent to us this morning on the grounds of total unsuitability. A Mr Parker, he said his name was.'

'Yes, go on,' she said, 'in what way was he unsuitable?'

'Much too good-looking, too intelligent, and too well endowed. Would have been a great pity to torment someone like that for an eternity in sulphurous fires, don't you think? Anyway, we sent him back to you.'

'Why are you telling me this?'

'Well, you see, Ms McDuff, it was rather warm down here, and we sent him back with a serious case of the hots.'

'Oh dear. I'd better go and see to him immediately.'

'Good idea.'

Some hours later Frankie and I picked up Wheezy outside Belsize Park tube station, and he took one look at me and groaned.

'Christ, Mr P, you're dressed like a bloody burglar!'

I was rather taken aback. I had indeed given some thought to my attire, and had ventured forth resplendent in brand new black tracksuit, black gloves, dark-coloured trainers and black beret. So as to blend into the darkness, you understand.

'What if we're stopped by the Bill, and they ask you where you're going at two o'clock in the morning, what would you say? "Oh, just home from an evening at Claridge's, Officer." Blimey, I tell ya, bleedin' amateurs are killing this business!'

I have to admit to feeling a little sheepish under such criticism, but there was no time for that. 'You bring the extra stuff I asked for?' I said. He made a derisive sniff, as if to say: I don't answer stupid questions like that.

The streets of Golders Green were deserted at that time of night and there was no one around when Frankie parked a few yards down the road from the house in Lemon Grove. Wheezy and I trod silently up the path to the front door.

'You sure there are no alarms?' he whispered.

'No alarms,' I confirmed. Well, none the last time I was here, but I didn't say that.

The front door had a Yale lock and it took Wheezy less than half a minute to get it open, and we were inside. No louds bells began ringing, and the first thing he did was check the edges of the door.

'What are you doing?' I whispered.

'Checking for alarm contacts. Just because we can't hear anything doesn't mean it's not ringing in some nick somewhere. No, there's nothing here.'

We moved through the short hallway and through a door on the right into the empty living-room. 'OK, let's have the black plastic,' I said.

Wheezy unfolded a large sheet of the plastic I had asked for, and we taped it around the window with wide masking tape, using a tiny torch so that we could see what we were doing. When I was sure that the blackout would be complete, I went to the light switch on the wall and turned it on, praying that the electricity had not been cut off. The light came on.

We set about a minute inch by inch search of the room. 'What are you looking for?' Wheezy said.

'I don't know. Anything and everything.'

It was fascinating to watch him at work. He ran his fingers along the worn old plaster and wallpaper, sometimes stopping to tap softly with the tips of his fingers. 'Checking for hollow bits,' he explained. He paid particular attention to the woodwork around the window and the two doors, the one we had come through and the one leading off to the kitchen. He also inspected the ceiling carefully. I took a small crowbar-type tool that I had asked him to bring and began levering off the skirting boards all around the room. Nothing.

Then I levered up a floorboard, and was astonished to find that the space underneath the wood had been filled with sand. It was hard packed sand, covered with a thick layer of dust, which had obviously been undisturbed since it was put there years before. We took up every second floorboard and found the same thing. Wheezy shrugged in puzzlement. 'I've never seen that before.'

But I had.

After about half an hour we moved back through the hall into the bedroom. We taped up the window and went through the same process. Nothing except more sand under the floorboards. In the bathroom we unscrewed all the plywood panels around the bath, virtually dismantled the toilet, checked the drains, demolished a built-in cupboard and unscrewed a mirror from the wall. Nothing. We took up the decaying and stinking lino from the floor and prised up a few floorboards. Sand.

The kitchen was next. Here we did everything but lift up the old-fashioned coal-burning Aga cooker, which must have weighed a couple of tons at least. We did take down the heavy cast-iron chimney flue that had been bolted to the wall, but it was, of course, filled only with ancient soot. And there was more sand under the floorboards.

We had been there two hours. 'That

leaves the basement,' I said, but I found the door locked.

Wheezy took one look at it and groaned: 'Oi, that's a serious door, Mr P.'

'What do you mean?'

'I mean it's not like the other ordinary Victorian doors in the 'ouse. This is a heavy security door reinforced by a sheet of steel between the two solid sides of wood, and its got a serious mortice lock.'

'Can you open it?

'I think so, but it will take some time.'

It took all of twenty minutes, with Wheezy sweating and cursing, and me wondering whether this was merely a crazy midnight escapade, before the lock yielded and the door opened inwards into the kitchen. 'Whoo, boy!' whistled Wheezy. 'I tell ya that was half luck, half accident, getting that sodding lock open. I wouldn't want to try that one again. One of me picks broke off in there, and I don't think it can be locked again.'

We looked down the steep wooden stairs into the total blackness below. There was a switch on the wall, and a large single bulb flooded the basement with harsh light. Half way down the stairs Wheezy stopped suddenly.

'Gawd,' he said.

'What?'

'The smell down here.'

'Yeah, I know, it stinks a bit, but it's not that bad.'

'No, it's what it smells of.'

'Which is what?'

'Prison.'

The word seemed to echo around the basement, getting louder and louder as it bounced off the walls and hit my ears again and again until the message finally penetrated my dim brain and the first stirrings of icy cold understanding began to wash through me. I felt a crushing weight of doom hit me between the shoulder-blades and it was all I could do to keep my trembling knees from buckling. I was gripping the stair rail so tightly that my knuckles were white, and the muscles were standing out like cords on my arms. I tried to resist the appalling ideas which flooded into my mind, but it was a losing battle, and the images which entered at will sapped the very wellspring of civilization in me. I felt a kernel of cold, hard fury and hatred form in my gut. For a moment I saw myself standing in that cemetery in Golders Green, listening to those icy words that had been spoken by Mrs Rosenberg. 'Oh yes, the person responsible had been punished.'

'You OK, Mr P?' Wheezy was standing at the bottom of the stairs, looking up at me in concern.

'Yeah, I'm OK.' I took some deep breaths, and continued to the bottom of the stairs. 'Tell me more about what you just said. About it smelling like prison.'

'I dunno.' He thought for a moment. 'It's pretty faint, but I guess it's the slopping out. Makes rooms with no lavatory smell like a toilet. After a while the stink gets into the brickwork and the plaster. It's also the smell of sweat and—and you might laugh at this—but there's a kind of smell of frustration and despair.'

I didn't laugh at all. I could smell the despair myself.

I looked around the cellar. Concrete floor, brick walls which one of the policemen had described as 'sixties or 'seventies on our first visit. One small skylight window double glazed with re-inforced glass on the inside and barred outside. A steel reinforced door. And a ceiling filled with sand to deaden any sound which may have wanted to emerge.

Outside, the garden was a dense tangle of weeds and prickly bramble which had been deliberately allowed to grow wild. And around it all a high and impenetrable hedge shielding the house from idle prying eyes. A better little prison with accommodation for one resident jailer could hardly have been purpose built.

'Come on, let's look. I'm sure there's something down here,' I said grimly.

But there weren't many places to look. The floor and ceiling were even and smooth, and the brickwork of the walls was also without apparent nook or cranny. We checked the little spaces between the staircase and the walls, and I even unscrewed the cover on the light switch. Nothing. We started to dismantle the little coal stove, looking up the chimney and underneath the base. Inside there were some charred pieces of wood, ash and part burned coal.

And a folded piece of paper.

I took it out, my heart beating. It was a torn-off top half of a front page of the *Hampstead Explorer* of about three months before. Convinced that this was some sort of message to me, I looked eagerly at the stories printed on the scrap of newsprint.

325

I remembered them all, and knew that none of them could have had the slightest relevance to anything in this cellar. Then I saw what the message was. The top masthead had been torn so that most of the title of the newspaper was missing. All that remained was: EXPLORE.

'Can we go now?' Wheezy said hopefully.

'No,' I said. I knew now that there was something down here. 'Come on, Wheezy. If you were stuck down here and you wanted to leave someone a message, where would you put it? Remember, you've got lots of time.'

'Like a letter, you mean?'

'Possibly, yes.'

We started looking again, going over the floor and paying particular attention to the corners.

'Was a carpet 'ere,' Wheezy said, pointing. 'Look, you can see an outline of the wooden gripper strip that had been nailed down there. And you can see the nail 'oles all around the edge of the floor. So if someone slipped something under the carpet, it would've been found by now.'

'No, it hasn't been found yet, if it exists.' Things were beginning to fall into place in my mind. 'Remember, you've got all the time in the world.'

'I s'pose I'd take a brick out. Dig out the cement.'

'All right, let's find it.' He took one wall, and I started on the other, checking the bricks one by one, tapping them hoping to hear the dull thud of a brick not properly cemented in. It was slow and frustrating, and more than once I had to repeat lines of bricks when I lost track of which ones I had inspected.

We'd been in the house for nearly three hours, and had been tapping the brickwork for about thirty-five minutes when Wheezy found it. Actually it wasn't a loose brick but a strip of pointing about six inches long that came away intact.

' 'Ere, Mr P,' he said softly.

We were looking at a hollowed out slot between the bricks, about six inches long, about half an inch high and some nine inches deep. Wheezy shone his little torch into the flat back hole and we saw three things. One was a twisted metal skewer, the kind of implement one would use for grilling kebabs, with a ring on one end. Its point was worn away entirely.

'That's what he dug the hole with,'

Wheezy said. The next thing he pulled out was a thin ballpoint pen refill. The third item was a little sheaf of papers, made up of individual sheets of toilet paper, held together by a rusty pin. Wheezy brought it out carefully, using a thin screwdriver, and handed it to me.

The papers were yellowed, dry and brittle, and the ballpoint writing on them was faded but still legible. In a shaky hand, on the first page, was written:

To Murdoch Finnegan
from Michael

I didn't try and read any more right then. My heart was thumping painfully, the emotions I was feeling clashing painfully with the knot of anger in my gut. I wrapped the papers carefully in some of the black plastic sheeting we had brought, sealed it tightly with masking tape and slipped the little parcel into the front of my black burglar's T-shirt.

We collected all our burglary tools, turned off the lights, retrieved the blackout masks from the windows and let ourselves quietly out of the front door. It was just after five o'clock in the morning and it was just beginning to get light. I opened the front gate quietly and was just about to step through when a loud, bell-like voice rang out.

' 'Morning, Mr Parker!'

I think my heart actually stopped, and my muscles certainly all turned to stone. Eventually I managed to turn towards the voice, and found Mavis Healey, Neighbourhood Watch Co-ordinator extraordinaire, standing in her woolly dressing-gown and beaming at me with hearty conspiracy in her eyes.

'Your lookout over there—' she pointed at Frankie's cab—'is fast asleep. So I thought I had better keep an eye out over here for you.' She winked. 'Everything's quiet, no one around. Just me.'

I looked at Wheezy, whose eyes were so wide with shock that I thought there might be a danger of his eyeballs falling out.

'Mrs Healey, this is serious business here!' I hissed at her. 'Go inside immediately!'

She smiled and winked at me again. 'Right-ho.' And off she went, back to her insomniac's lookout point, no doubt.

'Jeeeezuss wept! Who was that?' Wheezy whimpered.

'You don't want to know,' I replied. 'Just remember never to try a B&E within a mile of her house, or she'll have you for sure.'

We did indeed find Frankie fast asleep in the cab, and had to bang on the window before he woke with a start and unlocked the door.

'Fantastic lookout and getaway man you are!' I complained.

'Just resting my eyes, guv. Wasn't asleep,' he protested.

'Forget it. Let's take Wheezy home.'

My brain was buzzing and I felt wide awake. I sat in the cab planning the next skirmish with the enemy.

'Frankie, is that tape-recorder that I got from Mohan still in the boot?' I asked.

'Yes, guv.' That was a stroke of luck. Had I taken it home it would have been burned in the fire. The last few pieces of my plan fell into place.

'I'm going to need you guys again later today, OK?' Frankie shrugged, and Wheezy groaned. 'The money's good,' I added. The groaning stopped.

'Get some sleep, both of you, and meet me at the hotel at four o'clock. Wheezy, Frankie can pick you up on his way there. But don't be late.'

'What are we going to do, guv?' Frankie asked.

'We're going to catch a whole bunch of rats in a trap,' I said.

## CHAPTER 24

Michael Finnegan's last letter to Murdoch was a painful document. The handwriting was uneven, and almost impossible to decipher in places. The ink had faded, and in some parts the pressure of the ballpoint pen had torn the already flimsy paper. But the pain was seated in the almost childlike contents of the message.

What was immediately apparent was that Michael Finnegan had been deeply disturbed and terribly confused when he had written the document, but obviously aware enough that he had to find a secure hiding place for it.

It was a brief journey through his state of mind, fragments of memory, confusion and guilt. It wasn't very long.

To Murdoch,

You should know that Mrs Baker is very KIND to me. Who brings me food and plays me music on the radio. She takes my pail and when the doctor comes she does not tell him that I yelled. Sometimes screaming. The lady and the man come to holler at me. NEVER look at their eyes where the fire is. Mrs Baker always gives me my milk before. This is my room that I live in and listen to music. The old man said I have to stay here because of my trial and my verdict. I told them to ask you if I hurt that little girl but they said you could not come here. I do not REMEMBER the little girl, but sometimes she speaks to me in my room and tells me that I HURT her. The policeman hit me on my ears. He HURT me worse than those Ho Chi Minh boys and I see their EYES when they laugh. The policeman laughed. Did you come to my trial? I can't remember when it was. When Mrs Baker comes I put the pail at the top of the stairs and I have to go and stand on the bed without my shoes. Once my legs swelled up. I must always drink the milk that makes me sleepy. My friend Elliot helped me at my trial and sometimes he sends me magazines. But he had to go away because of President Reagan. I think of Mom and Pop when it's dark. Do they know about my trial? Can they come here? One day the pail fell down the stairs and Mrs Baker threw water on me. I hollered. The lady hollers at me and says I will stay here forever. But Mrs Baker say that I can go home next year. When she gets a phone she will call you collect to come for me. My one ear doesn't hear any more and my eyes hurt when Mrs Baker turns the light on. I heard about that little girl, but I don't remember her. I also heard a phone ring once when the door was open, but Mrs Baker said it wasn't hers. Say hello to Carol. I told Mrs Baker about the lake and the loons. Sometimes I hear them in my head. Mrs Baker cooks chicken stew on Sun

The ink in the pen had run out.

I sat for some time at the table in the living-room of our suite, the little lamp casting a pool of yellow light over Michael Finnegan's letter to his brother. I wondered whether Murdoch had found it and had left it hidden there for me to find, or whether it had lain there undisturbed for years. How many years? It was not dated, and there was only one clue: the reference to President Reagan meant that it had to have been written some time after 1980. Michael Finnegan had disappeared in 1973.

Murdoch must have found the letter, I decided, since it must have been he who left the 'Explore' message for me in the stove. But why had Murdoch taken no action himself? Was it because he was still gathering evidence? Or was he killed before he could do anything about it? There were still many puzzles, but at least I knew why Murdoch had bought the house, and perhaps why he had considered leaving it to me: in case something happened to him.

The monstrousness of it all made me tremble with rage. I knew that I should go straight to Theo Bernstein and tell him all I knew. But I knew, too, that I would not do that yet. Probably for the same reason that Murdoch hadn't gone to the police. The evidence was clear to me, but to a court of law it would be circumstantial in the extreme. Further evidence was required, and I had an idea about how to get that evidence.

I managed to shed my burglar clothes

without waking Samantha, and I lowered myself into a hot bath. I would have loved to get between the sheets, but I had a lot to do and there was no time for sleeping yet. Or anything else, for that matter.

It was before seven o'clock when I startled the restaurant staff by being the first guest to arrive for breakfast. I ordered scrambled eggs, lots of toast, marmalade and a large pot of strong black coffee, as well as all the daily newspapers.

I was pleased to see that *The Times*, the *Independent* and the *Guardian* all had short reports about my demise on inside home pages. The others hadn't thought my death was worth reporting. It was a safe bet, however, that the people I wanted to reach would have heard the news by now.

I drank as much coffee as I could without bursting, and then retired to Samantha's office where she had a word processor and laser printer for hotel correspondence and for producing menus and the like. I wrote, in large bold letters:

THE DEATH OF THE JOURNALIST
ADDS ANOTHER MURDER
TO THE LIST.
IT IS IMPERATIVE

WE MEET TONIGHT
TO DISCUSS FUTURE OPTIONS.
9PM AT LEMON GROVE.
IN THE CELLAR.
NO ABSENCE WILL BE TOLERATED.
DO NOT COMMUNICATE TODAY
OR DISCUSS THIS WITH *ANYONE!!*

I printed five copies of that on plain sheets of paper, and then, on the sixth, I added a sentence:

BRING THE TAPE CASSETTE,
*STILL SEALED.*

On that one, I also changed the time to nine-fifteen pm.

Using the word processor, I then addressed five envelopes: one to Mr and Mrs Rosenberg, one to the Jacobson brothers, one to Judge Rose, one to Dr Kaplan and one to former Chief Superintendent Gallacher. The slightly longer message went into an envelope addressed to the family solicitor Elliot Mandelstam, Michael Finnegan's 'friend'...

It was now about half past eight, and I went for a walk in the bright morning sunshine, down Chalk Farm Road with its trendy galleries and second-hand tat shops, towards Camden Town. I stopped at a hole in the wall cash dispenser and withdrew five hundred pounds with my new American Express card. In Bayham Street I knew there was the small office of a motorcycle courier company, and was pleased to find it already open and humming with activity.

I asked for the six letters to be delivered by hand, that morning, without fail. The man behind the counter looked at the six addresses, scribbled some calculations on a scrap of paper and said: 'You'll want our High Priority service which is £12.50 per item, and guarantees delivery within ninety minutes. That's seventy-five quid for the lot.'

I gave him the money. He began to write out a receipt. 'And the name, sir?'

'Arthur Daley.'

He lifted his head and looked me in the eye. The staring match went on for about half a minute. Then he said: 'Actually, I think you want our High Security Priority service. That's twenty quid per item.'

I handed him more money.

'Thank you, Mr...er...Daley. Is there any address?'

'I move around a lot.'

'I see. Well, that's OK, then.'

'They'll be delivered this morning?' I tried to add a steely glint to my stare.

'Without fail, by—' he checked his watch—'ten a.m. at the latest. Guaranteed.'

'I wouldn't want anything to go wrong, see.'

'Or else you'll send your minder round?' There was a slightly mocking but still vaguely respectful look on his face. I decided to quit while I was still dimly ahead, and I left.

I had told Frankie to catch up on his sleep, so I had to take a regular taxi through the rush hour to Mohan's shop off Tottenham Court Road. Having seen me alive the day before, Mohan had read the newspapers that morning with a healthy dose of scepticism.

'You're looking good for a dead person,' he remarked as I walked in through the door.

'Bloody journalists get everything wrong,' I said.

Mercifully, he knew me well enough not to ask a lot of difficult questions and, having seen the dark rings under my red eyes, put the kettle on. While the coffee brewed I explained to him precisely what I needed.

He listened carefully, asked a few questions about distances and location, and then set about putting together what I asked for. That, including some careful compatibility checks and frequency calibration, took about twenty minutes. Then he spent another half an hour demonstrating the equipment and making sure that I understood how to set and work the apparatus properly.

While I was there I took the opportunity of recording a message on a micro-cassette, using a device which Mohan assured me would give the sound of a strong echo-chamber effect.

When I asked him how much I owed him, he said, 'It depends on whether you bring it all back tomorrow, and what kind of condition it's in.' It sounded like a fair arrangement.

I got back to the hotel shortly after eleven o'clock, slipped in through the back entrance, took the service lift to the top floor, let myself quietly into the suite and was confronted by a stormy-faced Samantha McDuff who looked as if she was angry enough to break my back.

'What the hell is going on, Parker?'

'Nothing to worry your pretty little head about, my sweet!' I must have been light-headed from lack of sleep to make a stupid crack like that. She advanced on me alarmingly, her hands dropping into what I realized was a sort of unarmed combat position. I backed away somewhat more than hurriedly.

'Hey! Hey! Hey! Joke! A bad one admittedly, but a joke. Poor taste, I agree. I'm sorry! Really I am.' My back was against the wall now, and she was still advancing. I closed my eyes and resolved to take my punishment without whimpering too much, but when she reached me she just put her head against my chest. I folded my arms around her.

'Let's try this again. What's going on?' Her voice was soft, but just as insistent, and there was also a hint of strong emotion. 'You creep out of here in the middle of the night, dressed like some sort of amateur-night SAS imitation, intent on heaven knows what a mere two days after someone made a very determined and very professional attempt to kill you And me, for that matter.

'I lie awake for most of the night,

340

imagining the worst kind of things. And when I finally do sleep for a few hours, I wake up to find that you've been and gone again, without leaving any kind of message or explanation. Well, it's enough now. Either I am close enough to you to know what you're doing, or I'll just take the hint, pack up and get out of here. You choose. Now.'

I tightened my hold on her. 'You're not going anywhere, even if I have to break your arms.' That brought a kind of muffled giggle from somewhere in the folds of my shirt. I told her some of what we had found in the cellar the night before, and I outlined most of my plan for the coming afternoon and evening. She asked some questions. I answered them. Then she was silent for a time.

'Bastards! It's monstrous what they did.'

'Monstrous. My word exactly.'

'OK, Parker, just listen carefully, because I'm only going to say this once. I'm coming with you tonight.'

I drew in an involuntary breath to protest, but then thought better of it as I felt her leg-breaking muscles tense. I also remembered the way she had dealt with the two thugs in the street.

341

'OK,' I said simply.

'You never know,' she said, 'you might even get the chance to introduce me to some of them, and then we could shake hands.' There was a sinister edge to her voice which made me shudder slightly.

# CHAPTER 25

I managed to get some sleep over lunch-time, during which I dreamed like a baby, despite all the coffee and excitement. Samantha woke me at half past three, Frankie and Wheezy arrived on the dot at four o'clock and we set off again for Golders Green through the traffic building up to rush hour on a Wednesday afternoon.

The staff of the *Hampstead Explorer* would be frantically busy on the main stories for this week's issue before the printers took over in the morning. Arnie Bloch, I knew, would be wondering where the hell I was and just itching to fire me again when I got back.

I got Frankie to stop two blocks short

of Lemon Grove, and sent Samantha on ahead on foot to look around.

'You'll be a new face in the neighbourhood, so if there is anyone keeping an eye on the place, they won't recognize you,' I explained.

Ten minutes later she was back. 'All clear. There's no sign of anyone around, and in fact it wouldn't surprise me to discover that everyone in the street is dead.' I knew otherwise.

'OK, phase two. Wheezy and I go to plant the equipment in the house. You two wait here, and if we're not back by Friday, call in the SAS.'

'That's not funny,' Samantha said. The other two weren't laughing either. 'Seriously, how long do you think you'll be?'

'About thirty, forty minutes, maybe less.'

She looked at her watch. 'Right, off you go, and I'm counting.'

We walked the two blocks in what we hoped was a relaxed and inconspicuous manner, just two blokes carrying their shopping in Waitrose bags and chatting about this and that and one thing and another. You know, sex, football, arson, burglary, murder. Stuff like that.

Wheezy was nervous. 'I don't like this, Mr P. I mean a B&E in the dark is one thing, but it's bloody 'alf past four in the afternoon!'

'Think of it this way,' I said soothingly. 'We'll be doing it under cover of daylight. We'll look so innocent that no one will suspect anything.' I reminded him that a couple of gents dressed in white overalls had once spent an hour and a half calmly and authoritatively removing a whole range of fridges, freezers, washing machines, tumble dryers and dish washers from the window display of a major West End department store, and loaded them into a van parked outside. It had only been some hours later that the staff began to realize that no one knew who they were.

'Anyway, there's no alternative, we have to get this stuff into the house before the guests arrive this evening, and I don't want to leave it too late. Who knows, they might come early.' I hoped he was convinced. I wasn't.

We turned into the house briskly, as if we had been walking in there every day of our lives, and I shielded him from the street during the half a minute it took him

344

to open the front door. He was getting better at it.

Once inside, we went straight down into the basement, and I got to work. First I opened the back of the specially doctored tape-recorder, and carefully placed in it the micro-cassette that I had recorded that morning in Mohan's shop. Then I set it as he had shown me so that it would play what was on the little cassette, no matter what cassette was placed in the front of the machine. It would also simultaneously record that message on to the new cassette. Then I unwrapped the small microphone and radio transmitter that Mohan had supplied me with, switched it on and then taped it as instructed in the back of the machine. I screwed the back of the tape-recorder on, and left the machine on the floor in the middle of the room.

Next out of my shopping-bag was the radio receiver, which had been connected to a small voice-activated cassette recorder. I put the headphones on my head and switched it on. 'OK, Wheezy, say something near the ghetto blaster.'

'Gawd, Mr P, let's 'urry up and get outa here!' The words came through perfectly through the 'phones, and I saw the reels of the cassette begin to move. It was working, but I needed another test.

'Wait half a minute, and then say something else. I'm going outside.' Wheezy looked stricken, but I had to know whether the transmitter was strong enough to send a signal out of the cellar. I went upstairs, nonchalantly opened the front door and went for a stroll in the garden. Like any proud householder who loves his waist-high weeds and brambles.

Again I heard Wheezy's voice clearly through the headphones: 'Please, Mr P, come back and let's finish up 'ere.' I was more than satisfied.

I went back downstairs, checked that the receiver/recorder had actually recorded Wheezy's two sentences. It had.

'Can we go now?' he pleaded.

'Not yet. We need a back-up transmitter, Mohan says.' I took out another one, turned it on, checked that it was working and then looked around for somewhere to hide it. In the end I taped it under one of the treads of the open staircase leading down into the cellar, in a dark corner obscured by one of the supporting beams. A determined search of the room would reveal it, but I was banking on our guests not being that suspicious. I looked around carefully, checking that we had not left anything obviously suspicious behind—apart from the ghetto blaster, that is. Finally, I put a brand new hundred watt light bulb in the socket, after removing the old one with my handkerchief.

'What's that for?' Wheezy asked.

'I want to leave the light on for them, and I don't want some old light bulb to give up the ghost on us before they get here.'

Wheezy was becoming decidedly anxious to leave, but I had one more arrangement to make upstairs. In the kitchen I opened the fuse box, and removed all the old-fashioned plug-in fuses, except for the one marked 'Cellar'. I put them in my shopping-bag.

'What's that for?' my jumpy accomplice whispered. Honestly, I would have expected a seasoned burglar to be much more relaxed. But perhaps it was because I was in charge, and he clearly regarded me as a very dangerous amateur.

'It's to ensure that they hold their meeting downstairs,' I said. 'I don't want them talking where I can't hear them. *Now* we can go.'

'Thank Gawd!' he said, and led the way briskly.

We got into the street without mishap, and I looked at my watch. It was just over forty minutes since we had left the taxi, and I knew Samantha would be starting to claw at the seat covers.

'You go back to the taxi right away,' I told Wheezy. 'I want to do one more distance check on the transmitter. Tell them it all went smoothly, and I'll be there in a few minutes.' He needed no second bidding, and he scooted off gratefully.

I waited until he was around the corner, carried out my little errand, and then joined them ten minutes later.

'Well,' I said jovially, 'the trap is set and baited. Let's see if the guests come to dinner.' They all looked at me glumly, as if unable to understand why I was so cheerful.

The reason was, of course, that we had finally taken the initiative. After weeks of confusion, mystery and being on the receiving end of ambushes, I at last had a good idea of what was going on, and a fighting chance of securing a battleground victory. Not for me, but for Murdoch and Michael Finnegan.

'Right, the rest of the programme is as follows: First we drop Wheezy off at a convenient tube station, because his heroic role in this affair has now come to an end. Wheezy—' I turned to him—'your loot will be in the post, possibly with a bonus.' He was looking a lot happier.

'The three of us will then retire to some convivial hostelry where we will consume a few drinks, eat dinner and come back here at about half past eight.'

Personally I was ravenous, not having eaten anything since seven o'clock that morning. We went to the wonderful L'Aurent Tunisian restaurant in Finchley Road where we had their amazing brique a l'oeuf (the only starter), couscous with traditional chick-pea lamb stew and mixed grill, and stirring Tunisian red wine so thick you could almost stand a fork up in it.

Just the sort of sustenance needed for the strenuous night of intrigue ahead.

# CHAPTER 26

As arranged, the three of us were in place by half past eight, parked this time in a nicely shadowed spot under a tree in the next street down from Lemon Grove, where I estimated that we were less than fifty yards from the back of Murdoch's house.

I had explained virtually the whole plan again to the other two over dinner, and Frankie had asked one question. 'What's the point of this complicated business with the tape-recorded message you want them to hear?'

'The whole idea of all this is to get them talking about the Finnegan brothers, and about me if possible,' I explained, 'and that tape is a sort of catalyst to start them off in the right direction. They won't be able to explain it to themselves immediately, and the discussion will—hopefully—contain incriminating material, which we will get on tape. Voilà, rats trapped.'

Now I opened the window, extended the

receiver's aerial, put on the headphones and switched it on. I heard nothing but a static hiss. No guests yet.

'Boring night for you two, I'm afraid. There's only one set of headphones and I've got them,' I said. Samantha said something which I didn't hear. I took off the headphones. 'Pardon?'

'There's no need to shout at us,' she said. 'Remember, you're wearing headphones, and you'll have a tendency to raise your voice in order to hear yourself speak.'

So early in the escapade, and humiliated already. I nodded, as if to say: I know that. I put the headphones back on, and settled down to wait.

The first guests came at about quarter to nine. I suddenly heard a door slam, and my heart started pounding. I sat up abruptly.

Then I heard a voice call: 'What's happened to the fucking lights?' One of the Jacobson twins, I didn't know which. We are pleased to announce the arrival of Mr Morris and Mr Mervyn Jacobson. I checked the tape-recorder in my hands. The reels of the cassette had started turning. Bingo.

Another voice, similar, the other brother: 'I don't know.' Pause. 'There's a light on here. Who left this door unlocked?'

First voice: 'How the fuck should I know? They've all got keys, haven't they? One of them must have come earlier.' Voices louder now and the sound of feet descending the staircase, very loud as they passed the hidden mike.

First voice: 'What's that?'

Second voice: 'A tape-recorder.'

'Who put that there?'

'How the fuck should I know? Stop asking me stupid questions! No, better leave it. We don't know what it's there for.'

The two of them stood there for a few minutes being irritable with each other. I pictured them in my mind, and became aware again of the size of those ham-like fists. Then the sound of the door again, and more footsteps.

'Down here!' one of the Jacobsons called out.

Two pairs of feet getting louder, on the stairs, and then a woman's voice: 'Who are you?'

Please welcome Mr Julius and Mrs Debbie Rosenberg. I recognized her voice, and already some interesting information: the Rosenbergs don't know the Jacobsons.

'Morris and Mervyn Jacobson. We work for Judge Rose.' Aha!

'Debbie and Julius Rosenberg,' said a man's voice. 'Did you send that note round?'

'No, and presumably you didn't.'

Another door sound. Arrivals coming thick and fast now. A man's voice, with a Glaswegian accent. May we present former Chief Superintendent Paul Gallacher. ' 'Evenin' all,' he said. I swear he did. No one in the cellar laughed, but I giggled in the taxi. Samantha threw me a furious look.

'Don't complain. You were the one who insisted on coming tonight,' I said to her.

I realize we have more information: Gallacher *does* know the Jacobsons, as well as the Rosenbergs.

Next arrival, a single set of footsteps. ' 'Evenin' doctor,' says Gallacher. We are pleased to announce the arrival of Dr Gabriel Kaplan. He mutters something, and then Gallacher introduces him to the Jacobsons. So. He didn't know the terrible twins either.

Two minutes later, and now it's exactly nine o'clock, door noise again, another set of footsteps, and a distinctive, imperious voice. 'Who the devil sent that note to me at my chambers?' Pray silence, please, for His Honour Mr Justice Leonard Rose. A babble of denials.

'It must have been Elliot. He's the only one not here.' This from a voice I don't recognize. It has to be the good doctor.

There follows some discussion—sometimes difficult to hear since frequently more than one person talks at once—about the inconvenience of having to come tonight, about the presence of the tape-recorder (although, thankfully, no one feels the need to play with it), and Mrs Rosenberg is particularly perturbed abut the flowers with the note from the 'Masked Avenger'.

'If he was who we think he was, you don't have to worry about him again,' chuckled one of the Jacobsons. Suddenly I'm not finding this so amusing any more. That was clearly a reference to me, and the bastard is chuckling about it. It reminds me that we are dealing with serious stuff here, and I start to listen more intently.

Then Mandelstam, the family solicitor arrives, about five minutes early, but his timing couldn't have been better. The full cast is assembled. I pray that he hasn't forgotten the tape.

'Elliot!' booms the judge's best courtroom voice. 'Perhaps you can tell us what the devil is going on. You sent us the notes, didn't you?'

'Me? Of course I didn't! I assumed it was you.' Ah, Mr Mandelstam has a soothing, friendly, voice. He adds: 'Who are these two gentlemen?' There is a hint of concern in his voice, and I chalk up another guest who has not met the twins yet. They are introduced by Gallacher.

There is a moment's silence, and then Julius Rosenberg speaks up. 'If none of us sent that note, there's something very worrying going on, and I suspect that the best thing for us to do would be to get the hell out of here.' Clever man! My heart sinks. What if they all agree with him?

But Elliot saves the day. 'It may have something to do with this,' says the lawyer.

'What is that?' The Judge.

'Apparently it's a cassette tape. It arrived last Wednesday, delivered by hand by a taxi-driver, all sealed up like this with Sellotape, with instructions to put it in my safe without opening it. The note was sighed LR, so I assumed it was you.'

'Of course it wasn't me!' The Judge.

'Well, I didn't know that. In any event,

the note I received this morning instructed me to bring it with me. Obviously the intention is that we should all listen to it, since I see that there is a tape-recorder here. Who brought that?' A babble of denials.

'I think we should get out of here.' Julius Rosenberg again.

'No!' says the Judge. 'Listening to a tape can't do any harm. We need to know what all this is about. Let's hear it. Open it, Elliot.' The Judge has taken complete control.

I hear rustlings as Elliot struggles to get the sticky tape off the cassette, but eventually he manages it. 'Put it in the machine,' the Judge says. My heart is beating very fast now. I hear the cassette compartment slide open; I hear the cassette being inserted, and I hear the click of the play button being pressed. A moment later my own voice issues forth with a disembodied echoing sound as if speaking from the bottom of some sepulchral vault. The magnificent effect is magnified by the slight pause I inserted between each word.

*'This is the voice of Horatio T Parker —speaking to you from beyond the grave!'*

I had put in a long pause here to allow general consternation and comment.

But Julius Rosenberg shouted: 'This is nonsensical! Switch it off!' and there was a general murmur of agreement. My anxiety shot up: if they switched it off, even temporarily, the message would not come back on again. The special function needed to be re-set on each occasion.

'NO!' roared the Judge in a voice that brooked no opposition. 'We will listen! I want to know what is going on.'

*'I am here to inform you that the game is up. ALL is known. And to advise you that this is your best opportunity to confess your crimes while you are still in the position of being able to take the initiative in this matter. As Judge Rose will confirm, a voluntary confession to the police will act in your favour at your trial.*

*'It is KNOWN that you kidnapped Michael Finnegan,'* I boomed eerily from the machine. *'It is KNOWN that you held a trial. It is KNOWN that you imprisoned him unlawfully in this very cellar. It is KNOWN that you disposed of his body unlawfully. It is KNOWN that you plan to do bodily harm to me this coming Friday night, and it is KNOWN that when that fails you will*

*murder me by setting fire to my house on this coming Sunday night.* ALL THIS IS KNOWN AND DOCUMENTED.'

My voice went up a pitch: *As the Bible says, "Behold all ye that kindle a fire, that gird yourselves about with firebrands. Walk ye in the flame of your fire and among the brands ye have kindled.'*

I reached a crescendo of boom and intonation: 'NOW IS THE TIME YOU MUST CONFESS!

*'There will be no other opportunity. That is the end of this message.'*

There was a stunned silence in the cellar. Then someone muttered: 'Wait a second.' Clocks, the sound of a tape being rewound. Click. And the tape is played again. After hearing it for the second time, there is another silence.

'God Almighty!' breathes the Judge. 'Elliot, when did you say you received this tape?'

'Last Wednesday.' His voice is shaky. 'Look, I wrote the date on the envelope, and signed it too.'

'You're positive this is the same tape?'

'Absolutely!'

'Then something bizarre is going on! There is information here that didn't

EXIST last Wednesday!' Even the Judge sounding shaky now.

Then Debbie Rosenberg speaks: 'What did he mean about us murdering the brother, Murdoch, and the journalist? That had nothing to do with us, surely?

Here we get to it!

I was listening intently, eyes closed and straining to hear how she would be answered, when something hard touched my cheek. Something hard and cold and round. Startled, I turned my head suddenly and the perfect world began to crack and crumble like an empty eggshell as I realized that I was staring up the parallel barrels of a shotgun, behind which was leering one of the Jacobson twins. Samantha screamed briefly, and Frankie whipped round in his seat, and then everyone was still.

The thug leaned forward slowly and pushed the headphones away from my ears, keeping the gun steadily against my cheek. 'Well, well, well, well. Not quite so dead after all, it would seem,' he hissed slowly like some malevolent alligator. 'Or are you a ghost? Remember me? I'm one of the "low-life sleazeballs", as you so charmingly described us. What a stroke of luck that we meet again in this way!'

I could actually taste the bitterness of shock, despair and disappointment in my mouth, but for once I did the right thing: I said absolutely nothing. His nauseating smile widened, and he spoke very slowly.

'Nothing to say now, eh? Good, because if you say something smart or snappy, I may well just blow your fucking head off.' I said nothing.

'OK, let me tell you all what we are going to do. First of all, that scrawny little red-haired snot in front is going to get out of the cab, quiet like, and stand on the pavement over there. Then the short-arsed slut is going to join him. And if anyone does anything silly, you are going to end up without a head. Then you can be the headless ghost, hee hee.'

'Do it, folks, and quietly,' I said to Samantha and Frankie, and they got out of the cab, both looking pale and shocked. My knees were trembling.

'Now you,' he said to me, withdrawing the gun slightly so that I could open the door but not wavering his aim by one millimetre. I put the receiver/recorder on the seat and began to get out.

'No no no no no, my son. Let's bring that little toy with us, shall we?' I sighed and picked it up again. 'Right, now we're going to walk round the corner in a friendly little group, like a bunch of mates, see, me with my little shotgun under my jacket. Mr Parker here is going to be very close to me, in fact we're going to walk arm in arm. Let's go.' We walked with the shotgun pressing painfully into my armpit.

There is no way to describe the soundless consternation and bug-eyed astonishment that greeted out little procession down the steps into the cellar.

I cast my eye over the assembly. I knew them all by sight or photograph except for Elliot Mandelstam and Gabriel Kaplan, but I could hazard a shrewd guess that of the two unfamiliar faces that gawped at us, the man in the white coat and lapel name badge was probably Kaplan. I couldn't see the other Jacobson twin anywhere. There were now ten people in the confined space where Michael Finnegan had clearly spent some years of his life, and it had become crowded enough for me to be slightly more confident that there would be no wild shooting of shotguns.

'Good evening everyone. Please don't let

us interrupt your conversation,' I said as pleasantly as I could.

'Shut up!' barked the gunman, digging me in the ribs so hard with the gun that I knew he had drawn blood. I stumbled and nearly fell. 'I found them in a taxi around the corner. He was listening to this.' He held the receiver out to the Judge. 'It's a radio and tape-recorder, and I would be very surprised if every word spoken in this place tonight hasn't been recorded by our ghostly comedian here.'

I looked at the Judge's face and found a distinctly unjudicial mask of hatred and fury.

Jacobson prodded me again in the ribs with the gun. 'There is a bug in here, isn't there? Where is it?' I looked at him with contempt. 'Tell me, or I'll smash your little girlfriend's arm,' he rasped at me. His breath was terrible. I had no doubt that he would do it and enjoy it.

'It's in the tape-recorder,' I said. The Judge picked up the ghetto blaster and smashed it down on to the concrete floor with tremendous force, the impact breaking open the casing. 'There, it's that grey thing with the little aerial, taped on with masking tape.' Rose ripped off the transmitter and stamped on it until it was almost dust. Then he turned his attention to the rest of the broken machine, kicking and stamping on it like a man gone mad. He did the same thing with the radio receiver, and he shredded the tape cassette.

'How did you do that message...with the tape-recording?' Rose's voice grated. He was in such a state that tendons in his neck were beginning to twitch.

'Oh, simply a magician's trick. There was another tape-recorder inside the ghetto blaster. Did you enjoy my message from beyond the grave? It's all true you know?' That earned me another savage blow in the ribs.

I turned to the Rosenbergs. They were clutching each other in shock, and the woman particularly was as white as a sheet. 'You never thought it would come to this, did you?' I said harshly. 'Assault, arson, attempted murder and murder!'

'What are you talking about?' she keened in a high voice. 'We haven't assaulted or murdered anyone!' It was obvious that they knew nothing of recent events.

'Oh? Well, who do you think murdered Murdoch Finnegan? Who tried to have me beaten up? And when that failed, who tried to kill me in a fire? And for all I know your prisoner, Michael Finnegan, was murdered as well!'

'That's not true! Michael died from natural causes!' This was from Gabriel Kaplan.

I turned to him. 'Ah, up speaks the noble doctor who, in line with the high ethics of his profession and the requirements of his Hippocratic oath, came religiously once a week to check on the health of the prisoner. And to bring the jailer sedatives to put in his milk. What kind of natural conditions are these?' Jacobson was thumping me with the barrel of the gun, but I had to go on.

'Living terrified and alone in the dark with voices in his head, and unreasonable false guilt in his heart, with people coming regularly to scream abuse and retribution at him, shitting in a bucket, abused by his jailer and getting no exercise at all. Don't give me "natural causes"! I think you can add culpable homicide to the list of your crimes! When did he die, anyway?' I demanded angrily.

'Nineteen eighty-five,' Kaplan said.

'Shut up, Gabriel!' roared the Judge.

I turned to him, 'Ah yes, silence in

court! You were the judge at Michael Finnegan's kangaroo court trial, weren't you?' He said nothing. 'The distinguished judge, sworn to uphold the rule of law and to weigh the evidence while blind to prejudice and bias! What a precedent you've set for the legal profession! What a travesty of private justice you concocted here. I'm surprised you even bothered to hold a trial.'

'It *was* a trial!' Mandelstam protested.

'The defence counsel speaks!' I spat at him. 'The man with the brief to defend the victim and who failed him so spectacularly. Michael Finnegan actually thought you were his friend, do you know that? But after a while you couldn't bear to visit him here any more, so you abandoned him completely. Told him you were going to America, didn't you?'

Mandelstam looked stunned. 'How the hell do you know that?'

'I KNOW EVERYTHING!' I yelled at him. There was no stopping me now. I hardly felt the blows coming from Jacobson who was still trying to stop me speaking.

'I know that this deeply wounded family, suffering terribly from insufferable loss, felt cheated out of justice and retribution and the hoped-for comfort of revenge by what you saw as legal technicalities. So you took the law into your own hands and you condemned Michael Finnegan to twelve years of confusion, nightmares and torment in hell. Mrs Baker was the perfect jailer, wasn't she? She loved Rebecca too, and was only too pleased to go along with your plan. Apart from anything else, she got this house out of the deal, didn't she?

'But what puzzles me is why you didn't just kill him right away and be done with it!'

'I didn't *want* him killed!' burst out Debbie Rosenberg, now with feverish high points of colour on her cheeks. 'I wanted him *alive* so that he would be punished every single day of his life for what he did to my baby. Do you know what he did to Becky? He...' Her voice broke and she stopped for a moment. She knew she didn't have to spell it out.

'And I came every few weeks to remind him about what he'd done, just in case he was trying to forget. I would tell him when it was Becky's birthday, what she would have been doing, when she would have started secondary school. I reminded him that she should have been growing up, going out with boys, finishing school, going to university, getting married and having children of her own. I wanted him to feel the pain I felt every hour of every day since she was killed, and every time I remembered what he had done to her!'

'Except that he was innocent,' I said quietly. The thought of the effect this woman must have had on Michael Finnegan was unbearable.

'He was guilty! He confessed!' she shouted at me, almost hysterical. 'We heard it from his own lips, in this very room!'

'And what kind of confession was that?' I spat back contemptuously. 'A confession beaten out of a disturbed, vulnerable young man, who had already been through the hell of torture and interrogation by the North Vietnamese and had come to London in an attempt to escape the nightmares. A confession beaten out of him, no doubt by Mr former Chief Superintendent Paul Gallacher over there—who had been so justly humiliated by a *real* defence counsel at the committal hearing that he had to find a target for his rage. What role did he play at the trial, I wonder. Could it have been as the fine prosecuting counsel, protecting the nation from abuse and danger?' There was silence. Even Jacobson was listening.

I turned to Kaplan. 'Michael was deaf in one ear, wasn't he?'

'Yes, how did you know?'

'Never mind how I know. I also know that this was caused by Gallacher's beating! Go on, look him in the eye now and ask him to deny that. See if you believe what he says. He was the one person who knew everything there was to know about little Becky's disappearance, and was just the person to make sure that his victim 'remembered' the right things. What was your motivation in all this Gallacher? Money? Or were you just ingratiating yourself with this worthy family?' Nobody said anything. Gallacher looked stricken, but didn't say a word either.

Then the Judge spoke sharply. 'Right, that's enough of all this. You cannot hope to understand the terrible trauma we all lived through with the loss of Becky, and there is no point us wasting time trying to justify our actions to you. What we have to think about is what to do with you three.' The twitch on his face had become worse, and he looked positively deranged.

'The easiest thing would be to shoot all

three of us,' I suggested. I was pleased to hear Debbie Rosenberg gasp in horror. I turned to the couple. 'What about you, Mr Rosenberg? Have you worked out yet what has been happening, what has been going on over the last three or four weeks?' His face was ashen, but he made no reply.

The Judge spoke. 'No, shooting is not necessary. I've been thinking. There's a much better way. We'll leave you down here. When you are found eventually, it will be assumed that you broke in, got caught in the cellar and couldn't get out.'

'Do you think people would accept that we accidentally locked ourselves in with a mortice lock, and then lost the key?' I said mockingly.

He thought for a moment, and his wild eyes lit up. 'We won't lock the door with a key. We'll wedge it shut with the heavy chimney flue from the Aga which has come off the wall. You will have been trapped there by a freak accident. No one will have the faintest idea that we are involved.'

Kaplan said: 'Leonard, you can't do this, it's—'

'Shut up!' the Judge screamed loudly. 'Anyone who doesn't like the idea can stay down here with them. The alternative is to go to jail for thirty years! Any volunteers?' The fledgling opposition died an early death.

Then Frankie, who hadn't said a single word since we had been brought in, suddenly shouted: 'Oi! Police! Over there!' pointing to the top of the stairs.

Oh dear. It was, as they say, the oldest trick in the book, but the gunman couldn't nevertheless avoid snatching an instinctive glance over his shoulder, and for a fraction of a second, the gun moved away from my ribs.

That fraction of a second was quite long enough for Samantha, who must have been quietly organizing this move with Frankie during all the shouting and arguing. Her foot came up with frightening speed and caught Jacobson on the forearm. The sound of the bone snapping was clearly audible to everyone in the cellar, as was the loud clatter the shotgun made as it fell to the floor. In the same fluid movement she twisted her body round and the heel of her other foot plunged into his solar plexus. It was over in less than three or four seconds, the man was lying on the ground clutching his arm and trying desperately to breathe at the same time. I knew how he felt, but did not sympathize. 'Short-arsed slut, huh?' she said to him.

I stooped to pick up the shotgun which was lying next to him and said: 'Well, well, well. How the fortunes of man do change.'

But before I could actually lift the gun, a shot went off, and in that confined room it sounded as if a bomb had exploded. I looked up, shocked and with my ears ringing, to see the other Jacobson twin standing on the stairs. He had shot a large hole in the ceiling, and plaster and sand were pouring out of it. The gun was now pointing directly at Samantha.

'Drop it!' he snarled, 'or I'll shoot the slut first.' I looked at Samantha and could see despair begin to creep over her face. She knew that the chances of doing the same thing again were nil.

'No, *you* drop the gun, you bastard!' shouted a woman's voice, 'or I'll put a hole in your bloomin' head!'

Bewildered, we all looked up to the sight of Mrs Mavis Healey, Neighbourhood Watch Coordinator, standing behind the gunman on the stairs holding one of the biggest revolvers I have ever seen in my life.

371

But she was holding it steady, and there was a look on her face which suggested that she knew what to do with it. Jacobson hesitated. There was the unmistakable sound of the hammer of a revolver being cocked. 'I'm going to count to three, and then you're dead,' she warned him. He dropped the gun.

Seconds later Frankie and I were each holding a shotgun and the four of us were standing on the stairs looking down on eight shocked faces.

'There's still one thing I want to know,' I said. 'Which of you two low-life Jacobson sleazeballs killed Murdoch?' There was no answer, only baleful stares, and groans from the one on the floor. 'Not that it matters, of course. You're both equally guilty if you were both there.

'I suppose what happened was that Judge Rose somehow discovered that Murdoch had bought this house at auction, and he was rightly worried that if he had got this far, he was certain to work out the whole story before long. So he hired you two scum to 'persuade' him to sell the house back to the Judge, is that it?' No answers.

'Or did you just try and frighten him off? The only trouble was that Murdoch didn't frighten, did he? You didn't know he was a Vietnam veteran, did you? And when he stood up to you, one of you panicked and just blew him away in cold blood!

'And you nearly got away with it completely! All of you! The police would never have been able to find a connection between Murdoch Finnegan and the Jacobson brothers. And they had long since stopped looking for Michael Finnegan. You had covered your tracks perfectly, cleaned this place out, and as far as you were concerned, no one would ever know about your foray into dealing out perverted justice.

'Your mistake was to underestimate your enemy. Once Murdoch realized that you knew he was getting close to the truth, he also had the sense to realize that he was in danger. So he prepared a will, leaving the house, and its damning evidence, to one person he could be sure would continue asking questions. Me. I wasn't a great friend of his, but he knew I was a nosey bastard.

'And then when you found out that he had left the house to me, you had to do something about that as well, didn't you? I suppose you forged that signature on the new will?' No answer. 'And when I continued to be a nuisance, you two and the Judge decided that I had to be got rid of. You nearly managed that, too, but not quite. I'm sure the police will be able to work out all the details.

'It doesn't matter, though, because we are going to lock you all in here, using the Judge's ingenious idea, and let you rot in the dark! Let you experience for the first time what Michael Finnegan went through, see what persecution and anguish you inflicted on him.'

I will carry to my deathbed the mental picture of those loathsome people looking up at me with shocked, white faces. Let them believe they are going to die here, I thought.

'Don't forget, you can scream and shout as much as you like. The cellar has been made completely soundproof with all the sand in the ceiling. And of course there are no windows. The only way out is past this steel reinforced door. Enjoy the prison you built!'

We left the cellar, and there were screams and shouts as I slammed the door behind us. Then we wedged it shut with the chimney.

'We aren't really going to leave them there?' Samantha asked, wide-eyed.

'It's tempting, but no, of course, not. We're going to call the cops. But first, Mavis, did you get it all?'

'Yes, every word. Perfect, and it's all on tape,' the Neighbourhood Watch Coordinator said proudly.

'What are you talking about?' Frankie asked.

'Mohan's a great believer in back-up equipment, and he insisted on me having two receivers in case one failed. And who better to operate the second one than this superb woman who lives across the street! I knew her receiver was still running, which is why I was so determined to get the story out and get them to say damaging things. They'll have an impossible time denying the whole terrible conspiracy now.'

I had taken the equipment round to her house that afternoon, after Wheezy had gone back to the taxi. I had also taken the opportunity to confess to her that I was not a member of Special Branch, but a journalist. She was almost equally delighted, especially when I explained what I wanted her to do.

But then I turned to Mavis. 'You

375

disobeyed orders, though. You were supposed to ring the police if anything went wrong, not gallop over here yourself like Clint Eastwood with that huge gun. Where the hell did you get it, anyway?'

'It was my husband's; he brought it back from the war. I know I was supposed to call the police, but things suddenly sounded a bit desperate so I thought I would lend a hand first.'

Samantha asked: 'Would you really have shot him?'

'I would have, if I'd have had some bullets!'

'Thing I want to know,' said Frankie, 'is what they did with Michael Finnegan's body.'

'I strongly suspect the police will find it buried in the garden of this house,' I said. 'A nice deep grave underneath all the weeds and brambles. But, even if it's not here, the police will get the whole story out of them. The Rosenbergs, the lawyer and the doctor all seem the types to fall apart easily under tough questioning.'

'And what about little Rebecca? Who killed her?' Samantha asked.

'Who knows? The tragedy is that Gallacher's and the family's action probably let the real killer off the hook. Once they arrested Michael Finnegan, they stopped looking. The final irony is that their own obsessive desire for revenge may have denied them the real justice they were seeking.'

The last thing I did before we left the house was remove the last fuse from the box in the kitchen, plunging the cellar into utter blackness.

We went across the road to Mavis's house, where I had a terribly important decision to make. Who to call first, the police or Arnie Bloch?

'Oh come on,' I told myself. 'For once in your life get your priorities straight and do the right thing.'

I called Bloch at home. 'Arnie, hold the front page.'

The publishers hope that this book has
given you enjoyable reading. Large Print
Books are specially designed to be as easy
to see and hold as possible. If you wish
a complete list of our books, please ask
at your local library or write direct to:
Ulverscroft Large Print Books, Long Preston,
North Yorkshire, BD23 4ND, England.

# Other MAGNA Mystery Titles In Large Print

**WILLIAM HAGGARD**
The Vendettists

**C. F. ROE**
Death By Fire

**MARJORIE ECCLES**
Cast A Cold Eye

**KEITH MILES**
Bullet Hole

**PAULINE G. WINSLOW**
A Cry In The City

**DEAN KOONTZ**
Watchers

**KEN McCLURE**
Pestilence